DONE FOR THE BEST

A PRIDE AND PREJUDICE VARIATION

AMY D'ORAZIO

Edited by Katie Jackson and Jan Ashton

ISBN 978-1-963213-96-6 (ebook) and 978-1-963213-97-3 (paperback)

In loving memory of Lilly

CONTENTS

CHAPTER ONE

A SNAKE IN THE GRASS

April 1812

The morning dew made the grass slick beneath his boots as Darcy paced to and fro on the path Elizabeth most often walked. He passed his letter from one hand to the other, then replaced it in his pocket, then took it out again. At least a dozen times, he decided to return to Rosings and forgo this ridiculous idea entirely; a dozen and one, he decided he must adhere to his original plan of giving her a written explanation of his folly.

The sun was higher in the sky than when he usually met her, but she did not appear. Was she avoiding him? He prayed she would not, but certainly, she had every reason to do so.

He *ought* to have avoided her. After the harsh words they had exchanged in the parsonage last evening, he would have done best to leave her alone forever. But the charges she had laid at his door could not be ignored. The matter of Wickham would be bared before her, not only so she might understand the corruption within that man's character but also to protect her and her sisters.

Though it had enraged him to hear the hated name drop from her lips, to comprehend her sympathy for the dastard, in retrospect Darcy knew he could not have expected otherwise. Elizabeth Bennet had a sympathetic heart, and it was well within her nature to take up the cause for what she believed to be a pitiable creature. After all, had he not seen her fall to her knees to remove a burr from his own dog's paw? Heedless of the mud on her skirts, she removed the burr, then kissed Carlo's head, and Darcy witnessed a look of slavish devotion in Carlo's brown eyes that had before been reserved for himself alone.

He sighed, deeply. There was no end to her goodness it seemed, and it pained him anew to know what he had lost.

The sound of a horse approaching at a swift pace startled him, and he turned to see Fitzwilliam riding fast, his face set so grimly it appeared as though he was charging on Napoleon's troops. Darcy smiled faintly, prepared to tease him for it, but his mirth turned quickly to alarm at his cousin's words.

"Have you seen any sign of Miss Bennet? She has gone missing from the parsonage!"

"Missing?" Darcy demanded. "What do you mean?"

Fitzwilliam's eyes roamed the woods nearby while he bit out terse sentences. "Last anyone saw her was when the

Collinses left to come to Rosings last evening. I daresay that was about four."

"I saw her at, um, half past five."

Fitzwilliam cast him a look but said nothing in reply to that news.

"When the Collinses returned, they assumed she had retired. Mrs Collins does not habitually look in on her, and none of the servants had any idea of her having gone out. This morning, Mrs Collins sent her maid in with some powders, in the event Miss Bennet's headache yet lingered, and found the bedclothes straightened and no sign of the lady."

Darcy cursed. It was early April, and thankfully it had not rained the night before. Nevertheless, the woods were no place for a gently bred young lady to spend the night—presuming that was, in fact, what she had done. He prayed that her distress over his behaviour had not made her fool-hardy, even if all evidence suggested it had.

"I need that," he said, gesturing to Fitzwilliam's horse. "Come down."

Fitzwilliam's gaze narrowed on his cousin. "I was planning—"

"I am prepared to yank you right out of that seat," Darcy nearly shouted. "Let me have your horse!"

Fitzwilliam silently dismounted, and Darcy leapt into the saddle, barely remembering to mutter his thanks before setting off. In the distance, he heard the shouting of men—a search party, apparently. Fitzwilliam must have organised one early that morning.

He met his cousin again in one of the groves about two hours later. At Fitzwilliam's greeting, he swiped away the cold-sick sweat beaded on his forehead and dismounted. "Anything?" he asked.

Fitzwilliam shook his head. "Any man connected to Rosings or Hunsford is in these woods looking for her. She will be found."

To Darcy's ear, his cousin's voice lacked assurance. Bending down, he picked up a branch, then hurled it towards nothing, shouting her name with the full force of his frustration.

"Easy, old man."

Darcy rounded on his cousin immediately, demanding, "Where could she be?"

Fitzwilliam shrugged. "They have looked everywhere."

"Tell them to look everywhere again. A lady does not simply disappear!"

"No," Fitzwilliam agreed thoughtfully. "I have to imagine she went somewhere…different, I suppose. The trick is imagining where."

"Ide Hill." The words escaped Darcy before he could stop them. When his cousin looked at him curiously, he added, "Um, we had, ah, spoken of it lately. I told her it was particularly lovely at this time of year."

"That it is, but it is also above three miles. Unless you think it possible she rode out?"

Darcy shook his head. "Three miles is nothing to her, and the day is fine." *And she might have wished to go somewhere that she would not meet me.*

Fitzwilliam removed his hat, scratching his head. "I

cannot see it, Darcy. No lady walks so far on a morning's stroll."

"Miss Bennet would." The more Darcy considered it, the more possible it seemed. "I am positive she would. In the event I am wrong, carry on the search here—I will go to Ide Hill."

Without a syllable more, he remounted his cousin's horse and was off, riding as fast as he could while still searching along the way. Nevertheless, he arrived at the best vista without any sight of Elizabeth. His eyes roamed the landscape in front of him, hoping and praying for something, but there was nothing. Frustrated, he removed his hat and ran his hands through his hair. Could she have come another way? Perhaps been lost?

At once the futility of it struck him. There was a great deal of countryside around these parts that might appeal to a young lady who enjoyed nature. Paths branched and forked in all directions, and she might have taken any number of them—or struck off through a field somewhere. He felt a distinct chill come over him as he recognised the possibility that they might never find her.

He was about half of the way back to Rosings when suddenly his horse reared. He managed to remain seated, but the horse would not continue on, having become startled and restive. Dismounting, Darcy led him a short distance away and tied him, then returned to see what was the problem.

An adder lay amid the grasses by the road, sunning itself. No doubt its nest was close by.

He could still remember his father counselling him and Fitzwilliam, as boys, about the dangers of the venomous snake that had nearly killed an unnamed Rosings servant who inadvertently stumbled upon a nest once by the river. Such warnings, given in dire accents, had only stimulated their curiosity, and they had spent a good portion of their time diligently searching for them, heedless of the danger.

But now the understanding of the danger took on a different hue. Could Elizabeth have met one? Could she be, even now, breathing her last, succumbing to the venom?

He began a search of the area nearest the snake, which slithered away lazily in reply to Darcy's efforts. He knew not whether he more hoped or feared to find her.

No matter his feelings on the subject, he found her. He sucked in his breath at the sight of her, lying pale and still on the ground amid the taller vegetation nearby. He hastened to her side, dropping to the ground beside her and bending to listen if she breathed. It was a small relief to hear her respiration, faint and rough, although the icy coolness of her skin was alarming. "Elizabeth? Do you hear me?"

He saw her eyelids flutter, but they did not open. Putting her modesty aside, he pushed up her skirts to see her calves. He swallowed hard, seeing a telltale bite mark, which had torn through her stockings to, undoubtedly, pierce her skin.

When had it happened? He could not tell but would guess it had been very early this morning.

Removing his greatcoat, he wrapped her with as much gentleness as due haste would allow. She made some small sounds as he did it, which he hoped was an auspicious sign. "You are safe now," he told her. "I have you. I am going to get you back to the house."

He lifted her into his arms and pushed through the

hedgerow. "I will need to get you on my horse," he said, thinking aloud, wondering how best to go about that while still preserving her dignity.

It took some doing, but at length he managed to get them both mounted. He had placed her in front of him, reclined against him to minimise the bouncing and jostling she might experience. He clutched her tightly as he pushed his horse as fast as he dared while holding on to her. It was not easy; she was a dead weight, and gravity wished to pull her right back down to the ground. The appearance of the avenue leading to Rosings Park was an enormous relief.

He kept up a steady stream of the most comforting phrases he knew as they went, telling her she was beautiful, that she would be well, that she was, without any doubt, the handsomest, wittiest, most charming lady he had ever known. He continued to speak to her unconscious form as they arrived, seeing a small cluster of men, which included Mr Collins. "We may need to speak of marriage again after all," he told her with a wry chuckle, hoping no one was such a sapskull as to think there was any impropriety.

"Mr Darcy has someone!" one of the men shouted, and everyone turned to see them approaching. Darcy watched them begin scurrying about as he drew near. Even Lady Catherine deigned to emerge from the house in time to hear him shout out that Elizabeth had been bitten by an adder.

Mrs Collins came at a run to meet them, calling back over her shoulder to someone unseen to send for the apothecary. Lady Catherine was also quick to begin issuing orders, coming to him as quickly as dignity would allow her. "Marlowe," she said to the manservant behind her. "Have someone get word to Dr Hughes that he is needed at once." Dr Hughes was Anne's personal physician and lived in nearby Westerham.

Darcy stood by, seeing Elizabeth being taken off by others, unable to do anything but offer his sincerest prayers and wishes that her health would return.

CHAPTER TWO

AFFLICTION AND AFFECTION

The days following Elizabeth's accident were nothing short of dreadful. The adder had indeed struck her and had inflicted her with its venom; while that was not fatal, it led to a bout of mild apoplexy and constriction of her breathing. Just when that malady seemed to be resolving, the wound became infected, and she developed a fever that had her once again knocking on death's door.

Darcy found himself alternately numb with anguish and trapped in his own fevers, pacing, desperate to do something for her. He bargained with God, determined to right every wrong he had ever inflicted on another. He even bargained with Elizabeth herself, hoping his thoughts would somehow reach her within her unfortunate state in Collins's house. *I promise to be a man worthy of you. I will atone for the haughtiness you accused me of, my behaviour, which you thought so rude. I shall reconsider my thoughts about your family if you wish it. I shall improve for you if only you will survive this.*

His musings were interrupted by voices in the hall outside his door one morning.

"Susie says it be the missus what's taking all her time. Always needing someone to help her here or there, tea too hot, tea too cold, chair needing a blanket. Says it's lucky the girl is still asleep, for if the missus had her way, no one would even have time—Oh!"

Darcy pulled his door open, startling the two maids, whom he surmised were speaking of Mrs Bennet. Elizabeth's mother had arrived on the second day after her daughter was injured. It appeared that her object was not to help her daughter but rather to cause as great a tumult as she could.

The maids gasped in terror upon seeing him, alarmed to be caught gossiping. Immediately, they began to curtsey and apologise, edging down the hall with their eyes lowered.

"No! Wait! A moment, if you please!"

The taller one, a stout red-haired girl, said, "Mr Darcy, we are very sorry to have disturbed you, sir."

He waved that away. "Did I hear you say that things at the parsonage… Is Miss Bennet getting all the attention she needs?"

The two maids mumbled half-hearted assurances and more apologies for gossiping.

"No, no," he said impatiently. "The truth, now. I must know what is happening in the parsonage regarding Miss Bennet's care."

The taller girl flushed scarlet and stared at her feet but not before giving her companion a little poke. After a quick glance, the shorter maid admitted, "Forgive the impertinence, sir, but it's my sister who's over there, she's the maid-of-all-work for them Collinses, and she says that Mrs Bennet is running her off her feet."

"She has the nerves," the red-haired girl added. "So's they be having to take care of her as well as the young miss."

"Right." He considered briefly, then asked, "Who in the village is a nurse?"

An hour later, Darcy stood in the parsonage, having hired two nurses—one for day and one for night—and Mrs Collins was staring at him with profound relief in her eyes that plainly told of her exhaustion.

"Sir." She rubbed her hand across her head. "I do not know what to say. It…it is an unlooked-for kindness."

"It is nothing at all," he said fervently. "I wish I could do more."

"Do you?" She looked at him penetratingly and he, alas, did not look away quickly enough. She was perspicacious, and he winced, knowing she must see everything that he felt writ large on his countenance. Very mildly, she added, "It is much appreciated, I assure you."

"Do you think…?" His emotion crowded his throat, and he was required to pause. "Will she be well again?"

A fraction of a moment too late, Mrs Collins said, "Of course she will. To be sure." The troubled look in her eyes did not match her words.

"What else might we do?" he asked, frustrated. "Another physician perhaps?"

Mrs Collins shook her head. "I think she wants only for

time. She is young and strong. I do not know any lady who can boast equal strength."

"She simply must recover," he said softly.

"I will do all I can for her," she promised earnestly.

A FEW DAYS LATER, THE FEVER HAD DULLED BUT not wholly abated. Darcy had scarcely slept, and what he ate he knew not. Trays were put in front of him, and sometimes he partook of them and sometimes he barely recognised that they were there.

His conduct had been examined from every angle in his mind. He had made promise after promise—if she awoke, she would find him a better man, one without improper pride, one who did not stamp about meanly, looking down his nose and displeased by everyone he saw. He would reform himself; he would behave as a man who was truly in love with a woman worthy of being pleased.

At the end of the week, Fitzwilliam came looking for him. His cousin found him staring out of the library window in the direction of the parsonage. From this vantage, Darcy could see only a small portion of the roofline, but it was enough to engage his interest.

Fitzwilliam clapped his shoulder. "There you are, Darcy. Shall you join us tonight for dinner at Darlington Abbey?"

"I think not."

"Such a quick refusal! Perhaps you will change your mind when I tell you I suspect mysterious goings-on afoot."

"Why is that?"

"Our cousin has been conspicuously absent from the

drawing room these days. Mrs Jenkinson tells us she is unwell, but I daresay I have never seen her looking healthier."

"Mm," said Darcy disinterestedly.

After a short pause, Fitzwilliam said, "Perhaps it has something to do with a cousin of the Darlingtons who is in residence."

"Doubtful."

There was another pause before Fitzwilliam again tried to engage his interest, saying, "Only imagine if Anne were in love with someone over there!"

Darcy scoffed. "I would surely delight in any such attachment, but it seems unlikely."

He heard the sound of Fitzwilliam's footsteps retreating, but his cousin did not quit the room. Darcy glanced over his shoulder to see him settling into a chair across the room.

"Might I ask what the plan is, Darcy?"

Giving up on his study of the parsonage roof, Darcy went to sit in the chair adjacent to his cousin's. "Plan?"

"We were meant to depart two weeks ago, and now I am spending my days playing cards with your valet while you stare out of the window."

"Is that why Fields is so flush of late?"

Fitzwilliam chuckled, but it sounded more worried than amused. "It might well be. The man is not lacking in shrewdness."

"If you would like, I can send you back to London in my carriage."

"While you remain here?"

Darcy nodded. "My coachmen can return to Kent the day following."

There was a lengthy pause, during which he fancied he could almost hear his cousin's mind at work.

"The morning that we searched for Miss Bennet…"

Darcy leant back and crossed his legs, hoping he appeared nonchalant. There was a book on a table near him, and he picked it up and opened it to a random page.

"You mentioned that you had seen the lady well after Mr and Mrs Collins had left the parsonage."

"I wondered when you might ask me about that."

Fitzwilliam gave a half-smile. "As it stands, I already had some curiosity in that quarter. When the ladies withdrew from dinner that night, you did as well. I imagined you had gone to tend to the necessary and expected you back in some minutes. When you were not, I…I confess I thought to come and look for you."

"You did not find it agreeable to be left to entertain Mr Collins?" With a chuckle, Darcy stared at the page of the book and prayed his cousin would say no more.

"I did not. But the peculiarities of *that* gentleman were nothing to my wonderment at seeing you on your way down the path towards the parsonage, a certain—shall we say purpose?—in your steps."

Slowly, Darcy raised his eyes. His cousin's gaze was sharp and probing upon him. Still, he remained silent, determined to admit nothing.

"Why did you go to the parsonage in the middle of dinner when all the occupants of that house were present at Rosings —save for one?"

"I needed to speak to that one."

"As you already confessed you had seen her, then the question becomes whether you were indeed able to *speak* to her as you wished?"

"Why all the questions?" Darcy asked, imbuing his words with as much impatience as he could. "Am I not a grown man entitled to speak to whichever lady I choose?"

"Of course. But as a grown man, you are also well aware of the implied meaning of seeking a private audience with a lady."

"Yes, I am," Darcy confirmed softly. "And forgive me, but I am ill-prepared to speak more on this now, particularly not when the lady lies in the state she is in, her fate uncertain."

Fitzwilliam ran a hand across his mouth. "You do know that with these sorts of bites, these adders...well, I had heard of a lady who was just...not quite the same. And Miss Bennet had, you know, the difficulties breathing, the fit she suffered, the fever...she may have been outside all night—"

"I believe we have all already concluded that she began her walk at dawn. Adders, you know, are not active at night."

"The material point is that there is a possibility she will be...materially altered. She may never walk again, or she may have a limp. She may have no idea who you are, or she might—"

"I *know*," Darcy said, this time more emphatically. "Do you not think each of these dreaded outcomes has repeated itself, a litany of tragedy, endless in my mind for these weeks now? But I cannot abandon her; I cannot, and I shall not, no matter how long it takes for her to recover."

"*Abandon* her?" Fitzwilliam studied him for a long moment. "Darcy, are you…do you—"

Darcy looked away, swallowing hard in the bloated pause that followed. Finally, he admitted, "Yes," relieved to give voice to the feelings which had plagued him since last autumn.

At length, Fitzwilliam rose, leaning over to offer Darcy a light squeeze on the arm. He quit the room while Darcy again rose and went to the window, looking towards the house where she lay.

Charlotte Collins thought it a great piece of civility when Colonel Fitzwilliam called to bid her farewell. It seemed he was to return to London. "I only wish I might have accompanied Miss Lucas on her journey," he said agreeably, referring to her sister whom she had sent back to Hertfordshire after Eliza's accident. "I hate travelling alone!"

Charlotte waved her hand. "My husband was glad to accompany her to London, and my father got her from there. But what about Mr Darcy?"

"It was our original plan to travel together," Colonel Fitzwilliam told her soberly. "But, given the circumstances, I cannot be surprised he elects to remain. One can hardly decamp when one's betrothed lies in such a grievous state."

It took Charlotte several seconds to comprehend what she had heard. "I beg your pardon, but did you say…?"

"You did not know?" Colonel Fitzwilliam settled back; it was clear he relished being the bearer of some happy news.

"Evidently, while we were at dinner that evening—you must recall that Darcy was absent for a time?—he came here."

"I see. Mrs Davies did mention something of that to me."

Colonel Fitzwilliam smiled. "I daresay he is quite in love with your friend. I cannot say I am surprised—Mr Collins is the first parson Darcy has ever deigned to visit, and with all due respect, I soon recognised it was not interest in him that brought my cousin to your door."

"I cannot say it wholly shocks me either." On the colonel's look, Charlotte added, "I have always noticed that he stares at her when he thinks she does not see him. This has been his custom since last autumn."

"That is unusual indeed! They have been walking in the groves most mornings, you know."

"Eliza tends to keep her own counsel on such things," Charlotte told him. "We have been intimates since our girl-hoods, but she would not have dropped a word until things were settled—until her father knew, most likely."

"And now this," Colonel Fitzwilliam concluded sadly. "Merciful heavens, I do pray she awakes unaltered."

"As do I," Charlotte confirmed.

CHAPTER THREE

TEN MONTHS LOST

Consciousness returned in shadows and half-light. Elizabeth ached—her head, her legs, her stomach —and more often than not, it was easier to sink back into slumber than it was to face herself into the light. But at last, she felt enough mistress of herself to open her eyes and look about.

She found herself in a pretty room, simple but pleasant. Light streamed in through the window, which was framed by gauzy white curtains, and there was a painted table next to her bed upon which were a glass of water and multiple bottles of tinctures and potions. The walls had been painted a cheerful pale yellow, and the coverlet which lay over her was white with yellow flowers.

It was all quite sweet...but it was not hers. Of this, she was sure. She listened for the sounds of home, Mrs Hill's voice or the maids—but she heard nothing. She tried to sit up a little, feeling a hot pain sear her leg as she did so. *What happened to me? Where am I?*

She had a strange, muffled, confused feeling in her mind that she disliked heartily. It was as though she had awoken in the midst of a dream, but reacquainting herself with reality proved more difficult than it should.

She lay for a time, her eyes moving around the unfamiliar room, and tried to grasp on to the threads of memory that lay disordered in her mind. At last, she settled on a memory, an assembly at the rooms above the Merry Fox in Meryton.

She sorted through that memory as one might sift through the pages of a beloved book. Summertime… It had been very hot in the room with all the candles lit. Was it July? She had just had her twentieth birthday—no, it was the very night of her birthday. Late June, then. Kitty had teased that the assembly was given in her honour and that she was sure to meet the love of her life. She had teased her sister in return, 'Being that everyone there I shall have known for a decade at least, I doubt that!'

She had worn her ivory muslin with the rose-coloured sash, and Jane had on her pale-yellow silk, and Lydia and Kitty fought for who would wear a fawn tambour they both liked, but which Elizabeth privately thought made Lydia look sallow. Mary wished to remain home, and Mrs Bennet was too harried to argue with her about it. Elizabeth had danced a great deal that night, all the dances, twice with…what was his name? She could not quite remember it. He was Charlotte's cousin—Mr Stephen Lucas?—and he was very amiable if not very handsome. And Mr William Goulding had teased her about becoming an old maid, and she had teased him about his attempt to grow whiskers, which looked more like smudges on his cheeks.

Pulling herself from her memories, she looked around her. She was not at Longbourn, but it did not seem to be Gracechurch Street either. Was it still summer? How long had she been ill?

At length, the door opened very slowly, and a maid entered, an unknown maid. She clearly did not expect Elizabeth to be awake and went about the work of tidying the room. Elizabeth tried to speak to her but only a weak, hoarse "Pardon—" emerged.

The girl startled. "Oh! Oh, Miss Bennet! You're awake!"

Elizabeth, still clearing her throat, forced a smile to her painfully dry lips and nodded.

"I'll go and get Mrs Collins and Mrs Bennet. Don't you stir, I'll return in a wink!" She darted from the room too quickly for Elizabeth to ask who Mrs Collins was.

Minutes later, the door opened, and Charlotte entered, Mrs Bennet hard on her heels. Charlotte was instructing someone to 'call Dr Hughes at once and bring some tea and bread'. Elizabeth watched her with amazement. Whom was she ordering about, behaving as if she was mistress of the place?

Mrs Bennet bent over Elizabeth first, smoothing her hair and kissing her cheek. "Ah Lizzy, I confess it does my heart good to see you awake. We all wondered if we should ever know you again."

Elizabeth laughed, weakly. "What happened to me? I have some odd pains in my leg—is it broken?"

"You have been in a bad way," Charlotte informed her,

coming to sit on the bed. She explained about the snake and the fits and the fevers. It all sounded perfectly dreadful to Elizabeth.

"It seems I must be glad to be alive," she said. "Sounds like some dire times were had, and I am glad to have been insensible to them all. But Charlotte—where am I? This... this is not Longbourn. Where is Jane?"

"You are not at Longbourn," Charlotte replied with a glance at Mrs Bennet who had gasped theatrically. "This is Hunsford Parsonage in Kent, where you have been since the middle of March."

"March? But it cannot be March—"

"It is April, in fact."

"B-but...it is summer. My birthday..."

"When do you think your birthday is?" Charlotte asked.

"At the end of June," Elizabeth replied.

Charlotte and Mrs Bennet exchanged a glance before Mrs Bennet said, "Well done, Lizzy! Quite right!"

Evidently, I am to be lauded for knowing the date of my birth. Elizabeth looked round before asking, "Why am I in Kent? In Munsford—"

"Hunsford," Mrs Bennet corrected.

"Hunsford...Parsonage?"

"Because it is Mr Collins's house," Charlotte explained, a worried frown appearing on her forehead. "Where I live. You came to visit me."

Elizabeth began to chafe and twist her hands against the coverlet, a sensation of being unable to draw breath coming over her. A number of questions were churning about in her mind, but at last she settled on asking, "Who is Mr Collins?"

At this, Mrs Bennet threw up her hands and wailed loudly. "Oh! She has gone witless! Oh, she shall never marry now! No man wants a witless woman for a wife!"

"Mrs Bennet," Charlotte scolded. "Eliza has just a bit of confusion, she is not witless, and Mr Darcy is far too honourable to throw her over for some mild memory loss. I am sure that once she is better recovered—"

"Mr Darcy? Who is Mr Darcy?" Elizabeth interrupted.

But she could not receive an immediate answer, for Mrs Bennet had frozen. Still looking at Elizabeth, she said to Charlotte, "Mr Darcy has made her an offer of marriage?"

"Indeed he has," Charlotte said warmly. "And is much in love with her, from his cousin's own testimony. I suppose we should have guessed as much when he hired nurses to tend to her."

"Who hired nurses?" Elizabeth asked desperately. "Someone is in love with me? I do not know any Mr Darcy! Can someone please explain this to me?"

SOME HOURS LATER—AFTER THE PHYSICIAN HAD examined her and left, and the nursemaid had bathed and settled her—Elizabeth sat in shocked silence, blessedly alone in her bedchamber. Dr Hughes was on retainer by a wealthy and powerful widow who lived just across the lane in a beautiful house called Rosings Park. This lady had a nephew, Mr Darcy, who had proposed marriage to Elizabeth, and who loved her. Did she love him? She could not say, being that she had no notion of the man. Was he handsome? Witty? Was he fifty years old and missing his teeth? Did he have odd hairs sprouting from his ears? She suddenly felt as though she might cry and squeezed her eyes shut against it.

A year of my life is gone. Questioning by the physician in concert with her mother and Charlotte had determined that the last thing she recollected was the assembly given in late June of '11; it was presently April 1812, almost ten months later. She knew nothing of the events her mother and Charlotte had spoken of: Netherfield Park being let to a young bachelor called Mr Bingley who had two elegant sisters; Jane falling in love with this Mr Bingley; Charlotte getting married to Mr Bennet's cousin and heir, Mr Collins—what was he like? She did not remember him either.

For a girl who had long prided herself on her quickness, it was a blow, to say the least. She felt stupid and helpless, two things she disliked heartily. Charlotte had been exceedingly kind to her, tucking a shawl around her and promising her that she would do anything she could to get her friend well again.

Even her mother was treating her with unusual deference, only permitting herself a few dire proclamations about witlessness and being thrown over. It might have made Elizabeth laugh were she not so very much in need of a good cry. How she longed for her dear Jane! But her mother had not permitted her to come to Kent, insisting that she remain at Longbourn for reasons yet unclear to Elizabeth. She hoped Jane might disobey their mother and come anyway.

WHILE WELL-PLEASED THAT ELIZABETH HAD awoken, and with relatively little in the way of physical infirmity, Charlotte was nevertheless troubled by her friend's amnesia. She descended her stairs behind Mrs Bennet who moved very slowly.

When they reached the floor beneath, Charlotte opened her mouth to offer tea to Mrs Bennet only to have Eliza's mother announce grimly, "Come into the parlour, my dear, we need to have a talk."

"Very well." Charlotte followed Mrs Bennet into her parlour and closed the door as she had been urged to do. Mrs Bennet rounded on her as soon as the click of the door was heard.

"I do not suppose I need to tell you that no one can know about Elizabeth's madness," she announced.

"Madness? She is not mad!"

"Ladies have gone to Bedlam for far less. I worry that once Mr Darcy realises she has lost her quickness—" Mrs Bennet sliced one finger across her own neck and made a ghastly choking sound.

"Off with her head?" Charlotte asked, repressing a horrified chuckle. "I should think not."

"He particularly cannot know how grievously affected she is. These great men do not wish for half-wit wives! Whatever words have been spoken, you can trust he will work his way out of them. So pray, do not spread this abroad, this notion she has that Mr Darcy proposed to her!"

"Mr Darcy did propose to her," Charlotte reminded her. "I do not think you need to worry about him abandoning her— not if his cousin's understanding of the matter is any indication. The colonel said Mr Darcy is very much in love with her."

"He was in love with the woman she was," Mrs Bennet replied. "It remains to be seen if he will stand by her, such as she is."

"I really do not believe that—"

"Charlotte, a mother knows these things," Mrs Bennet insisted. Then, with a disdainful flick of her eyes over Charlotte's un-expanded waist, she said, "As you might understand some day for yourself."

Charlotte drew in a breath to summon patience even as she owned that she might not have been wise to tell her husband of the colonel's disclosures. "Very well. We will not mention this to anyone, and I shall tell Mr Collins not to write anything of it to anyone."

"Not even your mother," said Mrs Bennet firmly.

"Not my mother, not anyone in Hertfordshire. But what of Mr Darcy's family? We can surely have no sway over what they speak of and not."

"If they speak of it, then it is done. He will have to marry her then," Mrs Bennet declared.

Then, in a rare burst of maternal approbation, Mrs Bennet reached over to pat Charlotte's cheek. "You have always been dear to my girls, but I cannot help but feel an extra measure of gratitude for all you have done for our poor Lizzy."

She left the parlour, and Charlotte was left to stare at the door that closed behind her with the commingled exasperation and fondness that Mrs Bennet tended to inspire.

"A NOTE CAME FOR MAMA FROM THE PARSONAGE this morning," Anne informed Darcy as she came into the breakfast room. "Miss Bennet is awake."

A jolt of an emotion he could not name made Darcy sit straighter and lay his fork down. "Indeed?"

Mrs Jenkinson had just scurried into the room and was filling Anne's plate for her. Anne sat with her head held high and her back straight, not even deigning to tell the lady what suited her that morning.

"What did it say?"

"The note?" Anne shrugged, which caused her shawl to slip a bit. Mrs Jenkinson hastened to fix it. "I am sure I do not know any more than what I just said: Miss Bennet awoke."

Darcy fought the urge to leap to his feet and run to the parsonage. "Splendid news," was all he would say.

He forced himself to finish his meal, telling himself it would be perfectly natural that he, as an acquaintance, should call and ask after Elizabeth. But he must do so at a sedate pace, he determined, not go tearing off like a lunatic.

Leaving Rosings about half an hour later, Darcy strolled down the avenue, doing his best to appear unaffected and tame. He need not have worried, for soon enough—he imagined that it was the moment Mr Collins saw him—the door was flung wide, and the parson himself rushed out, wiping his mouth as he went. Apparently, he had been eating, if the napkin he was using to scrub himself was any indication. "Mr Darcy! Sir! We have some news of Cousin Elizabeth to share with you!"

Schooling his countenance to appear solemnly interested,

Darcy stopped. "Good day, Mr Collins. I hope I have not called you away from your breakfast?"

At this bit of mild civility, Mr Collins halted, looking as if Darcy had conferred great honour upon him. "Indeed you are too good, kind sir, but to put aside my own humble bodily requirements that I might impart upon you the most delightful news, indeed, our house may even be considered blessed above all—"

"I understand Miss Bennet has awoken? What of her fever?"

Mr Collins gave a slight nod. "She is not entirely well and suffers some confusion, but Dr Hughes has been to see her and pronounces her as well as could be expected."

"Mr Collins, you, Mrs Collins, and your household are to be commended for her excellent care." Darcy paused. He knew not what he had hoped for in coming to the parsonage, but he longed to see Elizabeth, to know for himself that she was well. Or at least on the way to being well. "You will send a note, I hope, when she is able to receive callers? I wish to—"

Mr Collins nodded vigorously. "You must wish to see her, of course! Alas, as soon as Dr Hughes had gone, Cousin Elizabeth settled into slumber."

"Of course. Best thing for her, no doubt." Darcy bade Mr Collins good day with a touch on the brim of his hat and left the good parson behind him, swollen and affixed in place by his own delighted importance.

When Darcy returned to Rosings, he was greeted by an exceedingly unusual sound: raised voices. Strident tones from his aunt were matched by shocking screeches from...

Anne? It had to be, for no one else would dare speak so to Lady Catherine, surely. He hastened his footsteps towards the parlour from whence the cacophony seemed to originate.

He entered to find Lady Catherine standing, her skin an alarming hue of puce and her walking stick shaking in time with her outrage. Anne sat in a posture of upright defiance; beside her sat an unknown gentleman, slight and concerned-looking. Darcy did not immediately place him but knew his face and believed they had been once introduced. This was confirmed when the man rose and came to him, bowing and saying, "Mr Darcy? We met at Lady Farmington's dinner last spring. I am Mr Roland Yardley."

"Yardley," his aunt scoffed from behind them. "Who are the Yardleys, I ask you!"

"I remember you, yes," said Darcy with a bow. Was this, then, the attachment Fitzwilliam had hinted about? He had given it little credence at the time, for Fitzwilliam saw clandestine romances everywhere he turned. It seemed in this case he had been correct. "Good to see you again, even if under somewhat…fractious circumstances? Anne, what is all this about?"

"Do you understand," Anne said, "that *I* am the owner of this house and all within it? Not you, Mother, me!"

"I have life tenancy!"

"But we both know you do not live from your jointure," Anne snapped. At this impertinence, Lady Catherine grew yet more purple.

"Ladies," said Darcy with a glance at Yardley. "Might we settle this peaceably?"

Lady Catherine laid down her walking stick, took a deep

breath, and came towards him, both hands outstretched even as she nearly elbowed Yardley out of the way. Yardley gave Darcy a small nod and returned to Anne. Darcy observed that he took Anne's hands in his own and believed he could surmise the rest of what was happening herein. "*You* are the victim here, Darcy," said Lady Catherine theatrically. "It is you who will have the greatest portion of the humiliation."

"Shall I?" he asked mildly. "How so?"

"Anne does not intend to fulfil your engagement!"

Darcy glanced over his aunt's shoulder to see that his cousin was now resting her head on Yardley's shoulder. "We are not engaged, Aunt, and if Anne's heart has led her otherwise—"

"Jilted!" Lady Catherine cried. "I could never imagine my own daughter being so ill-bred!"

"I did not jilt anyone!" Anne replied hotly. "Darcy and I were never engaged, and I love Yardley! I shall marry him, or I shan't marry!"

In a low tone, Darcy said, "Aunt, if some misplaced concern for my feelings is your only objection to the match—"

"He is a second son!" Lady Catherine hissed. "His father made his fortune in the navy!"

"My father *increased* his fortune in the navy, but the Yardleys have had land in Herefordshire for five generations," Yardley offered. "Eardisley Park is my father's home."

"Second sons should marry too," Darcy told his aunt. "With Anne's holdings, they will be quite comfortable indeed."

His aunt pointed a bejewelled finger at him. "You could

have been one of the wealthiest men in England. Your holdings would have rivalled that of any duke!"

"I daresay I shall just need to shift along as best I can without it," Darcy replied.

Lady Catherine's eyes narrowed to slits. "So you are saying you will not marry her?"

"I understand that my marriage to Anne was your wish—"

"And that of your mother!"

"So you say, but it was never said thus to me. Much as I hold my cousin in dear esteem, it has never been my intention to marry her, nor hers to marry me. Is that not true, Anne?" Darcy looked to his cousin.

"I told you that years ago, Mama," she said calmly, while Yardley squeezed her hand. "And Darcy as well."

Lady Catherine looked about, as if incredulous that the three younger people in the room did not intend to give way to her. *One can almost see the smoke coming from her ears,* Darcy thought, and bit the inside of his cheek to keep from grinning.

"Your generation is a disgrace," she spat finally and turned on her heel and stomped out of the room.

After a short silence, Anne spoke up, her tone considerably lighter than it had been only moments previous. "Would it be terribly peculiar if I asked you to give me away, Darcy?"

CHAPTER FOUR

FITS AND STARTS

L ady Catherine, angry at both her daughter and her daughter's suitor, left for London in a fit of pique, determined to punish them both by absenting herself.

For as much as it relieved the rest of those in the house, it placed Darcy in an uncomfortable spot. He ought to have left; his cousin, although his relation, was an unmarried woman, and he was an eligible bachelor. But he did not. Hang anyone who would speak against him—he was here for Elizabeth. In any case, Anne herself thought nothing of it and spent most of her days driving her phaeton to the neighbouring estate where Yardley stayed, or else entertaining Yardley in the drawing room while Mrs Jenkinson snored in her chair.

"My mother would be the one to insist on marriage to save my reputation, and she has already been doing that for years. People stopped paying her any mind a long time ago," she said. She had boasted a becoming pink hue to her complexion since Yardley's arrival and possessed a new straightness in her bearing. Darcy wondered, not for the first time, how much of her illness was due to the unrelenting shadow of her mother's iron fist. Anne was like a rose that had never before seen enough sun to really enjoy its bloom.

The next days passed with no little difficulty. It was easy enough to obtain news of Elizabeth; the moment Mr Collins spied him outside the parsonage, he rushed to speak to him, quick to supply whatever information he had, good or bad. The parson had determined it was his duty to report to Darcy, and Darcy did nothing to disabuse him of that notion.

Elizabeth's recovery seemed to proceed in fits and starts. One day she was mostly awake, talking, and eventually out of bed. The next day might find her once again faintly feverish with no energy to remove from her bed, or talk, or even wake.

When a week had elapsed since she woke, Mr Collins came into the breakfast room at Rosings to give his daily report to Darcy, who was sitting with Anne and Mrs Jenkinson at the table. Darcy immediately perceived that he was unsettled; he was twisting his hands, chafing them in front of him, and though he accepted the offer of coffee, he looked away when shown the plate of ham.

"Forgive me," he said when Anne raised her eyebrows, surprised by his demurral. "I cannot like…well, far be it from me…no, I cannot doubt the wise counsel…dear Lady Catherine with her superior comprehension must surely have hired a man of advanced understanding of the workings of—"

"Mr Collins, what is it?" Darcy asked quickly. "Something concerning Miss Bennet?"

"Indeed," Mr Collins said gravely. He quickly went on to explain—with a countenance that grew paler with every syllable—that Dr Hughes felt, given Elizabeth's poor appetite and continued exhaustion, that her humours were imbalanced. "He has recommended a course of…of purgatives and bloodletting."

Darcy felt his heart plunge into his boots, and his hands suddenly clenched his fork very tightly. He remembered still, with painful clarity, the effects such treatments had had on his mother when she was ill. He was certainly not medically trained, but he had always felt that the treatments had hastened her demise; in any case, they had certainly not cured her of anything.

"I cannot allow that," he blurted.

Mr Collins looked about uncertainly. "The good doctor does feel strongly that Cousin Elizabeth is in need of it, and I am very certain that if Lady Catherine were here, she would recommend—"

"No." Anne had gone very still, but her voice was louder and firmer than Darcy had ever heard it. "No matter what my mother might think of it, such a treatment will not help Miss Bennet. I should stake my own health on it."

"Do you truly think so?" Darcy knew Anne had, herself, been the subject of frequent similar treatments.

"Have you ever suffered such a regimen? If one is not near death before it, you can be sure one will be afterwards. Darcy, you must stop Dr Hughes immediately."

Scarcely were the words fallen from Anne's mouth than

Darcy was on his feet. "Excuse me," he said and strode from the room.

The breeze through his hair reminded him he had exited without hat or gloves, but as he was already halfway down the lane, he disregarded that. When he arrived at the parsonage, he was glad he had not spared the moments required to retrieve them. The maid took him to the parlour wherein sat only Mrs Bennet, twisting her handkerchief in her lap.

"Oh! Mr Darcy, sir."

"Has Dr Hughes—"

"The doctor is with my poor girl even now!" Mrs Bennet cried out. "Oh, how her poor addled wits can withstand such a treatment—"

Darcy heard no more. "Mrs Bennet, pray, stop him at once."

She stopped her wailing rant and gaped at him.

"Pray, go! Send him to me directly."

Shocked, the lady only continued to stare, and Darcy, aware that at any moment a foul leech might be placed on Elizabeth's delicate skin, turned and moved towards the stairs. He was not insensible to the impropriety of his actions, nor was he unaware that he had no understanding of where her bedchamber might be; nevertheless, he plunged ahead.

"Hughes!" He took the stairs two at a time, shouting with no concern for decorum. "Hughes, a moment please! Desist in your actions, man, I must speak to you!"

He could hear sounds behind one of the doors and, taking a chance, he stopped and pounded loudly. "Hughes?"

There was a pause, and the door was pulled open by Mrs

Collins who, while white-faced, appeared resolute. "Mr Darcy?"

"I must speak to the doctor, madam, if you please."

A male voice from within the room rumbled a few syllables, and over it, Darcy said, firmly, "I would speak to him at once, Mrs Collins."

Dr Hughes—a portly gentleman of advanced years— appeared behind Mrs Collins. "Mr Darcy, this is highly irregular. We were about to begin treatment on Miss Bennet."

"I cannot authorise it." Darcy spoke firmly. "I fear it will do her more harm than good."

"Authorise?" Mrs Collins looked at the doctor and then at Darcy.

The doctor nodded towards her. "Mrs Collins, stay with Miss Bennet please." He stepped outside of the room and motioned for Mrs Collins to close the door behind him. She did as she was bidden, leaving the men in the hall, alone.

"I will not see Miss Bennet bled," Darcy said, imbuing every ounce of authority he could summon into his tone. "I do not think it will benefit her and may, in fact, be quite detrimental to her recovery."

"With all due respect, I cannot agree with you, sir," Dr Hughes replied. "Miss Bennet has refused nearly all food, her skin is pale and dull, and her fever has not wholly abated. These are all signs of generalised inflammation that might encompass the kidneys, the heart, the stomach—all manner of problems which can be cured by a reduction in the amount of blood she has. With the leeches, along with a purgative—"

"I disagree," Darcy said with a little frown. The sound of his own blood roared in his ears, and he gave the older man his haughtiest glare. "My cousin has said she has been bled and had purgatives many times and suffers greatly when she does."

"Miss de Bourgh has not suffered an attack by an adder," Dr Hughes replied calmly, unruffled by Darcy's demands. With gentle insistence, he added, "Sir, you must understand that Miss Bennet might not have eliminated the venom fully and even now it might be causing further injury."

The two men eyed one another. Dr Hughes seemed as determined as Darcy felt that his was the correct course.

"One more day will surely not make a difference," Darcy said firmly. "I insist. I will see to it that she eats something."

"One day could be the difference between permanent damage and not," Dr Hughes warned. The man had to be at least sixty years old. No doubt he had been trained when bloodletting and vomiting were the most recent advances.

"One more day," Darcy repeated.

Dr Hughes offered one last weak protest. "Lady Catherine would not—"

"Lady Catherine is not here. I am, and I wish you to give Miss Bennet one more day. She will eat, sir, I assure you of that. You will find her in better vigour tomorrow, or you may apply the leeches to me alongside her."

"One day," said Dr Hughes with a resigned sigh. "I give you one day."

"Thank you," Darcy said, profound relief coursing through him.

"And she must not be subjected to commotion! None of

this shouting or pounding on doors; certainly no news to shock her system. She is in a highly delicate state!"

"You have my word." Darcy extended his hand to the doctor who, obviously surprised, shook it. "No shouting, no shocking, no commotion."

With a curt nod, Dr Hughes took himself back into Elizabeth's bedchamber, and Darcy, feeling as if he wished to sag against the wall, instead moved slowly back down the stairs, to the room where Mrs Bennet still sat. She looked up with eyes wide with fear, her handkerchief clutched in her fist.

"He will wait one day," Darcy said. "We must make Miss Bennet eat something for him, and we must keep her calm and peaceful."

There was a piercing wail, part nerves and part elation, and before he could understand it, Mrs Bennet had leapt from her chair and come and kissed his cheek. He was so startled, it was over before he realised it had begun.

"Dear boy! Dear, dear boy!" she exclaimed. Then in a lower voice, she said, "I was in terror, remembering my own experience with it—it was right after my dear girl Lydia was born. I had a little fever, nothing so very dreadful, and Mr Jones... Was it Mr Jones? Or was that back when Mr Wilton was still in Meryton?" She tapped one finger on her cheek, considering it. "Old Mrs Percy was the midwife, and she hated Mr Wilton, thought him quite a brute and never wished anything to do with him, but I daresay if I was ill enough, she might have called on him. Of course, Mr Bennet did nothing but sit in his study smoking, he was quite attached to his pipe in those days...in any case, it was the most dreadful experience of my life. Leeches all over me, draining me nearly dry, and the purgatives! Oh, the purgatives were the worst of it! I could not stand for a fortnight after that!"

On and on she went, telling him far too many details, certainly much more than he ever should have known of any woman; and in the midst of it, Mrs Collins entered looking uncertain. "Sir, Eliza has asked if you will…if you would wait and allow her to speak to you."

His heart leapt. "Yes, of course I will."

"I shall bring her in here," said Mrs Collins.

"She will need a fire," Mrs Bennet said. "I shall get your girl in here to set it." With that, she bustled off.

Mrs Collins watched the door close behind Mrs Bennet, then turned back to Darcy. "Sir, the fever has left Eliza with some confusion."

"What sort of confusion?"

"She seems to have forgotten a great many things," Mrs Collins explained. "Pray do not think she's gone witless! No, nothing of that sort! She remembers some things very well, but others…not at all. Lady Catherine's physician questioned her thoroughly. She has every idea of who she is and where she is from, and she did not forget any of her family, save for my husband. She had no idea who Mr Collins was or why she should be in Kent, a guest at his house."

"I see."

"Her last memories—her last clear memories—were of June of '11, or thereabouts. She remembers being at an assembly at that time."

"N-not the assembly that I—that we, Mr Bingley and I—"

"The assembly where she was deemed tolerable but not

handsome enough to tempt you?" Mrs Collins cast a reproving grin at him. "No, not that one."

Darcy chuckled uncomfortably.

"As for the rest of your acquaintance, we have…well, we have told her a little bit. Not everything, of course, as it seems there is a great deal that none of us knew."

"But she has no true recollection of me?"

"Do not distress yourself for that," said Mrs Collins, her grey eyes earnest. "Dr Hughes says all is not lost, not yet. She may still recover some of her memories."

CHAPTER FIVE

UNKNOWING

While Darcy waited for Elizabeth to arrive, he looked around him at the room where he had been received only once before—the morning he had come upon her alone, the other ladies having gone to the village. It was the back parlour, a smaller, less formal space but very neatly furnished and comfortable. Most importantly, it was *not* the scene of his ill-fated addresses, and for that he was most grateful.

What would he say to her? She had no remembrance of him—but how to say, 'By the bye, you despise me, but I love you.' Perhaps they might begin anew?

Shortly thereafter, he heard them in the hall, Elizabeth saying, "Charlotte, I assure you, I can walk," just before the door creaked open and the ladies entered.

She was beautiful in her renascent state. Pale, as would be expected, and thinner, but the delicacy only enhanced her loveliness to him. She had grey shadows of fatigue beneath her eyes, and her hair was very simply done—a plait wound up and pinned—but she was walking, even if she needed to lean heavily upon her friend to do it.

He moved to assist them, but Mrs Collins quickly had her situated on a small but comfortable-looking sofa, so he contented himself with bringing over a little footstool. Mrs Collins gave him a quick, grateful smile, but Elizabeth only looked a little dazed.

"I brought your blanket," Mrs Collins said while he returned to his position by the mantel.

"I am not cold, thank you."

"Pray, put the blanket over your legs, at least. The last thing we need at present is for you to take a chill."

"I assure you, I am far more apt to break into a sweat than to take a chill." While she spoke, Elizabeth's eyes had moved away from her friend and fixed upon Darcy. He felt pinned, like a moth to a tray, as her eyes roved over his countenance. He smiled at her, but she did not smile back. She seemed frightened and uncertain, despite her firm words to her friend.

He cleared his throat lightly. "The rain we had yesterday has made it exceedingly damp today, and likely you should have the blanket to ward off any chill."

This earned him a searching look from her, followed by a small smile. "Very well."

Mrs Collins busily exchanged Elizabeth's shawl—which she deemed too thin—for her own which was thicker. Throughout her friend's fussing and fretting, Elizabeth sent quick, darting glances in Darcy's direction, examining him it seemed.

"Charlotte, I daresay I am swaddled enough."

Mrs Collins gave the shawl one final tweak over Elizabeth's shoulders. "Shall I send for some tea?"

Elizabeth, in a low voice, said to her friend, "No, I do not want tea, I just wish to speak to Mr Darcy, if you please."

"I will leave shortly; I only wish to see to your comfort."

"I am comfortable, I promise you. Please?"

Mrs Collins sighed and said, "Very well." She cast one last glance between them and then left, leaving the door slightly ajar. The sudden stillness of the room was alarming. Darcy felt his heart pound, wondering what he should say, but Elizabeth spoke first.

"Thank you." Tears had welled up in her eyes. "Thank you for the...the doctor. I was so frightened when he brought out his jar and...and I simply could not bear the thought of it, of enduring such a thing. Thrice a day, he said! I did not see how I would bear it even once!"

"Shh," he said, trying to soothe her as he joined her on the sofa. "Of course, think nothing of that. But we must get some food in you, something nourishing. Otherwise, he and his jar might come back tomorrow, and I fear I have exhausted all my persuasive charms upon him today."

This made her laugh, a tinkling, unpractised sound, even as she wiped away one of the tears which had fallen. "My trouble is that everything sounds so...so disgusting. I try to imagine eating something, and it just feels like my throat closes."

He thought for a moment. "Mrs Reynolds, my housekeeper, used to feed me bread soaked in tea when I was ill.

It…it just sort of melts away in your mouth. Could you manage that?"

She smiled at him, genuine and warm. "I think I could, yes."

He rose and went to the bell; Mrs Collins herself replied to the summons. He explained quickly what was needed, and she went off to see it prepared for her friend, obvious relief in her eyes. Darcy then returned to Elizabeth.

"I must tell you, sir, I have searched my mind, very diligently, and alas I must say I truly have no recollection of you." She offered an apologetic smile to him. "The only thing I could summon up was…"

She paused, an enchanting pink blush rising on her cheeks. More quietly, she said, "I seem to recall you saying that you 'ardently admired and loved' me. When I heard you speaking to Dr Hughes outside of my bedchamber, the sound of your voice seemed to stir that recollection. Is it faithful… that memory?"

"Um." He swallowed. "Yes, that memory is true. I did say those words to you… And I do…I do love you. It has been dreadful these past weeks, being fearful for your safety. I… the thought that you might not…"

He stopped, unable to go on. He turned his head away from her but turned back, startled, upon feeling her gentle touch on his shoulder.

She was smiling, beguiling and playful. "But I did. So those fears, terrifying as they might have been, were unfounded. I am hale and whole."

He found himself smiling back. She was intoxicating, her delicate bewilderment slowly ebbing away, leaving an ease and friendliness that was everything he had ever imagined and more. "I do not think that as yet we can declare you hale, but you *are* as lovely as ever."

"I suppose it will be some time before I can call myself hale, and my memory, for certain, is not whole." Her good humour dimmed a bit. "Memory loss is a strange thing. You do not know what is lost until you have reason to look for it."

Then, shockingly and suddenly, she began crying. She pulled up the edge of the shawl to cover her face, and her slender shoulders shook. Darcy hesitated one moment, then placed a hand on her back. He longed to pull her into his chest but restrained himself.

"I despise feeling so…so confused, so stupid!" She leant against him, and his heart leapt.

"You are not stupid," he consoled her. "Very likely you will remember it all one day; you are still recovering."

"I cannot even recall your proposal," she said into his chest. Then she pulled back, looking up at him, her face damp and small tears clinging to her eyelashes. "You did propose to me—did you not?"

"I did," Darcy said.

And then she was weeping again, apologising to him for not remembering it, apologising for being so mercurial with her emotions. He soothed her with inane mutterings—"There, there, think nothing of it"—all the while thinking what a relief it was that she did not seem to recall the bitter exchange they had had or the fact that she had despised him from the first moment of their acquaintance.

She had only just stopped weeping when the maid

entered bearing a tea tray and the bread, prepared just as he had requested. Elizabeth regarded it with a faint look of revulsion but then said, "Well, 'tis this or the leeches I suppose," and tucked in to it. He felt inordinately pleased watching her.

While she was thus occupied, he asked, with careful nonchalance, "Do you recall anything of the matter with your sister and Bingley?"

"I am afraid I do not have the faintest recollection of Mr Bingley," she said with a smile over her teacup. "Charlotte told me that Jane wanted to come to me here, from London, but my mother insisted that she return to Longbourn. Evidently a report had gone round the neighbourhood that Mr Bingley would be coming to Netherfield."

"Did he? I am afraid he has not replied to my recent—"

She set down her cup. "Charlotte says Jane is violently in love with him, so I have already decided I shall like him."

Surprise made him chuckle. "Bingley is very easy to like. Perhaps you will remember him when you see him again."

"Perhaps I shall," she said, tearing off a little piece of bread. She had consumed almost an entire slice, he noted with satisfaction.

"And he has two sisters as well. Miss Bingley, who is of an age with you, and Mrs Hurst who is the elder sister. She would be, um, I believe, four- or five-and-twenty."

Elizabeth considered that while she ate another small bit of bread. "Were they friends of mine?"

Darcy winced. "Um…they are both the sort of ladies who are really only friends to themselves." Cautiously, he asked,

"There was a regiment quartered in Meryton last autumn. Do you remember them?"

She tilted her head as she pondered the question.

"Colonel Forster was the head of it and a Captain Carter. Then there were some various lieutenants who came to the parties—Denny, Chamberlain…a Mr Wickham."

"Wickham," she echoed faintly. "No, I am afraid I do not remember any of them."

This gave him a great deal of satisfaction.

"Do you recall anything of the last night we were together, here? Besides when I said that I loved you?"

"Is that when you said it?" She shook her head. "No. I cannot say I recall anything but that, and I only recollected that when I heard your voice in the hall. Why?" She took a sip of the tea, giving him a mischievous look over her teacup. "Did we have a dreadful quarrel?"

He laughed, too loudly, then admitted, "In fact, yes, we did."

"Was it something you did? Or was it me?"

You said I was the last man in the world you could ever imagine marrying. You said I had behaved in an ungentleman-like manner. "It was me, wholly and completely my fault."

"How fortunate then that this accident erased all traces of it from my mind!" She smiled. "You are pardoned and exonerated, with me none the wiser. It seems it was the ideal moment for a vicious row." Her giggle as she concluded her sentence showed she thought it was of no consequence.

"I daresay it was," he acknowledged. "But I do want you to know this. I am sorry for how I hurt you, and your reproofs are tended to, even if you do not remember what they were."

"That sounds very serious." She said so in a deepened voice with a mocking little frown that was endearing. "From all Charlotte has told me, you are much to be admired. In any case, I surely would not have accepted an offer of marriage from someone so bereft of good character!"

The last she said lightly, but it gave him a jolt. She believed she had accepted him; she believed they were engaged. He opened his mouth, intent on correcting her, but just then Mrs Bennet bustled in, with Mrs Collins hard on her heels.

"Excellent news, Lizzy! Mr Bingley has made a purchase offer for Netherfield Park!"

NEARLY AN HOUR LATER, DARCY STOPPED ON THE lane between Rosings Park and Hunsford Parsonage. What had he done? Why had he not corrected her misapprehension?

'Disguise of every sort is my abhorrence'. The memory of his own voice, rich with arrogance and self-importance, taunted him.

Turning back towards the parsonage, he took one step forwards. It had been a torturous temptation, Elizabeth, sweet and loving, allowing *him* to care for her, turning to *him* for comfort and affection—just the way he had always imagined it might be for them. An unbearable enticement for any man.

He took another step towards the parsonage.

But she had been retiring when he left, shadows having deepened beneath her eyes and a weakness afflicting her bearing. She must surely be in her bed by now, perhaps already asleep.

The words of the doctor returned to him: *'No news to shock her system. She is in a highly delicate state'*. What might the news that, no, they were not engaged, do to her?

He could not do it to her now, not with the threat of Dr Hughes and his purgatives looming. She needed to rest, to be calm and to gain her strength. He would explain it all later.

"CHARLOTTE, YOU ARE TRULY TOO GOOD TO ME." Charlotte bustled about the room, making sure Elizabeth had everything she needed, though in truth, Elizabeth knew a long and deep nap was due shortly, so in fact, she required little.

Her friend smiled at her. "I confess, the duty has been made much easier by the nurses Mr Darcy hired."

"You have no idea how relieved I am that he stopped the doctor from bleeding me."

"As am I," Charlotte admitted with a laugh. "I wished to do what was needed for you, but I am still not sure I could have applied those leeches to you. My hands were already shaking at the thought of merely touching them!"

Elizabeth shuddered. "I was doing my best to hold fast to my courage, but I could not imagine how I would get past the hour much less the days to come. But I shall not think of that; I am well aware Dr Hughes might be back tomorrow."

"He will have to go through Mr Darcy first," said Charlotte with a little laugh.

"He is the protective sort, is he not?"

"That is putting it mildly."

"And handsome," Elizabeth added. "I confess I feared he might be forty-five and bald, but he is...almost shockingly handsome. And so tall!"

"That he is. Everyone in Hertfordshire thought him a fine figure of a man." Charlotte smiled down at her where she lay in the bed. "I am putting some barley water over there if you feel you can manage something more."

"Thank you, but I doubt I will be awake enough to drink it. Are we...are we in love?"

"You and I?" Charlotte asked teasingly. "You know I have always been fond of you."

Elizabeth smiled wanly even as she felt sleep tugging her away. "Mr Darcy and I...I just...I have no remembrance of him, just one faint recollection of him saying he ardently admired and loved me. He said that he told me so the night before this...this mishap of mine, but then he also said we quarrelled. How does one go from such declarations to quarrelling?"

"I am hardly his confidante, so I really cannot say," Charlotte said. "Perhaps the declaration came after the quarrel? As you made up?"

"That would make sense."

"I may not have known everything of your attachment to him—you do tend to keep things close, Eliza, and he even more so—but I had suspected that he had a tendre for you

49

months back—he watched you all the time, and singled you out for dancing at his friend's ball."

"Is that so remarkable?"

"I do not think he danced with anyone else from the neighbourhood."

"Not even Jane?"

Charlotte shook her head.

Elizabeth felt her eyes drifting closed amid the guilty pleasure of that. "Dear Jane. I have not even been able to look at the letters she has sent me, much less write some of my own."

"Do not worry about that. I told her you were as yet unable to read or write, but she misses you so, she says she will just carry on writing to you. You will read them all soon, I am sure, and be able to reply."

Elizabeth hoped that was true. Her memory being what it was, she felt as if she had not seen her sister in nearly a year, not merely the weeks she was told they had been apart. She hoped Jane was enjoying the society of Mr Bingley; it would make it wholly worthwhile.

Sleep was overcoming her, and her last thought, as she drifted off, was whether this Mr Bingley would propose and, if so, if she and Jane might have a double wedding.

CHAPTER SIX

A PROMISE OF RETURNING HEALTH

To Darcy's great pleasure, the food Elizabeth ate improved her enough to satisfy Dr Hughes that her humours were not so dangerously imbalanced and that the leeches were unneeded. Elizabeth's relief, as well as that of Mrs Collins and Mrs Bennet, was accompanied by an excess of gratitude for his intervention.

"I told him the same myself," Mrs Bennet said. "But no one listens to me! A mother does know, no matter what these doctors might think! I knew Lizzy could never survive such a treatment! It would have killed her right there while we all stood by!"

From his position by the window, Darcy offered a faint smile, though Mrs Bennet was not looking in his direction and not likely to see it. She was a silly woman—his opinion of her in that regard had not changed—but in one very important matter they were alike: they both loved Elizabeth.

He had never before thought of it, how a mother's

apparent greed might be rooted in love for her daughters. The Bennet ladies held a precarious position in life; when Mr Bennet died, their status would be lost. Good marriages were their only hope. Was it any wonder Mrs Bennet had rejoiced at the appearance of wealthy bachelors in their little town?

"Dr Hughes was just so certain it was necessary," said Mrs Collins. "How can one argue against a learned man in such a way? We are grateful you were here, Mr Darcy, to stop him."

"Oh yes. Yes! Without Mr Darcy, I do not doubt that we would be standing over my poor girl's grave even now!" Mrs Bennet cried out.

Elizabeth laughed. "Would I have been buried in Kent? Or would we have required Charlotte to come back to Hertfordshire and stare at my grave there?"

Having eaten increasing amounts over the course of three days, Elizabeth's energy was undoubtedly returning. Her chair had been tugged close to the window by which Darcy stood; together they beheld a brilliant spring morning with birds singing and flowers blooming.

As Mrs Collins and Mrs Bennet continued their discussion on bloodletting and purgatives and Elizabeth's near demise, she looked up at him and whispered, "I have endured this conversation no less than four times. None of it grows any more interesting in the retelling."

Darcy smiled down at her, readily perceiving, from the sag in her shoulders, that it pained her to remain indoors as they were. "I am certain your restlessness is a promising sign of returning health."

"Is it?" She smiled wanly. "Must I start screaming from the tedium before we may pronounce me healed?"

"My cousin Anne hit upon an idea this morning that I think you might like."

"Oh? What is it?"

"She has a phaeton, and a pair of ponies to pull it. I wonder if a slow drive around the avenue might—"

"Yes!" Elizabeth shot to her feet, her shawls and blankets dropping from her shoulders onto the floor. "Now?"

"What are you talking of?" Mrs Collins immediately rose and came to them.

"Mr Darcy and I are going to drive out in Miss de Bourgh's phaeton," Elizabeth said hurriedly, extricating her skirts from the blankets and shawls which were now at her feet. "I shall need my boots."

"I do not know if you are ready for that, my dear. Perhaps we ought to ask—"

"Fie on Dr Hughes, Charlotte, I need to get some fresh air." Elizabeth turned to Darcy, released from her swaddling, her eyes shining and her countenance as happy as he had seen since her accident. "Surely a short, slow drive can do me no harm? Indeed, I think it might do me a lot of good!"

"Absolutely not," cried Mrs Bennet. "You will certainly catch a fever out there, and that will kill you for sure!"

A heated disagreement ensued. Mrs Bennet thought Elizabeth ought to remain indoors, while Elizabeth believed that remaining indoors for even one minute more would send her gibbering mad. Mrs Collins, while cautious, tended to agree with Elizabeth, that the fresh air might help her. Darcy himself forbore from offering any opinion, but it mattered not; Elizabeth, having seen a potential for reprieve, would not be dissuaded. Darcy offered many reassurances and promises to the two other ladies before running across the lane to Rosings's stable. He soon had the phaeton brought up to the parsonage door.

Elizabeth found a great deal to admire in the ponies as well as Anne's little conveyance and amid exclamations of delight was soon comfortably situated beside him. He drove them along at a comfortable pace, enjoying the spring sunshine on their faces and the faint scent of apple and cherry blossoms in the air.

They passed Rosings and then went out on the avenue towards the park. He could tell Elizabeth was enjoying herself; she looked about eagerly, as if every sight was magical and new. He supposed to her, it was.

"I believe that you, sir, are my hero," she said at length. "I could not have remained in that room for even one more minute."

He laughed. "It does please me to relieve your suffering, in whatever small ways I can."

She answered him with a smile that could only be described as loving—it made him catch his breath. He knew he returned her look with his own emotion plain in his eyes, but hard on its heels came a prick of his conscience. He needed to tell her that she had refused his offer, but the words of Dr Hughes echoed in his mind. Would it be too shocking to tell her now? She had improved, but he had no wish to set her back.

His inner debate was silenced by her question: "Will you tell me about yourself?"

"Tell you about myself?" Darcy chuckled, prodding the ponies to take a left turn. There was a beautiful field of wildflowers that would likely not quite be in bloom but would be pleasant to check upon. "What do you want to know?"

"Everything, I suppose. I do not really know anything about you." She said it lightly but there was a small note of anxiety in her tone, and he resolved to put aside his innate reluctance to speak of himself.

"Very well, but you must tell me immediately if I grow tiresome. Where to begin? Um…well, my estate is called Pemberley, and it is in Derbyshire."

"Derbyshire? Oh!—I presumed it was nearby."

He smiled at her before continuing. "My parents are deceased—"

"They are? I am so sorry," she said with genuine feeling in her eyes. "Recently?"

"No, it has been some years now. I was fourteen, and my sister, Georgiana, was only two when our mother died, and our father died just above five years ago, when I had only lately finished at university."

"You became master of your estate so young!" Elizabeth exclaimed.

"Master of Pemberley and guardian to Georgiana, ill-qualified as I was for both," he said with a rueful chuckle. In truth, he did not much like to recollect those days when a dark cloud of uncertainty and sorrow had seemed to encapsulate him.

"She was quite young—and is much younger than you are, it seems? Is it only the two of you?"

"Only the two of us," he confirmed. "She is sixteen years old."

"Is Georgiana…does she…" Elizabeth paused.

"Does she what?"

"Does she like me?"

"Ah, well, she does not know you yet, but she does send her regards and best wishes for your health."

"That is very kind of her." Elizabeth looked thoughtful. "What did you…how did you manage it? Raising her, I mean."

"She went to my aunt for a bit, we hired a governess for her, of course, but then my aunt became very busy bringing out my cousin Aurelia, and Georgiana seemed to be…in the way. She was twelve then, so we thought school would do her some good." He shook his head. "In truth, I have never felt I did well by her. I always looked at her as a child and then suddenly one day she was a child no more."

He glanced at Elizabeth, wondering if more would be too shocking. "I was reminded rather painfully last summer of how she was no longer a child."

"Oh?"

He fixed his gaze on the ponies. At length he said, "You recall I once mentioned a Mr Wickham to you?"

"A man in the militia, yes?"

Darcy nodded and continued, telling her of Mr Wickham's association with Pemberley and their family, and then, more painfully, of what he had done to Georgiana. When he finished, Elizabeth's mouth was agape.

"Poor, poor girl!" she exclaimed. "And you! I cannot

imagine what you must have felt for a good friend to have betrayed you like that!"

"It was terrible, but in retrospect, not entirely unexpected. I had denied him money, you see, and no doubt it was on that day that his scheme was formed. Georgiana has a fortune of thirty thousand, and that was clearly his first object."

"The scoundrel! But—this man is roaming about Hertfordshire? Does my father know? He allows them too much liberty...he ought to know so he can have a care with Kitty and Lydia. Have you met them?"

"I have indeed."

Elizabeth grimaced. "They are full young and ought not to be out. Lydia *is* out, is she not?"

"Yes, she certainly seemed to be when I was there."

She shook her head. "I knew my mother could not long withstand her entreaties. She is only fifteen! The most dangerous young ladies are those who cannot wait to prove themselves grown. You take someone like this Wickham person and heedless, impulsive girls like my younger sisters, and you have the sure ingredients for disaster."

"I shall write to your father about it tomorrow. Forgive me, it should have been done long before, only I..." Darcy paused, shame flooding him. "I did not wish to lay bare my troubles."

"You scarcely knew us," Elizabeth said absently. "Still, you may trust my father's discretion, particularly if you ask him for it."

"If I can reassure you on one point. Wickham, and men like him, do tend to prey on wealthy young ladies."

"Then my sisters, and indeed all the ladies in Meryton, shall have no fear." She turned that loving smile on him again, but it was short-lived. A shadow passed over her face. "You *do* know that I have no fortune of my own?"

He nodded. "You know how it is these days; one can scarcely enter a room without everyone immediately wishing to examine their accounts."

She laughed. "Too true. I am glad to hear that you are aware that you have made an impractical choice."

"I do not consider it impractical."

She turned to look at him, a question in her eyes. The ponies were trotting along well, so he took one hand off the reins and gently brushed her cheek with his fingers. "What price can be placed on love? A man who has found it is the wealthiest man alive."

That made her blush, deeply, and she lowered her gaze only to jerk it upwards, eyes wide, moments later. "Oh! But if your sister—Georgiana?—if she has thirty thousand pounds, then Pemberley...you..." She sent him an awkward look, then asked, "Are you very wealthy?"

Unsure how to answer, he paused; he had just opened his mouth to reply when she cried out, "Wait! Do not answer me. That is to say, clearly I know, from seeing your aunt's house and your sister's fortune and the like that you have means, but...allow me to know you in the absence of your income."

Then she smiled, a little tremulously, and said, "I know, already, how well I like you. You are good and kind and protective and...and I see a turn of our minds that is very similar. I just wish to not have those practical considerations in my mind as I become reacquainted with you. Is that silly?"

"It is charming," he told her. Then he again released the reins, reaching over to squeeze her gloved hand. "Utterly charming."

He kept his hand on hers too long; it inspired within him a powerful, almost irresistible urge to kiss her, a kiss that he knew instinctively she would not rebuke. Indeed, she seemed almost to invite it, looking at him with a faint smile on her lips, the air between them increasingly charged.

He forced himself to tear his hand away and turn his attention back to the ponies, remarking over some trifling thing on the ground they travelled, even though there was nothing, and the ponies were plodding along as sedately as they had been before. The danger, of course, was hardly beneath the ponies' hooves; the danger was right there in the phaeton and took some time to dissipate.

This was not real, no matter how it felt. Elizabeth needed to be told that she did not love him, and had not accepted him, and it was horrid that he had not done so thus far. Kissing her could only compound his sins, no matter how tempting it might be to do so.

He glanced back at her and was immediately alarmed by her appearance. She had grown paler and seemed to be sagging a little in her seat. "Forgive me, you are grown tired."

"I confess I am, though I am enjoying our discussion. I have struggled against it, but I fear it is getting the better of me. Perhaps we will continue another day? I am eager to hear how it was that we fell in love."

"Next time," he promised, and again, the moment of truth went by him.

CHAPTER SEVEN

FALLING IN LOVE WITH HIM

Elizabeth settled into her nap with thoughts of Darcy in her head, and she woke the same way. She lay there for a time, thinking of what she knew of him and recollecting the sweetness of their drive.

His sister has thirty thousand, which means Pemberley must be extraordinary. Astonishing, she thought, *to imagine such a man to be in my power.*

Did he truly love her? Why? She had never imagined herself making a brilliant match. She was not a great beauty, nor did she have the education or fortune or talents to impress a man. She was too clever, and did not hide it well enough. She was too apt to give her opinion and disinclined to flatter a man's genius simply because he was a man.

It was not that she lacked confidence, only that she knew herself. If she had awoken from her illness to find that Jane had attracted such a man as Darcy, it might have made sense, but herself? No.

And yet, it did seem he loved her, and with each hour spent with him, she was falling more in love with him, too. Though her mind remembered nothing of him, it seemed her heart recalled their attachment very well.

She was fortunate, it seemed, to have earned the regard of a man who was, in disposition and talents, well matched to her; a man who could be her friend, her suitor, and—one day not so distant—her husband. "And he is handsome and wealthy." She shook her head. It all felt too good to be true.

What is wrong with you, Lizzy? Have more faith in yourself, more belief that you are as capable as any lady of attracting a worthy gentleman.

She could not quite shake it, however, the niggling sense that surely all of this was too fantastic to be real. Perhaps she was looking a gift horse in the mouth but only because she was fearful it was about to bite her.

If I knew more, perhaps I could worry less, she reasoned, and to that end resolved to begin asking him about the time they had known one another. *I must learn how it was that we fell in love.*

SHE IMPROVED A BIT EACH DAY. THE DRIVES SHE took with Darcy were the best part of any day and soon became a regular occurrence. Darcy would call in the morning and take her on a little drive and then later, when she had slept, call again and either sit or walk out with her.

She hoped she did not flatter herself unduly that the bloom was returning to her countenance, her fatigue was abating, and her energy was returning. She remained quick to tire when she exerted herself, and headaches were common, but all of it steadily lessened even though her memory showed no sign of returning. It seemed a year of her life—an important year—would be forever lost to her. Darcy, she realised, was the means by which some of it might be returned. She hoped he would not grow weary with her questions about their acquaintance. She wanted to know everything, every moment of what seemed to have been an excessively important autumn and winter, and yet every question begat more questions. She wished to learn not only the bare facts, but also the feelings and impressions and shades of meaning that went along with those facts. Happily, Darcy never seemed to grow impatient explaining things to her, even when she required second and third explanations.

"You came with Mr Bingley in October, with Mr Bingley's sisters and—"

"Mr Hurst," he told her. "He is married to Louisa who is Bingley's elder sister, and Miss Caroline Bingley is his younger sister."

"Miss Bingley is my age?"

"She has just reached her majority."

"Is she pretty?"

To this, Darcy replied with only a sidelong glance.

"Is she?" Elizabeth persisted.

"Her outward appearance is too often contradicted by her...mean-spirited tendencies." Darcy grimaced. "I know her too well to think her pretty."

"She must have had hopes for you," Elizabeth mused. "Being an intimate of her brother as you are."

To this, Darcy replied with a satisfying shudder and an

unintelligible sound that clearly communicated his distaste for that notion.

"An assembly in Meryton," was his reply to her question about their first meeting. "Though we did not dance together at that one. I danced only with Bingley's sisters, for I did not know anyone else."

He had, apparently, asked her to dance while she stayed at Netherfield, nursing Jane through an illness, however. "I said no to you?" she asked with no little amazement. "How…rude of me."

"I cannot fault you your refusal," he said. "You had every reason to. In fact, you had refused me once before as well."

"Had I?" Elizabeth laughed. "My mother must have been fit to be tied."

Slowly he shook his head, his eyes trained on the path they walked. He seemed too dismayed about the matter, which she had been prepared to treat with levity, and it concerned her. After a short pause, she slid her hand into the crook of his elbow. "Is there more to the story than that? You appear unduly distressed for what seems to me an impertinent lady's refusal of a dance."

"There is…" She watched as he swallowed hard. "There is a great deal more to the story, in fact."

Her hand still rested on his arm, and she gently squeezed it through his greatcoat. "You certainly must tell me all, then. After all, what can it matter now?"

He did not immediately reply, but his steps slowed and he stopped walking, turning to face her. Elizabeth removed her hand from his arm, folding her hands in front of her.

"The first night we met, I, um, well I was feeling prodigious uncivil. The situation with Georgiana that I mentioned before…"

She nodded, and he continued, "It was very recent, and the pain associated with it was still acute. Being in a different society than I am accustomed to is never easy for me, but that night it was positively intolerable. So much so that I declined to be introduced to you and your sisters. Your mother was not pleased by that."

Elizabeth smiled. "I do not doubt that. Was she very unkind to you?"

He shook his head. "She…well, she said a great many things that I easily overheard. Indeed, most of the assembly overheard her, and it did nothing to improve my mood or my feelings towards her or your family. So then when Bingley began urging me to ask you to dance, I…I reacted badly. I believed that, like your mother, you were, um—"

"Presumptuous? A bit vulgar? Insolent?" Elizabeth smiled again. "I love my mother, but I do know how she is perceived by others, particularly when a new bachelor is come to town."

He dipped his head to one side but still did not meet her gaze or share her light humour. "I was vexed with her, and with you by extension, for I assumed that like mother so must the daughter be. I was also angry with Bingley; he seemed to me to be wilfully uncomprehending of my feelings, and I could not like his imprudence with regards to your sister. They had danced twice by then, and I did not doubt he wished me out of the way so he could ask for a third without my disapproving stares. So I said, in reply to his urgings—"

He swallowed hard again. "She is tolerable; but not handsome enough to tempt *me*; and I am in no humour at present to give consequence to young ladies who are slighted by other men."

Elizabeth laughed. "Badly done!" she exclaimed mockscoldingly. "And what did I do in reply? Did I say something dreadfully impertinent to you? Stamp on your foot, or slap your cheek perhaps?" She knew she would have done no such thing, but in the face of such a woebegone expression, she wanted to make him laugh, or at least relax a little.

"Would that you had!" He took one of her hands in his. "I deserved no less. You were and are too good, only rising to walk past me and go to your friends. You all laughed moments later, and I was left to burn with the shame of being an object of ridicule."

"Oh no," she said softly, reaching over to stroke the skin of his cheek with the gloved fingertips of her free hand. "How ghastly of me."

He finally allowed a small smile. "And yet it was the seed. How could I not grow to love such a woman? Any other lady might have run off crying or been enraged. You were so very singular, in that as in nearly every other circumstance in which I have known you since."

His admiration of her was so clearly overflowing, so plain in his eyes, that it made her blush. It felt, in every way, like a kiss *must* surely happen. She felt it in the air between them, a peculiar charge, and she lifted her chin slightly, held his hand more tightly, willing him to just do it.

A sound like a stick cracking made them both startle, and Darcy immediately stepped away from her. "We had better get you back to the parsonage. I fear we have walked too long."

AN HOUR LATER, DARCY CROSSED THE PATH FROM the stables to the manor house with long strides, angrily tugging his gloves from his hands. A footman met him at the door to collect his coat and hat, and he reminded himself to be civil. It was not the footman's fault that Darcy was behaving like a reprobate. Wickham had nothing on him!

With each moment spent with Elizabeth, his love for her grew. He had always believed they had similarity in the turn of their minds, and their drives and walks proved it. With their prejudices and quarrels set aside—or, in her case, forgot—it was easy to be lovers.

He retired immediately to his apartment, closing the door firmly and then standing, not knowing what to do with himself. It could not go on, this deception of her, and he *was* deceiving her. He could not prevaricate with himself. No matter what Dr Hughes had said about shocks or upset...he was lying to her.

A mirror stood nearby, and he glared into it. "A liar. You are a liar."

Clearly, she was curious about the year of her life that had gone missing from her memory. She asked question after question, and he spoke honestly, but not once had he ever so much as mentioned, 'By the bye, you have loathed me since last October. You thought me ungentleman-like and rude, arrogant and uncivil up to and including the hour I proposed to you. You had no design on me—no matter what I thought

—and rejected my offer in no uncertain terms, and if a snake-bite-induced apoplexy had not ejected all of that from your remembrances, I would have been long gone from Kent, and we likely would not have known one another again.'

Darcy shook his head, disgusted with himself. This was, without a doubt, the worst of all his sins against her, to allow her to believe them in love. He sank into a chair, sighing heavily. Therein was the difficulty. He did love her, and he believed, in these past weeks, she had begun falling in love with him too. It was, as many things contrived of fairy dust were, sheer perfection.

What temptation it did present! A second chance in every sense of the word.

I can be a man worthy of her. Have I not learnt what it might have cost me, my pride, my selfishness? I have changed and will continue to change. No, I shall never be a Bingley, who beamingly embraces anyone he meets, but neither will I disdain those I do not know. The shades in my character that she admonished, though she does not remember them, will be remedied.

But still, I must tell her.

She had laughed about his insult of her. Perhaps she would be equally amused by the contentions and misunder-standings of their past.

He hoped rather than believed it to be true.

CHAPTER EIGHT

AN EXCELLENT READER

Some hours later, Darcy called at the parsonage, his heart encased in lead in his chest but determined to do what was right, to speak the truth to Elizabeth. Mr Collins met him in the vestibule.

"Cousin Eliza has awoken in a difficult temper," he said.

"A difficult temper? What do you mean, sir?"

Mr Collins went on a long-winded discussion of his opinion that ladies ought to be trained in the art of staying home, of tending the hearth, because ladies given too much freedom and exposed to the outdoors suffered irreversible harm to their dispositions. Darcy's own cousin Anne was held up as Mr Collins's model of ideal womanhood.

Darcy regarded him with some amusement. He might previously have been offended or tempted to make a cutting remark to him, but he had taken good care of Elizabeth, offering her every convenience unstintingly. Mr Collins was a man of weak understanding, but he did right by his family—

or tried to. *He has done better by her than you have*, his conscience reminded him.

"So what you are saying, Mr Collins, is that a woman ought to be raised up as if she suffers illness so in the event she does fall grievously ill, she will be better able to bear it?"

Mr Collins opened his mouth to answer then paused, considering it; and into this pause arrived Mrs Collins. She had a smile on her lips though worry had bent grooves into her forehead. "Eliza is in the drawing room, sir. She is very tired and headachy this afternoon."

"Then let us hope I might suitably divert her," he said, but it was ill-timed for just then he heard it, the soft patter of a spring rain against the window. He turned to look behind him and saw that the quiet grey of the morning had given way to a gentle but steady rain shower.

Mrs Collins seemed to read his mind. "Indoor diversions have never been Eliza's delight," she said with a small laugh. "But perhaps you will hit upon something the rest of us have not thought of."

Darcy found Elizabeth in the drawing room, and from the strained white of her countenance and the pink hue of her eyes, he deduced she had been crying.

"I am being the absolute worst sort of patient," she told him. "Ungrateful and wretched. Charlotte ought to just save herself the trouble and toss me out into the rain."

"Mrs Collins said nothing of that," he told her, taking a seat next to her on the small worn settee. "Only that you were tired and had a headache. I hope our ride this morning was not to blame."

She shook her head. "I have found myself struggling

terribly with the tedium. I should imagine it is a good problem to have; it must mean my health is improving, and yet it is still too poor to do the things I wish to do."

"You have always seemed to me the active sort."

"Much to my mother's dismay," she said with a smile. "She did not think it was ladylike that I was so often rambling about."

"I knew almost immediately of your fondness for a walk when you came to Netherfield to nurse your sister," he said. "On foot."

She laughed, lightly, at this mention. "I am not a horse-woman," she said. "I never have been. So the choices are to become a good walker or stay at home."

"With the exception of reading—it seemed to me you were fond of reading."

"I confess I am, although it is rather difficult for me now, more's the pity. An ideal activity for convalescing, save for those in whom the activity results in an aching head. More than a few pages and the words begin to swim before my eyes."

"Shall I read to you, then?"

"Would you?"

He smiled. "I would be honoured." Her return smile lit her eyes, and he was, as always, pulled immediately into her thrall.

"What will you read to me?"

"Whatever you would like."

"Truly? What if I select some insipid novel?"

He laughed. "Then we will groan and complain over it together."

They stood, the pair of them, before the shelves in Mr Collins's study, eyes scanning the shelves for something that would do. Mr Collins had limited taste and interests, it seemed, for his scant few books were nearly all of two subjects—religious instruction and gardening. Every now and again, Elizabeth would take one of the tomes and examine it hopefully before putting it back; Darcy occasionally did likewise.

"Do you like these sorts of books?" Elizabeth asked eventually.

"These do appear a bit too ponderous for the diversion of a spring afternoon."

"Perhaps we might find something more appealing at Rosings?"

It was a disinterested suggestion; Rosings Park's library had often been neglected. Sir Lewis de Bourgh had not been interested in reading overmuch, and what he had read, most often, was designed to titillate rather than inform or entertain. Nevertheless, Darcy thought it might do better than what he saw in Mr Collins's book-room.

A quick glance at the window reminded him of the rain. "What if I ran across to Rosings and brought back a selection for you. Would that do?"

"I hate to ask you to go out into the rain," Elizabeth said with a worried glance at the window.

He waved his hand. "Think nothing of that. It will be the work of a moment."

He turned then, intending to be off, but she had further surprises for him: she grabbed his hand, forestalling his progress and sending a lightning bolt of warmth through him. With her gaze fixed on his countenance, she said, "You are too good to me."

"You deserve far better," he murmured, giving her hand a little squeeze. How delicate it felt within his own!

She edged closer into the slight distance between them. "Impossible."

It would have been so easy to kiss her; indeed, she nearly invited it with her lips, tilted into the slightest of smiles, angled towards his own, her dainty, yet strong, fingers grasping his hand. He had never wished to kiss her more.

With great effort, acting against every base inclination he had, he pulled their joined hands towards his lips and gently kissed the backs of her fingers. "I shall be back directly," he said in a low voice, and then he left her.

THE COOL SPRING RAIN WAS RELIEF AGAINST HIS face and neck. He crossed the small lane in quick paces, wishing he had a rock to throw or an opponent that he might box or fence; the untamed frustration within him begged for release.

There was no one about at Rosings, which was further relief, as he should not have liked to account for his agitation. Within the library, he leant against the bookshelves and swore. Every day he was in deeper and deeper, and the lies mounted. He needed to make a clean breast of things!

His respirations came quickly. His mind was in tumult—he wanted, no *deeply desired*, to kiss her, to take her in his arms and press her body against his own, to ravish her, to taste her, to make her his own. But he knew his own guilt.

What he did was bad enough, but to take liberties as well? It would be unconscionable. "Everything you are doing is unconscionable," he growled into the empty room.

When he was with her, when the warmth in her eyes and the smile on her lips were for him—it was everything he had ever wished for from her, and it proved impossible to deny himself. How was a man to begin a confession which would rob him of his heart's true desire?

He took several deep breaths, determinedly bringing himself under regulation, forcing himself into more wholesome musings. At length, he turned his attentions to the shelves to look for a book, choosing several that were lying about, one of which was his own—*Gulliver's Travels*. It seemed like one she might like.

He wondered briefly how it had come to be on the shelf in Rosings' library but then recalled he had read it on the day he found her. Rather he stared at it uncomprehending, fearing the worst for her.

Recalling that day reminded him that it was decidedly a blessing that she walked and talked among them now. *She must be told the plain truth,* his conscience urged him.

Walking back to the parsonage, he was reminded of his father. 'When you must do something difficult, set a time for yourself', had been his father's counsel. 'Never plan to do something at some point distant; choose your moment and adhere to it faithfully'.

Darcy nodded. Very well, then. Not today—she was feeling unwell. But tomorrow, during their ride, it would be done.

CHAPTER NINE

THE THINGS UNKNOWN

While Darcy was across the lane retrieving a book to read to her, Elizabeth rang for some tea and settled herself onto a little sofa. Charlotte herself came in with the tea.

"Where has Mr Darcy got to?" she asked, placing the tray down on the table.

"He has gone to retrieve a book from Rosings. I did not see anything on Mr Collins's shelves that was not—"

"Akin to *Fordyce's Sermons?*" Charlotte laughed, her eyes on the things she was setting out on the table. "My husband does favour ponderous reading material. I often think a novel might do him well."

Elizabeth laughed with her but then said, "I cannot laugh at him too much, Charlotte, for he and you have been so very good to me. 'Tis a strange thing, particularly as I only know him as much as what I have learnt of him here, since my illness."

"It is certainly to my good fortune that he came to Longbourn when he did." Charlotte bent over her friend, busily tucking Elizabeth's shawl around her. "I had quite resolved myself to being the spinster aunt, shuffled about between my brothers' houses. Fortunate for me that you did not take a liking to him, and that he extended his offer to me instead!"

"What do you mean?"

"Oh!" Charlotte straightened, finished with her ministrations. She tucked one piece of escaped hair behind her ear and admitted, "I forgot that you would have forgotten it. Mr Collins proposed to you before he offered for me. The day after Mr Bingley's ball, in fact."

"Mr Bingley's ball…that was at the end of November? The one where…"

"Where of all the ladies from the neighbourhood, Mr Darcy asked you, and only you, to dance. He danced with his hostess too, of course."

"Of course," Elizabeth echoed. "And then what happened?"

"You danced with some of the men in the militia, and—"

"No, I do not mean that. The day after the ball. My cousin proposed to *me*?"

Charlotte's face had flushed, and she looked decidedly ill at ease. "He did. He felt it a right thing, being that you and your sisters would lose your home on Mr Bennet's death, to make an offer for one of you, and you were the one he selected."

"And he did that despite Mr Darcy's preference?" Elizabeth shook her head, frustrated. "It all seems so odd to me!

From what I have heard, it seems that both Jane and I ought to have been engaged last winter."

"Perhaps you would have been, had they all not left immediately after the ball." Charlotte bit the corner of her lip, then sat, and sighed heavily. "Mr Bingley's party returned to town, and Miss Bingley sent a note to Jane informing her that they would not return and hinting at an engagement between Mr Darcy's sister and Mr Bingley."

"I see." Elizabeth considered that. "I daresay Mr Darcy and I must not have been in love then, else he should have remained."

"I really cannot say when you and Mr Darcy fell in love. Perhaps this meeting in Kent was something of a second chance for you."

"It seems that is how it went," Elizabeth owned. "I wonder when exactly I fell in love with him. Was I bereft all winter, longing for his return? Heartbroken?"

Charlotte gave a little laugh, then leant over the table, straightening the teacups and saucers in a useless sort of way. "Jane was, to be sure, but you are made of sturdier stuff, Eliza, you know that. You keep your own counsel in these things."

Charlotte excused herself, saying she believed she heard Darcy in the hall, and Elizabeth was left to ponder the meaning of it all. Had Darcy perhaps been attached to someone else and thus she and he had carried on in quiet? Or maybe a London lady believed she had a claim on him, and thus had he scampered off after the ball, intending to end things?

There is more to this story that I do not know, and only Darcy can tell me. Time and enough to get an answer to the question of how we fell in love.

DARCY ENTERED THE ROOM WITH THE SCENT OF spring behind him. He was strangely hurried and seemed to have something on his mind; Elizabeth thus forbore to ask her questions in favour of setting him more at ease.

"*Gulliver's Travels!*" she exclaimed delightedly, gesturing towards the tome in his hand. "I have not read it for such a time but own it has always been a favourite. Like so many great works, it improves on further acquaintance."

"Indeed it does," Darcy agreed warmly. "The more basic elements of plot can be readily grasped, even by children, but as one familiarises oneself with it, the more complex elements of theme and satire become evident."

"Evident—and debatable. The enigmatic Mr Swift has not always been clear in his meaning, which is ever more diverting as it allows us room to discuss." She smiled. "An ideal choice, sir."

"You know," he said tentatively, "you once said to me that you were sure we never read the same things, or if we did, that we surely had different feelings on them."

"Did I? I should hope we would not have the exact same feelings on things. How dull that would be! I should be far more amused if we could engage ourselves in lively debate on what we read."

He laughed. "Yes, I imagine you would. In fact, I once accused you of expressing opinions that were not wholly your own to provoke lively discussion."

"I wish I could say that was not true but alas, it is." She grinned. "You have my measure, sir. I am very fond of debate and discussion and see no point in all of us just nodding and agreeing with one another."

"It was one of the things I liked best at university—the chance to not only learn but to critically analyse my own opinions."

"It is the only way to be sure of something, I daresay. To look at it from every angle, even through another's lens, so that we may have a rational answer for our beliefs."

She poured him tea then; she had learnt the way he liked to take it and made it just so. He opened the book and settled himself onto the sofa and began to read.

The story came back to her with ease, much to her relief. Familiarity in anything was prized by now. He read it very well, his voice mellifluous and his pace ideal for the listener. There was something pleasing about his mouth when he spoke, and dignity in his countenance; and with an awkward blush, Elizabeth found herself awash in admiration of him, her former questions quite forgotten in favour of admiring her beau.

I wish he would kiss me. She wondered, often, why he never did. He was, she already knew, a very proper gentleman, but surely engaged people could kiss. Everyone did! And there were opportunities aplenty. Charlotte was a haphazard chaperon at best; the Collinses had only their housekeeper and one maid-of-all-work, and they were both far too busy to worry about the goings-on in the parlour. And her mother? No one could worry less for a daughter's reputation than Mrs Bennet. In any case, Mrs Bennet had found some like-minded friends in Hunsford village and was enjoying her days very well playing cards and hearing the local gossip.

Darcy read to her for quite some time. When they reached a point at which it seemed natural to stop, they did, but he left his book behind, promising more on the morrow.

"I am eager for it," she said as he rose to his feet. She rose as well, and he bowed over her hand as he customarily did when leaving. On an impulse, she said, "When was it that you decided to propose to me?"

He seemed to grow very still before enquiring, "When?"

She nodded.

"The very day I actually did it," he admitted. "It just... came upon me. I knew I loved you and could not live without you and next I knew I was walking the path as fast as my feet could take me, intent on making you mine."

A sweet answer, and it made her blush with pleasure, her confusion rendering her unable to ask further questions.

CHAPTER TEN

ARGUMENTS AND ABSTINENCE

A letter had come from Jane at Longbourn containing news that was mightily dissatisfying to Mrs Bennet. Mr Bingley had purchased Netherfield Park for his permanent home, but there was no indication that he meant to live there anytime soon. Mrs Bennet found this exceedingly odd behaviour, and Jane had been cast into despair anew over it.

"What does this man mean, buying a place and then not living in it?" Mrs Bennet demanded angrily of Elizabeth and Charlotte over breakfast. "If he wishes to settle down, then he ought to settle down!"

Elizabeth exchanged a glance with Charlotte. An earlier conversation between them had revealed to Elizabeth that Mr Bingley was quite young; furthermore, Charlotte believed he had taken Netherfield, at least initially, not as any great foray into land ownership, but as a place to entertain his friends with fishing, shooting, balls, and parties. His purchase might have been nothing more than a sound invest-ment and to his credit in Society. One could not truly be part of the landed gentry without, well, *land*, and now Mr Bingley would have that. Nothing that Charlotte had told Elizabeth suggested that Mr Bingley was a man wishing to 'settle down'.

Jane, on the other hand, very much wished to marry, and though she had not said so to her mother, Elizabeth wondered at her sister's wisdom in placing hopes on a man so young, quite lately out of university.

"Perhaps he has pressing engagements elsewhere this summer," Elizabeth suggested and then winced at her use of the word engagement.

Mrs Bennet huffed disgustedly. "I cannot say anything about that, but Lady Lucas says these young bucks make a dreadful scene in London, racing about in curricles, staying out all night drinking… I say, if that is what he wishes to do, then do it and leave Hertfordshire society out of it!"

It seemed to Elizabeth that was precisely what the gentleman was doing, but she did not offer the opin-ion. Without thinking too much of it, she mentioned, "Per-haps we might see him in London and speak to him directly of the matter."

It was an idea that had been tossing about in Elizabeth's mind of late. She longed to see her aunt and uncle Gardiner, having no recollection of recent visits, and she thought it might be interesting to see Darcy's town house and meet his sister. If they could chase down Mr Bingley while they were at it, so much the better!

"London?" Mrs Bennet looked interested. "I confess I had not thought of it."

"We might stay with my uncle, perhaps even shop a little."

"Eliza, *you* cannot be thinking of gadding about London, surely," Charlotte said, her eyes on a piece of toast she was buttering. "You are not nearly healthy enough for such exertions. You must remain here for a few weeks more, at least."

A few weeks more? It had been above a month since Elizabeth's injury, and from what she understood, she had been in Kent for a month prior to that. Much as she appreciated all Charlotte had done for her, she longed to be somewhere else. "Surely we have imposed on your hospitality long enough, Charlotte."

"You have done too much, my dear," Mrs Bennet agreed.

Charlotte looked up with an unexpected countenance; there was almost—disappointment?—in her eyes. Elizabeth could understand it, somewhat. She imagined that Charlotte's life, when she did not have visitors, was difficult. Mr Collins had been good to her, but he was a foolish man, and Lady Catherine, from what she had heard, was overbearing and officious. Her ladyship had gone away in a pique due to Miss de Bourgh's engagement and no one, not even Miss de Bourgh, seemed to repine her absence.

But Elizabeth could not remain in Kent just to entertain her friend. These days she felt as though the walls of the cosy parsonage were closing in around her—days on which she was impatient to resume the life she had had and learn more about what she had 'missed'. She wished to know Darcy better, understand the man he was within his own sphere, not in this place where he, too, was a visitor. She tired easily, yes, but otherwise what was to stop her?

"I am not thinking of gadding about London," she conceded. "But I have wedding preparations to see to, do I not? A trousseau to amass, things of that nature?"

She had her mother's attention. Mrs Bennet had a gleam in her eye as she said, "Oh yes! For the bride of such a great man as Mr Darcy...well, your wedding gown alone!" She quickly rose from the table. "I am going to go and send word to Dr Hughes. Let us summon him here and see when he thinks Lizzy will be fit for travel."

Charlotte's look had gone from mere disappointment to a shocked sort of hurt. "You surely do not mean to leave so hastily?"

"We must!" Mrs Bennet cried out, already half out of the room. "'Tis the Season, all the modistes will be busy, the fabrics half gone! These grand ladies get a new gown every day; we will be fortunate to find anything!"

After the door closed behind Mrs Bennet, there was a strained silence. With an uneasy chuckle, Elizabeth said, "Oh dear, what have I done? She will have me at every warehouse in London, just to make sure my gown is fine enough."

Charlotte did not laugh. "You do mean to marry him, then?"

"Yes, of course, I do," Elizabeth replied, thinking what a peculiar question it was. "I would be a strange creature to be engaged to a man without meaning to marry him, would I not?"

"I should have asked whether you meant to marry him *soon*," Charlotte said.

Elizabeth shrugged. "I really cannot say. We have never actually discussed a date."

"I think you ought to take some time. You scarcely know him."

"I know him enough."

"Do you, though?"

"And did *you* know Mr Collins so well when you married him?"

Charlotte laid her hand over Elizabeth's, a pacifying gesture that was mightily exasperating. "No, I did not. But that was a different circumstance. I was not ill or addled—"

Elizabeth fought the urge to yank her hand away. "And neither am I," she shot back.

"Yes, you are, and I think it would be foolish of you to bind yourself to someone you cannot remember half the time!"

"Is this because he is so wealthy?"

Charlotte looked as if she had been slapped. "Of course not. I am satisfied with my own choices and only wish to see that you do not regret yours."

"Why should I regret being married to a handsome, charming gentleman who seems, in every way, to suit me?"

"That is often the trouble with regrets—they are unanticipated. I just think you ought to take your time and not be rushing off to London and rushing into marriage."

"I thank you for your advice." Elizabeth rose to her feet. Tears threatened, but she hoped to restrain them. "Pray, summon me when Dr Hughes arrives."

"Ate up with jealousy," Mrs Bennet pronounced minutes later.

"I cannot think that is true," Elizabeth replied. It was not generally her custom to go to her mother when she was distressed, but Mrs Bennet had come upon her while she wept angry tears in her bedchamber and demanded explanation.

"Lizzy, Mr Darcy is a very great man. Charlotte will not be the first to show jealousy towards you for securing him."

"But she seemed to think it foolish of me to move ahead with wedding plans and the like." Elizabeth sighed and wiped her eyes. "I suppose if nothing else I ought to get Papa's permission before too much else happens. You have said nothing of any of this to him?"

"It is Mr Darcy's place to go to your father, not mine." Mrs Bennet sniffed. "But yes, I daresay it would be the right thing. Have your father sign the articles and whatnot. But…I have had more reasons than only that to keep the news from our neighbours."

"What do you mean?"

"I confess that I have had some concern," said Mrs Bennet carefully, "that he might not remain true."

"You thought he might jilt me?" Elizabeth threw up her hands. "Does Charlotte think so too?"

"I do not think it *now*," said Mrs Bennet. "I only feared what might happen, in the beginning, when you were not yourself. I merely asked Charlotte to not write to her mother about it because you know how that is. I declare there is no woman I know with less to do with her time than Lady Lucas. She would see you ruined—"

"Then you did think he might throw me over," Elizabeth concluded angrily.

"No, no," said Mrs Bennet. "But I have seen these things go off for far less reason than…" She made a swirling gesture encompassing Elizabeth's head.

"I am not mad, Mama, nor am I suddenly an imbecile."

"I know, and Mr Darcy does as well. And I confess, no matter how often I have tested him—"

"Tested him!"

"Talking of wedding plans. I thought, if he is going to jilt my girl, let him understand her family has expectations of him. But he has not seemed in any way bothered; indeed, he seems quite willing to make plans." Mrs Bennet giggled girlishly and then said, "Oh my dear Lizzy, how great you will be! The carriages you shall have, the pin money!"

"But do you think he loves me?"

"Anyone with eyes in their head can see that the pair of you are exceedingly well matched."

"Do you think so because of these last weeks? Or did you suspect something in Hertfordshire as well?"

Mrs Bennet pursed her lips, seeming to consider that. Then, very assuredly, she said, "I have known it since the very beginning!"

"The very beginning? Was that not the assembly where he insulted us all by refusing the introduction?"

Mrs Bennet waved that aside. "The next time, then. No one cares about that silly assembly nonsense! The point is that he showed you clear preference in Hertfordshire—you were the only lady he asked to dance at Mr Bingley's ball, you know."

"So I have heard. And yet, did not Mr Collins propose to me the very next day? How did *he* not see it?"

"In case you have not noticed, my dear…" Mrs Bennet made a great show of looking round the room, even though they were in Elizabeth's guest bedroom with the door securely closed. "Mr Collins is an idiot."

Elizabeth giggled, delighted by her mother's irreverent jest. She could not be easy knowing that everyone around them was just watching to see them falter, but she supposed it must be some relief to know that her attachment to Darcy was not the work of a moment. She knew him well enough, and he was proving true to her. She just did not remember it all very well. *Hang Charlotte and her opinions!*

It was a surprise to Darcy to find Dr Hughes in the parsonage when he called and still greater a surprise to find the ladies making plans to depart for London. Not an unwelcome surprise, for he would far rather be in London than to spend more time in Kent. Pleasant images of walking in the park with Elizabeth, showing her Darcy House, introducing her to Georgiana, quite carried him away. He stood at the parlour window, gazing out and allowing such happy notions to carry him away right up until Elizabeth entered the room, clear evidence of tear stains on her face.

"Darling, what is it?" he asked, the endearment slipping easily from his lips.

"Nothing. I am only tired of being ill—or rather being treated as though I were ill or mad or a child or…or anything like that." Elizabeth sighed heavily and then, without pause, thrust herself into his arms. She laid her head against his chest and fell silent.

He had carefully eschewed such forms of physical contact with her, not wishing to do anything that would constitute taking liberties, not wanting to provoke his own desires, which were scarcely containable as it was. *But she did this,* he reminded himself. *Not I.* Even as he thought it, he allowed one hand to slowly rub her back.

No different from the way I would soothe Georgiana. Then again, Georgiana is my relation. I would certainly not have caressed Elizabeth in this way a month ago. But it is still innocent. I am not kissing her, am I? I am not so much a libertine as that.

I must tell her. I must! Surely by now—he inhaled deeply, drawing in the sweet warmth of her—*surely by now it will not signify? She sees now how I love her, how I respect her friends and family.* She had laughed off his insult of her. Could not she also laugh at his dreadfully rendered proposal?

The sounds of Mrs Bennet bidding farewell to the physician pulled him reluctantly from his thoughts. "Excuse me," he murmured into her hair. "I must speak to Dr Hughes."

Elizabeth scoffed as she stepped away from him. "If you wrote down everything that man knows about medicine, you would still have two-thirds of the page left."

He chuckled as he hurried from the room and down the hall to the front door. "Dr Hughes? A word, please." Darcy strode rapidly towards the man, who had been about to enter his carriage.

"What may I do for you, Mr Darcy?" Dr Hughes stepped back from his carriage, turning towards him.

"Um." Having gained the man's attention, Darcy faltered,

unsure how best to say what he wished to say. "You mentioned before that any shocks to Miss Bennet were to be avoided."

The physician nodded gravely, then said, "I still do, most assuredly. Let us not shout halloo before we leave the woods, sir."

Darcy furrowed his brow. "I have not the pleasure of understanding you."

"I mean to say that Miss Bennet is not wholly out of danger just yet."

"Do you think her well enough to travel?"

He sighed reluctantly. "She insists that she is, and her mother does not gainsay her. I cannot like these fits she seems to have."

"Fits?" Darcy's brow wrinkled. "How do you mean?"

"Laughing one moment, crying the next, restiveness. Excessively fearful of even the most commonplace treatments."

"The leeches?" Darcy's brow rose. "I do not think any gently bred lady greets the notion of leeches with equanimity."

Dr Hughes inclined his head, conceding the point. "Be that as it may…I presume Miss Bennet was previously a sensible girl? Even-tempered?"

"Of course."

"So these fits of ill-humour, bursts of tears or laughter… Uncommon, yes?"

"I do not think she is behaving in a manner inconsistent with the trial she is facing," Darcy said. He had a suspicion that it was Mr Collins who reported that Elizabeth had 'fits'.

The man seemed to see a storm in every raindrop. "It is grievous indeed to feel yourself out of your wits, particularly for someone so clever."

"Exactly," Dr Hughes said warmly, to Darcy's bemusement. "She is not yet herself, correct?"

"No, not yet."

"Precisely." Dr Hughes splayed his fingers across his waistcoat, no doubt imagining himself professorial. "Mr Darcy, a woman's mind is not like a man's. Her thoughts and feelings are…entwined in a manner that we may not wholly comprehend. But what I do know is that Miss Bennet is…at something of a crossroads. One path leads to health. The other may lead to hysteria, even madness. That road is one we wish to avoid, clearly."

"I think that is coming it strong," Darcy said with a frown.

"I hope it is," Dr Hughes said, again surprising him by agreeing. "But that is a physician's task, sir, to not only heal that which is ill, but to prevent potential illness ahead. I only want to see Miss Bennet restored to her former equanimity, as I am sure you do as well."

To this Darcy had to nod.

"Was there something in particular you were concerned might shock her?" Dr Hughes drummed the fingers that still rested on his waistcoat, looking as though he meant to get some sort of confession from Darcy.

Wary, Darcy asked, "Nothing very particular, no."

Giving Darcy a piercing look, the doctor said, "I understand that you and the young lady are engaged. When is the happy day?"

"We had not yet determined—"

"You do not mean to jilt her, surely?"

"Good Lord!" Darcy exclaimed. "Of course not. Miss Bennet may name any day she chooses, as soon as she is well enough, and I shall be at the altar posthaste."

Dr Hughes nodded. "Good, good. All this talk of shocks and concerns for her wits… She is a lovely young woman. I should not like to see her health endangered for the vagaries of a man."

"You need have no concern there," Darcy replied stiffly. "I would marry her yet today if it were possible."

Dr Hughes smiled blandly. "I wish you the best, sir. And do not fear—she will be the lady you once knew soon enough, I am sure of it."

CHAPTER ELEVEN

MILES OF GOOD ROAD

To Elizabeth's further relief, Charlotte did not let their quarrel stand. She came to her immediately after Darcy left, apologising and explaining it was merely disappointment at imagining them gone so soon.

"You cannot know how much I have enjoyed you being here," she told Elizabeth. "I suppose I had it in my head that you would remain all summer, which is silly. Of course you would not wish to be away from home so long, wedding or not."

Elizabeth had imagined it would require some days to arrange travel; it was what she was accustomed to, time spent considering post chaise schedules and when this man or that could retrieve them from here or there. How easy it was to merely climb into Darcy's very luxurious carriage and wait to arrive on Gracechurch Street!

"I assure you that your wealth is not why I wish to marry

you," Elizabeth teased Darcy as the carriage rolled away from the parsonage, "but to travel with such ease, such comfort— that is well worth marrying a man for!"

It was just above thirty miles to London, according to Darcy, and his horses could do it in about four hours—in usual circumstances. "We will go slower than usual," he told her. "I do not wish for you to be rattled and jostled about."

It would prove a punishment to him, for evidently Mrs Bennet felt it would be an ideal use of the time to discuss each and every detail of their forthcoming wedding, from the sort of lace on Elizabeth's gown to what foods would be served at the breakfast. Elizabeth knew not how Darcy felt about it, but for herself, the sound of her mother's voice rapidly produced a headache. When her legs began to ache as well, she could bear the noise of it no more and begged her mother to stop.

"My father has not yet given his consent, Mama. We ought to at least allow him that before we present him with a bill for lace."

She hoped it would be a matter Darcy attended to forth-with, once they were returned to town. She wondered that he had not written to Mr Bennet or done something of that sort, but she trusted that he would have his reasons and that they were good ones.

Mrs Bennet gave Darcy an odd, penetrating look that Elizabeth wondered about, then quickly turned the subject to something more pointed: Mr Bingley's strange behaviour. She did not care that Darcy had not seen his friend in above two months; she was sure that he would know Mr Bingley's intentions for Netherfield—and for Jane.

"He and Jane were so well-suited! And now with you marrying Lizzy... What could be finer than two friends married to sisters?"

"Nothing at all, madam, but I am not certain Bingley knows I proposed to Elizabeth," Darcy assured her. Elizabeth noticed signs of impatience on his countenance.

Alas, mention of his proposal returned the conversation to the wedding. It was thus with great relief that Elizabeth recognised the familiar sights and sounds of Cheapside and knew Gracechurch Street was near. Inasmuch as she was delighted to arrive at the Gardiners' residence, she noticed that Darcy appeared to withdraw into himself a little, appearing uneasy. *Is Cheapside so distressing to him? Is it because my uncle is a man of occupation?*

He glanced up and down the street as he helped her and her mother out of the carriage, saying nothing as the door to the Gardiners' grand home opened, and Mrs Gardiner exited hard on the heels of her housekeeper.

"Oh, my dear Lizzy! You cannot know how I have worried about you!"

Concerns for Darcy were lost in the wash of her dear aunt's affection, followed rapidly by the appearance of her little cousins, Elspeth and Grace with little Henry toddling unsteadily out behind them.

"Did you catch the snake?" Grace enquired immediately. "Or did someone shoot it?"

"Shoot a snake!" Mrs Bennet threw her hands up. "What a notion!"

Elizabeth laughed. "No, no one shot it, and I do not think anyone caught it." Tweaking the girl's button nose, she said,

"I was too busy almost dying to ask about the snake, but in fairness, I must have intruded upon his home. He was only defending himself."

"They have been eager to know the fate of the snake since the moment they learnt our Lizzy had been injured," Mrs Gardiner explained. "But let us not stand here on the street! Come in, come in!"

Darcy had moved to the back of his carriage, ostensibly overseeing the footmen who were removing the trunks. When he perceived Elizabeth looking at him, he came near and said, for Elizabeth's ears only, "Pray expect a note from my sister tomorrow or the next day. She will be eager to meet you. I shall send my carriage to bring you to Mayfair."

He did not seem to wish for an introduction to Mrs Gardiner; indeed, he glanced at her only briefly before turning his gaze. Mrs Gardiner stood a beat too long, looking expectant, but she was too well-mannered to allow an awkward moment to continue. She quickly turned to move the children back inside, and to link arms with Mrs Bennet and guide her along behind them.

Elizabeth knew that her emotions had been somewhat mercurial since her illness, yet the surge of dismay that brought a lump to her throat seemed warranted. "I daresay my aunt's carriage will do well enough for the journey."

"As you wish," he said and appeared about to say more but then did not. With a small bow, he entered his carriage again and left.

Elizabeth followed behind her aunt and mother, more than a little bewildered by his odd change in demeanour. She said nothing more of the scene to Mrs Gardiner. There was much to do, settling into rooms and refreshing themselves, then arguing over whether Elizabeth was strong enough to be in the drawing room as opposed to her bedchamber. Elizabeth adamantly believed she would do perfectly well without a nap, but her aunt ultimately prevailed, insisting that she lie down for a short time.

When Elizabeth descended into the drawing room an hour later, Mrs Gardiner was alone. "Ah, Lizzy," she said on seeing her niece. "You do look better. You were so very pale when you stepped out of the carriage!"

"Was I?" Elizabeth laughed lightly as she took a seat in the chair next to her aunt. "I confess the trip was more difficult than I imagined it would be, despite Mr Darcy's efforts to make me comfortable."

"How surprised I was when your mother wrote and told me the happy news!" Mrs Gardiner nodded to the housekeeper who had just entered with tea. "And even more surprised when she told me I must say nothing of it to anyone."

"Certainly you could have been no more surprised than I was to wake from the worst of my illness to learn the happy news myself."

"He must have improved on further acquaintance," Mrs Gardiner said with a knowing smile as she handed Elizabeth her cup.

"What do you mean?"

"Oh! Only that...well, I had the impression that...but never mind that. You are engaged! When do you think you will marry?"

"What impression did you have?" Elizabeth urged,

leaning forwards. "Aunt, I cannot tell you how…dismaying it is to have been ill as I have and suddenly find myself engaged to a stranger!"

"You have nothing to fear on that account. He comes from an excellent family. His father was all that was good, and I am sure the son cannot be too far from his principles," Mrs Gardiner replied. "You do know Pemberley is quite near Lambton?"

"The town where you grew up?"

Mrs Gardiner nodded. "Obviously we did not move in the Darcy's circle, but the region owed its prosperity to the family."

"I was a little taken aback by his behaviour outside. To my knowledge, he has not generally been so…" 'Proud' was what she wished to say but waited instead for her aunt to draw her own conclusion.

"It is the way of the world," said Mrs Gardiner. "He is very high, my dear, and you will be too once you are married to him."

Elizabeth nibbled on her lip while she considered that.

"In fact," Mrs Gardiner said tentatively, "you might wish to…well, he may have some strictures on time that we spend together. I do not doubt, seeing him today, that he might well wish to forget you have relations in trade."

"You are not merely relations in trade," Elizabeth retorted staunchly. "You are the dearest people in the world to me, and surely the gentleman who has spent a month utterly devoted to my care would not wish to make me unhappy?"

"I should think not," Mrs Gardiner said, reaching out to give Elizabeth's hand a conciliatory squeeze.

"Likely he was only tired from the travel and wished to be home."

"Very likely indeed," Mrs Gardiner agreed, although her eyes did not speak the same.

CHAPTER TWELVE

DARCY'S FAMILY CONNEXIONS

The morning following their arrival, Miss Darcy sent a note to Gracechurch Street, inviting Elizabeth to call on her at Darcy House in Grosvenor Square the next day. Elizabeth felt a short pulse of trepidation on seeing it; everything about it announced wealth, from the thickness of the paper to the evenness of the ink and the fine penmanship. *I hope she likes me,* she thought anxiously. *What if she is the sort of sister who cannot bear to share her brother's attention? What if she has no wish to cede her position as lady of the house?*

Elizabeth did all she could to rest herself that day, not wishing to appear ill and wan before her soon-to-be sister. Unfortunately, she did not have a good night's sleep—she was far too anxious for that—and awoke in the morning feeling grainy-eyed and tired. *Nothing for it now,* she decided as Mrs Gardiner's maid, Norris, finished arranging her hair.

Darcy had sent his carriage and one of his maids to escort her to his home, despite the fact that Elizabeth had told him the Gardiners' carriage would do. It was a fine conveyance and very comfortable; the maid, Sally, was sweet, and although apparently very curious about her, certainly knew her place.

A short time later, Elizabeth alit from the carriage in front of an undeniably impressive town house in Mayfair and paused. Darcy's house was very wide, much wider than the ones it was situated beside, and seemed somehow taller as well. There were symmetrically placed arched windows and elaborate wrought iron balconies. The neighbourhood had a sort of genteel hush to it with trees and green spaces that belied the fact one was *not* in the country. Even the air smelt better here; she supposed with the park to the west of them, the breeze was more refreshing.

Looking at the grand edifice before her, Elizabeth immediately felt shabby, even if she was dressed in her finest day gown. *Ladies of the* ton *have day gowns that far surpass my best ball gown,* she reminded herself. *I cannot compete with them, and evidently I do not have to. Darcy likes me in my country attire.*

"This way, miss," said the maid and escorted her into the vestibule where a housekeeper awaited them.

"Miss Bennet?" the lady said with what seemed to be a smile of genuine warmth. "I am Mrs Hobbs, the Darcy's housekeeper. Mr Darcy has asked me to bring you to the parlour, if you will come with me. Sally, you may go."

Elizabeth followed the woman down the hall, their steps ringing loud on the marble floor. It could not be denied that this was a home of someone wealthy—the thick rugs, gilt frames on portraiture, and sheer size of the place informed her of that—and she found herself a bit awestruck. Surely she, little Lizzy Bennet from Longbourn Village, could not become the lady of the house for such a place as this!

Outside the parlour, a young footman sprang into action to open the door for them, after which Mrs Hobbs said, "I shall go and retrieve the refreshments Mr Darcy wished for."

"Thank you," Elizabeth told her and entered the room.

She had expected Darcy would be there to meet her; instead, an impeccably garbed man with golden hair and an imperious air stood by the mantel. He locked his gaze upon hers instantly, and before she could react, he strode across the room, crying out, "My darling!"

He was nearly bent in half as he bowed to her, raising her hand to his lips to kiss reverently. "Come, let us sit. It has been an age I have stood here awaiting you! Did those coachmen drive you all over London?"

As he led her across the room towards the fireplace, she managed to say, "N-no, sir, but I, ah—"

"Sit," he urged, having arrived at a cream-coloured sofa. When she had, he took a seat so close to her, their thighs nearly touched. He then grabbed both of her hands in his own. With a warmth that bespoke an acquaintance of the most intimate sort, he said, "They said you lost your memory, but I knew it could not mean you forgot *me*, or *us*."

What? Elizabeth felt her heart constrict painfully. "Um, sir, I fear there has been—"

"If you tell me you have forgotten me, I shall die. By my own hand! I promise you!" His deep blue eyes bored into hers. "Darling, sweet Elizabeth, do you not know what these last weeks have done to me? I have been tormented, terrified that all of our plans—"

"Our plans?" Beginning to feel a little panicky, Elizabeth attempted to pull back her hands. "Sir, th-there has been some mistake."

"Are you trying to tell me you no longer love me?" He squeezed tighter. "Pray do not say it!"

Elizabeth's heart thudded as she prayed, desperately, for some sort of escape. "I...I cannot recall—"

"You and I have shared something that no one else could ever—"

There was a clicking sound as the door opened to reveal Darcy. He strode into the room, pausing to look at Elizabeth and the man on the sofa. Elizabeth stared at him, hoping he would comprehend her wordless plea for assistance. His gaze immediately narrowed on the man beside her, and he finished traversing the room with quick paces.

He gave the man a fierce scowl. "Saye, what nonsense is this?"

The man, Saye, released her hands and met Darcy's gaze. Then he burst into loud laughter and pointed one elegant finger at Elizabeth. "You should see your face! You look positively appalled!" he crowed to Elizabeth, as she sagged with relief, one hand pressed to her chest as if it might help slow the rapid thudding of her heart.

"Absolutely unforgivable," Darcy hissed at him. "And I do not even know what precisely you have done."

"She has to forgive me, for evidently we are to be family," the blond man replied cheerfully. "Cousins! I am from the Fitzwilliam side, Lord Saye...you may call me Saye."

"Th-thank you?" Elizabeth replied uncertainly.

"What did he do to you?" Darcy asked her. "Do you need a glass of wine? You do look very distressed."

"No, I am not distressed," she said and tried to smile. Alas tears, the accursed tears that seemed always at the ready, had begun to sting her eyes. They were not unnoticed by Darcy.

"I ought to knock you into Thursday next." Darcy had gone pale with anger, and he glared at his cousin. "Move away from her and tell me what you have done."

With a sigh, Saye moved to a chair across from her. "I pretended she and I were in love. I thought it should be wildly amusing if she believed that she and I had had some hidden tryst to conceal from you."

"You are going to pay for this, Saye." Darcy's fists were clenched by his side, and he ground his words from between gritted teeth. It would have made Elizabeth smile had she not been on the verge of stupid, silly tears. She turned her head away, knowing her eyes were shiny and hating appearing to be one of those ladies who wept at the least provocation.

"You are not going to cry about it, are you?" asked Saye. Half-rising from the chair, he extended his handkerchief into the space between them.

Darcy reached down and knocked it from his hand, then handed Elizabeth his own as he took a seat beside her.

"No, no, I am not crying," Elizabeth assured them, dabbing at her eyes. "It is only…well, I suppose my illness has left me a bit…half-witted—"

"If there is a half-wit here, he is sitting across from us." Darcy took Elizabeth's hand very tenderly, but his words were anything but tender as he said to his cousin. "You are despicable, Saye."

"It is not so distressing as all that, I assure you. I enjoy a joke, I do!"

"You have never even met him before," Darcy explained gently, "and likely wish not to know him now."

"Not know me?" Saye exclaimed with indignation. Then to Elizabeth he said, "You *will* wish to know me. I am the fun cousin."

"I am certain you are," she told him, relieved that the tears had stopped. She sniffed a bit to clear her nose.

"Do you hear that, Saye? She is crying. Not five minutes since she met you and she is reduced to tears."

"It was a joke! Miss Bennet, I throw myself upon your mercy!" Saye cried out theatrically, though he remained very much at ease, lolling comfortably in the chair he had tossed himself into. "I shall offer myself to do a penance. What would you like?"

"Revenge," Darcy inserted. "Something painful, preferably. She is yet unwell, Saye, and you made a mockery of her. Nothing short of a public dressing down will do."

"Dressing down?" Saye looked up at Darcy with one brow raised. "You mean like nudity? I am not opposed, but one must await the proper audience."

At this, Elizabeth burst out laughing, even as part of her marvelled at the capriciousness of her spirits. One minute crying, the next laughing...would it ever end?

"See there? Now she laughs." Saye gave Darcy a smug grin. "Miss Bennet, my fate lies in your hands. Shall I dash naked around Grosvenor Square for you? Drop my breeches at Almack's?"

"None of that will do, because you would enjoy it too much," Darcy replied grimly. "Elizabeth will think of something suitable, I am sure."

A fraction of a second too late, Elizabeth roused her spirits enough to reply, with a smile, "Of course, all the best revenge involves things unexpected and sorely anticipated."

"Ah-ha!" Saye nodded with approval. "I like your girl, Darcy. She will do very well."

The door again clicked open then, and Elizabeth looked up to see a girl, very finely dressed, about Lydia's or Kitty's age, standing there with an uncertain smile on her face. Elizabeth smiled at her, and she came to where they all sat. Elizabeth rose and the gentlemen rose with her, Darcy's introduction confirming that this was his young sister, Georgiana.

Georgiana Darcy was shy but sweet, and Elizabeth liked her immediately. She had imagined that for a girl with such a fortune, and such connexions, she would feel superior to a young lady from the country who had an obvious lack of such things. Instead, the opposite appeared to be true; Georgiana appeared almost desperate to please Elizabeth, starting with the light repast she served them all: fresh fruits of every variety and in vast quantity.

"What is this?" Saye looked at the spread of fruits in front of him with undisguised horror. "Are we meant to starve?"

Georgiana blushed scarlet but managed to say, "There is bread right there, Saye. I remember my brother writing from

Netherfield last year and mentioning, Miss Bennet, that you do not eat meat during the day?"

"Good Lord! Only fruit? Is it some sort of religious conviction?" Saye asked, turning his dismay towards Elizabeth.

She had already taken a large bite of a strawberry and so could not immediately reply. Instead, she was treated to the sight of Darcy himself blushing.

"I only ever saw you eat fresh fruit during the day while your sister was ill," he explained hastily. "I think I might have thought—"

"I had been having some trouble with spots," Georgiana inserted. "He said that you had a flawless complexion and that your hair shone with good health and said he felt it might be due to your diet in which you ate only fruit in the day."

"Indeed?" Saye had gone from scornful to interested. "I once heard an excess of fruit leads to ruddy hues. Something about an imbalance of blood. But what has it done to your hair? I am excessively worried about hair loss. I should rather be dead than bald."

Elizabeth had finally swallowed her strawberry. "As I have no recollection of my time at Netherfield, I really cannot say why I ate only fruit during the day. I do like fruit, and my mother does not often serve it, save in jams or stewed preparations, so I might have been indulging only because it was uncommon to me. But this is all quite wonderful, and I thank you both for considering my tastes."

She gave both Georgiana and Darcy warm smiles; Georgiana smiled in reply, and Darcy gave her a look which caused her heart to flutter.

"Yes, yes, we are all charming people. But I daresay our new cousin may have a point about this fruit business. It is decided! Only fruit, all day," Saye declared.

"I cannot boast to following an all-fruit diet, sir," Elizabeth explained.

"But you *do* seem to have a great deal of hair," he replied. "How long have you adhered to this diet?"

Smothering a grin, Elizabeth said, "I do not maintain an all-fruit diet, but if one had to, well, I suppose it would need to be life long."

"Oh yes," Darcy said gravely. "It would need to be a permanent change else the hair would immediately begin to fall out again."

Saye winced, then asked, "What about wine? Is wine a fruit? Is brandy fruit?"

Elizabeth pressed her lips together to hide her smile as Darcy told his cousin not to be a numbskull and that obviously brandy was not fruit.

"Actually," Georgiana offered, "I do believe it is made from fruit. Fermented or something like that?"

"A-ha!" Saye cried out. "Now who is the numbskull, Darcy? I believe 'tis you! But very well! This seems a plan I can adhere to!"

AS SHE PREPARED FOR BED THAT EVENING, Elizabeth gave the day, particularly her time at Darcy House, more consideration. Saye, for all his eccentricity, was amusing, and Georgiana was delightful. Elizabeth had liked her very well and had to admire Darcy for her upbringing. His sister had obviously been well cared-for, no matter her youthful missteps, right down to seeking advice from her brother when she feared her skin had got spotty. It was sweet.

His diligence in caring for others is one of the things I love best about him, she mused and then stopped herself. Did she love him? Was she in love? *Do you really need to ask yourself such a silly question?*

Even in her younger days, Elizabeth was not so foolish as to have expected some grand romance in her life. Kitty and Lydia always went about swearing how their husbands would be passionate lovers, but she and Jane understood their position in life too well to spout such nonsense. An admirable man, one who did not lie or cheat or steal, run them into debt, hit them or their children, and who provided a reasonable living would do well enough.

Except that I seem to have done a great deal better for myself. She knew that, despite her practicality, she would not have accepted Darcy merely because he was wealthy. She closed her eyes, thinking of him. He was so undeniably handsome, so very tall, and with such a commanding air about him. His character was unimpeachable and yes, his wealth was an inducement as well. Not that she needed fine gowns and jewels, but she should be a fool to deny that she would enjoy them. What lady would not?

Saye had teased her about it a little, earlier in the day. "You do know how rich he is, hm?"

"He is?" she had exclaimed with mocking surprise. "I thought everyone in London lived in such a house as this."

"This?" Saye gave a dismissive flick of his hand. "This is nothing to Pemberley. I daresay this entire place would fit neatly into Pemberley's drawing room."

Elizabeth had noticed that Darcy did not disclaim his cousin's teasing. At least she hoped Saye had been teasing. To imagine herself mistress of such an estate! She hardly knew if she was equal to such a thing.

Darcy was far beyond any man she had ever dared to dream of, and on top of all the material comforts he offered her, he loved her. That much she knew—that he truly did love her.

She thought about the way he was always on her mind, the way sunshine seemed to erupt within her whenever she beheld him...the way she longed, almost painfully, to be kissed and held by him.

Because I love him. The thought settled on her like a soft blanket. *I do. I love him.*

Not that she had ever told him. Or at least not at a time that resided within her memory. Sudden dismay struck her. Perhaps she had told him so regularly before her injury and then not at all since. Was the poor man suffering under the belief that she no longer cared for him as she once had? What grief would come from losing someone's love in such a way! She could not imagine the pain she might feel if it were the other way round, if he was injured and sustained the loss of all memory...including his memories of *her*. She had not before considered that pain, but doing so now felt like an agony.

Perhaps that is why he never kissed me? Because he did not know my feelings? The thought sank her. Poor, dear man, pained by the weight of uncertainty, thinking he might have lost her love to the bite of a snake! And yet how good of him to behave so honourably when so many times he might have kissed her with not only her acquiescence, but her encouragement!

I should write him a letter. A love letter. The thought made her cringe with humiliation, terrified her, and electrified her all at once. It was an excellent notion, a love letter to assuage whatever griefs and fears her injury must have caused him. She would do it tomorrow.

CHAPTER THIRTEEN

MR BINGLEY CALLS AT GRACECHURCH STREET

The writing of a love letter proved far more difficult than Elizabeth had imagined it would be. Even the salutation was cause for debate. Should she write 'my dearest' or 'my darling'? Call him Fitzwilliam? Darcy? Or —heaven forbid—Fitz?

She was still at the escritoire, with scarcely a sentence she liked written, when a caller for her was announced. 'Mr Charles Bingley,' she read from the card and closed her eyes briefly, glad he had called while her mother was out shopping. Elizabeth wondered how much he knew of her affliction and whether he was the sort to be offended by being forgot.

She need not have worried. She knew within moments of his entry into her aunt's drawing room that Mr Bingley would be hard-pressed to be offended by anything. He greeted her warmly, then chastised himself for the familiarity he impressed upon her.

"I understand," he said as they sat, "that you have not much recollection of…well, any of our acquaintance!"

"None at all, in fact," Elizabeth told him with a smile. "About nine or ten months has gone missing from my memory, and I am afraid you and—your sisters, I believe it was?—arrived squarely in the midst of those months."

"I do hope I hold up under a second first impression," he said jovially. "What an unfortunate thing it would be if you decided I was not worth knowing, for I daresay we were friends before all this!"

Mr Bingley was well worth knowing, Elizabeth decided very quickly. He was amiable and kind and had nothing of the pretensions she despised in most wealthy young gentlemen. He was exceedingly charming to Mrs Gardiner, causing her to blush in reply to his effusive compliments to her home and even to the little girls who could not resist the urge to peep in at them.

It was into all of this agreeability that Mrs Bennet intruded, having returned from the warehouses. "Mr Bingley! Why, how very good of you to call upon our poor dear Lizzy!" She bustled in, chastising Elizabeth for not serving him her uncle's port.

"Coffee does very well for me, ma'am," he said with a laugh. His complexion had turned ruddy at the sight of her mother, and Elizabeth hoped it did not mean that Mrs Bennet had a history of embarrassing the gentleman. Or that she might do so now.

"I understand you have decided to purchase Netherfield Park. You must sorely miss it after all these months you stayed away," Mrs Bennet said. "A fine, fine home! When shall you be in residence there?"

"Ah…yes. Yes, I did. And we expect to reside there very soon."

Mrs Bennet cried out as if the raptures of such a statement could not be constrained by words or syllables. But Elizabeth observed the gentleman closely, and although she could see his pleasure in the announcement, beneath it was discomfort.

"The neighbourhood will be very glad to have you there," she said.

"I hope they will," he said very slowly, looking down into his coffee cup. "My…wife and I should depend upon it."

Mrs Bennet's effusions were cut off mid-syllable, and she only stared at him.

Elizabeth very delicately enquired, "Are you married, sir?"

"I shall be soon," he said, with an awkward look towards her mother. "Another month."

Mrs Bennet's lips were pressed into a thin, hard line, but she remained blessedly silent. Hurriedly, Elizabeth congratulated him.

"Thank you," he said, then lowered his gaze to stare at his shoes. "You are too good."

With nothing further said, Mrs Bennet rose from her chair. She did not bid Mr Bingley farewell, nor did she make any excuses, but merely swept from the room with the air of a duchess, pulling the door closed behind her with a loud bang. Mr Bingley again hung his head.

"Forgive her," Elizabeth said quickly. "She…she had her own hopes, of course, based on those of my sister. But it cannot signify. You have followed your heart, and it was not for Jane. We can hardly wish you ill for that, nor will any of our neighbours."

"You say so because you do not recollect how I abandoned her." Mr Bingley raised his head, and Elizabeth was struck by the torment in his eyes.

"Did you? And just when I was forming a new opinion of you being such an amiable fellow." She said it lightly, not wishing to censure him too much but, as ever, loyal to Jane.

He ran his hand through his hair and sighed heavily. "I…I was in love with your sister. I believe it was from the first night I ever saw her. We were like two halves of a whole, finally united. I could scarcely believe my good fortune—I had very nearly leased a house in Derbyshire! I might never have known her!"

"From my understanding, Jane felt likewise for you." Elizabeth cleared her throat. "It all seems very promising. How did it go so sadly awry?"

He repeated his gesture from before, running his hand through his hair. "I returned to London after having given a ball. My sisters and Darcy were meant to remain; I had only an appointment with an architect—for Netherfield!—and I had a notion for surprising Darcy and bringing Miss Darcy back with me. Imagine my surprise when I called at Darcy House and there was Darcy, telling me that my sisters were in Grosvenor Street. Darcy told me that my sisters and Hurst would be at his house for dinner later and very nearly commanded my attendance as well. So naturally I went, only to be greeted with…well, one might call it a complete upheaval of all the happy thoughts and plans which had been in my head since meeting Jane...um, Miss Bennet, that is."

In surprise, Elizabeth said, "They spoke against Jane? Mr Darcy did as well?"

"Do understand that I hold myself fully accountable for my actions. It is no one's fault but my own," he said with an urgency that spoke to the truth.

"But you were persuaded against her," Elizabeth said flatly. "By Mr Darcy?"

"Understand I do not wish to injure you or your charming family. They were so warm, so welcoming to us all!" Mr Bingley sighed heavily. "My sisters wished for me to make a match with a lady of...well, someone who boasted...um... something on the order of—"

"Fortune? Connexions?"

"Yes," Mr Bingley said. "Forgive me, I ought not to speak so."

"Do not think of it, sir. I am well aware of the modesty of my circumstances, and your sisters would not be the first to wish their brother to marry in an exalted way," Elizabeth reassured him.

"I did not give a fig for any of that. I am wealthy enough to marry where I like, and I was in love! Nothing else was of any concern," he exclaimed. "But then...but then Darcy said he did not believe she loved me. He believed she only tolerated my attentions."

"What?" Elizabeth shot to her feet. "That is absurd. Jane would never pretend to affections she did not truly feel!"

Mr Bingley rose too, and Elizabeth recognised, belatedly, that he was being polite. She sat again and he did likewise.

"My own inherent modesty has made me too much reliant on Darcy's opinions. You must understand that he has been, for some time now, something of an elder brother to me. One I look up to a great deal. His character is unimpeachable. You are marrying a most excellent gentleman."

Elizabeth knew not what to say about that.

"I was much affected by his judgment. I was deeply embarrassed, imagining that all of Meryton had witnessed me behaving like a mooncalf for a woman who did not love me. That embarrassment was what kept me away when I ought to have gone back and seen for myself how it was. A terrible, terrible mistake which I then compounded with another."

"Which was?"

"To propose marriage to the first lady of good fortune and family who looked my way," he said, his unhappiness with the arrangement obvious.

"I see," Elizabeth said gently. After a short pause, she added, "I hope you will be very happy together."

"She is my sister's friend," he replied glumly. "Or rather someone my sister hoped would be a friend. Miss Sophie Roberts. Her uncle is the duke of something or other and moves in circles with the Prince Regent. I once saw her kick a dog out of her way and…if I am being honest, if someone kicked one of my dogs, I…I do not know. How does one behave so despicably?"

Elizabeth had no idea what to say and only made a small sympathetic noise.

He rubbed his eyes roughly. "But pray do not think ill of

Darcy. His intentions were good if misplaced. Darcy is like that, always wanting to take care of people."

"I have seen a great deal of that for myself this past month."

"I have no one to blame but myself. Your mother, your family…if they despise me, I have earned it."

"Once I am married, I shall make it my first object to see my sister settled too," Elizabeth said, trying for cheer. "The neighbourhood will surely hold nothing against you then."

She had meant to be humorous, but it was the wrong thing to say. Mr Bingley gave her a look of pure agony. "I had not thought of that," he said bleakly. "The notion of Jane…of attending her wedding…"

He groaned, sounding like he was in utter despair; then he rose. "I have stayed too long and have surely made you despise me."

"I do not despise you," she said quickly. "Love…love can get twisted about sometimes. Jane will recover, and you will be happy with Miss Roberts."

"Perhaps you are right. I do truly wish every happiness to your sister. She deserves"—he swallowed—"she deserves every good thing." He bowed to her. "I thank you, Miss Elizabeth, for your kindness."

CHAPTER FOURTEEN

MR DARCY'S LETTER

Agitation kept Elizabeth from concentrating on her letter after Mr Bingley departed. Such an amiable man! Everything a gentleman ought to be! Even on so short an acquaintance, she could see how ideally suited he might have been for Jane. At length, she abandoned the effort, reasoning it would be for another day; today she would ask Mrs Gardiner for the use of her carriage and her maid. There were questions which needed answering.

"For what, Lizzy?" Mrs Gardiner enquired.

"I need to call on Mr Darcy," Elizabeth explained. "There is, um, something I must speak to him about."

Mrs Gardiner looked curious, but as Elizabeth kept her countenance neutral, she did not press for more. She granted the use of her carriage, and before too long, Elizabeth found herself on the way to Mayfair, hoping she did not presume too much to call unbidden.

She was admitted to the house by a butler whose name

escaped her. He surely knew her well enough, for he took her directly to a parlour and informed her that the master would be there posthaste. And to Darcy's credit, he was.

"This is a wonderful surprise," he said, possessing himself of her hands and squeezing them gently but warmly before releasing her.

"I hope I am not interrupting you?"

"Of course not. I was only replying to some letters from my steward, and those can wait. What can I get you? Shall I ring for tea?"

"No, I do not require anything at all." She wished, suddenly, she had thought more about just what she needed to say. Her most acute agitation had abated, a little, but she still felt all the distress of knowing her dear sister suffered.

He invited her to sit, gesturing towards a sofa nearby. Alas, Elizabeth had only just taken her seat when Mrs Hobbs intruded on them, looking mightily regretful. "Forgive me, sir, but your solicitor is here and insists he must have a few minutes with you. He promises it will not be long."

"Tell him he must wait," Darcy replied, his gaze not moving from Elizabeth.

"Oh no," Elizabeth said. "It is I who am interrupting your day. Do go to him, and I shall wait here."

Darcy grimaced and then sighed. "Five minutes, at the most."

"Of course."

Elizabeth was glad of the reprieve. Seeing him, hearing the tenderness in his accents and the amiability in his looks, it seemed impossible to imagine him speaking against Jane. Jane—who would soon be his sister as well! Elizabeth had no recollection of how things were, but she knew her sister, and Jane would never pretend to an affection she did not truly, wholly feel. It seemed Mr Bingley had been likewise attached to Jane. So why had Darcy contributed to parting them?

He was gone for longer than ten minutes. As the mantel clock inched past a quarter of an hour, Elizabeth decided to stretch her legs and take a turn about the room. On a small table next to the chair by the window, she saw a familiar sight. *Gulliver's Travels,* the book Darcy had read to her in Kent. Was it the same book? She believed it might be due to the marks on the cover. *He must have brought it back with him.*

She picked it up from the table and then sank into the chair. Happy recollections immediately arose. Their courtship, marred as it was by her illness, had been wonderful, and this small reminder of that time was a delight. She began to leaf through the pages, but a noise elsewhere in the house startled her. She dropped the book, giving a little sigh of dismay when she saw several pages slide out from within.

"Oh no!" She bent to retrieve them and was reassured to see the pages were not from the book itself but were, rather, a letter—a letter addressed to *her.* She did not yet know Darcy's hand, but it was a man's writing, firm and clever-looking, and she knew at once that it must be his.

Elizabeth smiled, feeling her cheeks grow pink with the anticipation of a love note. *Did he write a love letter to me? And perhaps forget to give it to me?* She desperately wanted to read it, although it was hard to know whether she ought to or not. He had not given it to her yet, but it was sealed and addressed to her.

At length, curiosity—and the belief of benign sweetness

within—proved too great to overcome. She unfolded the pages with a brief, guilty glance towards the door. *He will surely understand that I could not resist the temptation of reading a letter addressed to me.* Felicity turned to bewilderment, however, as the substance of it soon revealed itself to be the furthest thing from a love letter.

> *I write without any intention of paining you, or humbling myself, by dwelling on wishes, which, for the happiness of both, cannot be too soon forgotten…*

> *Here again I shall give you pain—to what degree you only can tell. But whatever may be the sentiments which Mr Wickham has created, a suspicion of their nature shall not prevent me from unfolding his real character…*

> *If your abhorrence of me should make my assertions valueless…*

Abhorrence of him? Elizabeth looked up, staring into the expanse of the room. *What is this about?*

Her brow furrowed as she returned her gaze to the letter. Staring at it did not make it yield greater sense. It was addressed from Rosings Park, dated from the morning of her accident—which he had told her happened the very morning after he proposed to her.

It was certainly not any note between lovers. An astonishing spirit of bitterness pervaded it; he appeared to suppose that she hated him and had some sort of tender feeling for Mr Wickham. The ending of it, while charitable, sounded as if he never meant to see her again.

As she had so many times before, she searched the dark recesses of her mind, willing some remembrance of Darcy's proposal to come forth. As before, there was little to be retrieved save for five words—'ardently admire and love you'. She could still hear those words, uttered in his voice.

Those words are surely promising, she told herself. *Who knows what the rest of this nonsense is!* He had told her they had quarrelled, had he not? *This certainly seems like a great deal more than a quarrel between engaged people.*

But the feeling that she did not truly know all the circumstances around her engagement to Darcy would not be so easily set aside. Indeed, she had, too often, pushed such concerns away in the beginning of their betrothal. She had assured herself it was nothing, for he so obviously loved her that it could not signify.

But what if it did?

This letter sounds as if I was in love with that Wickham character, and Darcy and I ended by despising one another and meaning never to see one another again. Another read through the letter strengthened these suppositions...and subsequently left her even more puzzled than she had been before.

But puzzlement was not the only feeling which remained. She had, evidently, already argued with him for his actions against Jane, and he had responded in a manner she could not like.

To convince him, therefore, that he had deceived himself, was no very difficult point. To persuade him against returning into Hertfordshire, when that conviction had been given, was scarcely the work of a moment—I cannot blame myself for having done thus much.

"On this point we must disagree," she said, feeling anger

rise within her. Could not blame himself? Who, then, could he blame? It seemed very much like he had acted a principal role in the matter!

It was a form of hell to have a year of one's life gone from memory, any year, but most particularly a year in which she had met so many new people, fallen in love, agreed to marry someone. She had made a concerted effort to put aside the inconsistencies and vague shadows, reasoning that they could only drive her mad. But now the hour was upon her to ask the difficult questions. This time, she could not be distracted by his handsome face or kindly manner; she needed the *truth*.

Sitting felt odd, so she stood once again and moved a little closer to the window, looking down upon the street. It was a busy day in Mayfair, elegant carriages clattering to and fro, but they could not distract her from her dismay. She knew not how long she stood there, uncertainty twisting in her gut, before the click of the door opening informed her that he had returned.

"Forgive me, I have kept you waiting," he said. "My solicitor had several questions about—"

"I must ask you about something." Elizabeth crossed the room in rapid paces, all the while extending the letter towards him. "I was looking for something to read and came upon *Gulliver's Travels*. I dropped it, by accident, and this, these pages, came out. It is dated on the morning of my accident."

Having dropped his gaze to see the proffered pages, the smile dropped from Darcy's lips. He went utterly still and pale. Seeing him thus seemed to hollow her out. Her chest felt very tight, but she managed to add, "It was addressed to me, so I thought it was…I thought perhaps you wrote me a love letter. Alas it seems it is anything but that."

Darcy had always been, in her view, an assured man. When he spoke, on even the most inconsequential of matters, his voice carried authority, perhaps even a touch of arrogance. Thus, was it doubly alarming that he sounded so uncertain, that he looked almost ill as he said, "I can explain this."

CHAPTER FIFTEEN

THE LETTER EXPLAINED

"An explanation would be splendid," Elizabeth said, her voice quivering a little. "I think it is long overdue for me to have some sense made of any of this."

Darcy took the pages from her hand, briefly glanced at them, and then slowly folded them again. Elizabeth extended her hand, wishing to have them returned to her, and he complied. He seemed unable to meet her gaze. His pallor truly alarmed her, so she suggested, "Perhaps we ought to sit."

He did not reply, but she turned and went to a sofa. He followed and sat next to her.

"The night before my accident, you proposed to me. Yes?" she asked.

"Yes, I did." With a deep breath he said, "I told you I ardently admired and loved you and begged you to relieve my suffering and become my wife."

There was a long pause until she said, "That sounds very prettily done."

"No." He leapt to his feet and ran a hand through his hair. "No, it was not prettily done, not at all. There were other things, concerns and considerations…things which *did* merit consideration but should never have been a part of any proposal. Certainly not."

She folded her arms over her chest. "Such as a dislike for my sister."

"A dislike for…? I do not dislike your sister, any of your sisters."

"Then why did you persuade Mr Bingley to abandon her?" She held up the pages. "And apparently conceal her presence in London from him. Did it not occur to you that in marrying me, Jane would be *your* sister too?"

He walked towards the mantel, leaning one hand against it. "Elizabeth. I love you and I believe…I think you love me too. I cannot deny I have made many mistakes—"

"No!" Her voice rang out more loudly than she had intended. She modulated it but remained firm as she said, "I will not be put aside again. It is too frustrating, too distressing to be walking about feeling like the main character in a book someone else wrote. I want to know all."

"What good can that do? If our past was not always… amicable…what can it—"

"What precisely were the concerns and considerations you spoke of?" Elizabeth said sharply. "And what would provoke you to enumerate them while proposing?"

"I suppose some part of me thought that you might feel… feel the weight of distinction more keenly if you knew of the obstacles I had overcome to…to…offer…" He heaved a sigh. "The expectation for Mrs Darcy has always been a woman of wealth, of status…perhaps a lady who is titled. My mother was the daughter of an earl, as you know."

"Whereas I am the daughter of a minor landowner and a woman he raised from trade."

"And I wish I had never given the least thought to any of that, but much as it shames me to acknowledge it, I did. I spent a great deal of time last autumn discouraging any… pretensions you might have had towards me."

Elizabeth had no idea what to say to that. She could not imagine herself having *pretensions* towards any man, but perhaps she had.

Darcy turned from the mantel to look at her. "Alas the joke was on me, for what I perceived as interest on your part was merely…I know not what. Nothing. In any case, when I met you at Rosings Park, I knew I was lost. I had barely been able to remove from Hertfordshire without declaring myself madly in love with you. To see you again, by such coincidence…it felt as if Providence was telling me to throw aside all else and make you my wife. I believed you understood the nature of my intentions towards you. We had been walking the grove…you had teased me about taking the trouble to practise conversation with you—I believed it an invitation to further attentions."

Had she been pleased by his attentions? She had no idea.

"When I came to you, that night, I somehow felt that the differences between us…these matters of station and fortune, ought to be discussed." He had begun to pace, slow steps towards and away from the mantel. He did not look at

her as he said, "I also mentioned the fact that your sisters…
your mother…they can be somewhat…untamed in…in
company."

To hear him say that so plainly still stung. Yes, they had
spoken of it before and yes, she had made light of it, but
somehow, in this context, it pained her.

"You grew angry, as I did too. In fact"—he rubbed a hand
over his brow—"you were already angry with me when I
came into the room."

"Why?"

"You had learnt, earlier that day—unbeknownst to me of
course—that I…" He paced away again, looking at anything
but her, and licked his lips. "About my role in separating my
friend from your sister."

"So you admit it."

He nodded. "When did you speak to Bingley?"

"He called on me at Gracechurch Street. Evidently, he did
not think it would irreparably damage him to be civil to my
aunt and uncle."

Darcy looked down but said nothing to that.

"Jane loved him," Elizabeth said earnestly. "She loves him
still. Is my family so disgusting to you that you would make
your friend unhappy by telling him the woman he loved had
no regard for him?"

"I believed it to be true!" He paced while he explained
how he had led his friend away from Netherfield Park, and
yes, had even gone so far as to hide her sister's presence in
London, believing his friend ought not to be involved with
Jane. The pain of that made her tremble, but she could not
fully consider it, not yet.

"I truly did not think your sister's heart was touched by him. I believed that she was perhaps tolerating him in hopes of gaining a wealthy husband."

"My sister is not mercenary," she said immediately. She might have forgotten many things, but Jane's good character was still fast in her mind.

"I know. I know I was wrong, and it was presumptuous of me, who barely knew her, to make any judgment of her feelings for my friend."

"Did I think she loved him? That night, I mean."

He nodded. "Yes, you were quite certain of it. Miss Bennet was terribly distraught by his leaving, and you were pained by her continued distress, even in April."

"I am told she remains distressed now," Elizabeth said flatly. "In May. But he has found another, so there is nothing for it."

To this Darcy could only sigh heavily.

"And this Mr Wickham—from this it would seem you thought I had a tender regard for him? But you offered for me anyway? Thinking I was in love with another man?"

Again turning from her, Darcy slowly walked to the window where he leant heavily against the sill. "I...I did not think you were in love with him when I proposed. I thought so...afterwards."

"After what?"

"There are things I have done to Wickham, things you felt revealed a general cruelty in my character. You did not, at the time, know about Georgiana, or understand the truth of his nature."

"Clearly not, for surely I could not defend such a creature, certainly not to you."

"But what you *did* know was that I had behaved unkindly nearly throughout my entire stay at Netherfield. I perceived the society of Meryton to be far beneath me and did not exert myself to be friendly to any of them, including your family. Including even you."

She watched his shoulders rise and fall as he drew a deep breath. He reminded her then how he had refused to stand up with her the first night they met. "The worst of it was that I knew, quite well, that you had overheard me and yet I failed to apologise to you."

Elizabeth remembered laughing about his insult previously. Somehow it was not at all amusing now.

"You said I had a selfish disdain for the feelings of others, and you accused me of having injured your sister with regard to Bingley. In truth, the fact that I accused you of being in love with Wickham was, in itself, a slight against you, because it ignored all else that you so justly tasked me with."

She recognised that she was twisting her hands and forced them to still. She had hoped the truth would make her feel...if not better at least less confused. But she was still confused, still unable to reconcile her present reality to the brackishness of the past.

"I still cannot understand why it is that after such a row, we would somehow find ourselves engaged. And that you would write this letter to me...the ending of which seems like you would never know me again, if we were not..."

Her voice trailed off as the comprehension at last dawned. "We were never engaged."

His gaze was locked on hers for several excruciatingly long moments until at last, he shook his head and dropped his eyes. "The last thing you said to me was"—he swallowed audibly—"that I was the last man in the world you could ever be prevailed upon to marry."

She gasped, and her hand flew up to land on her chest.

"I left the parsonage that night with your rejection echoing in my ears, and heard you begin to cry as I closed the door behind me. I went back to Rosings where I spent a sleepless night writing you that letter and intended to wait for you in the grove the next morning, hoping to place it in your hands. Then I learnt you had gone missing from the parsonage, the search ensued...the next I saw of you was when I found you, unconscious."

"The last man in the world..." Elizabeth echoed him faintly. It was too difficult to grasp the meaning in it all. How thoroughly she had been deceived! How blatantly everyone had lied to her!

He crossed the room to come to her in two quick paces. "I intended to tell you, truly I did. I thought I would tell you and offer a proper proposal this time, one worthy of you—"

A piercing pain shot across Elizabeth's head. She pinched the bridge of her nose, feeling panicked confusion mount. "You were disgusted by me, appalled by my family...and then I went to Kent and all of this...this disdain for me somehow turned into tender regard?"

"No," he said immediately. "I was in love with you long before that. In truth I cannot say where or when exactly, but it certainly began in Hertfordshire, fairly early on."

"Early on? How can you say so? You left Hertfordshire,

and could not have known if or when you would see me again! You behaved so...so unfeelingly towards me and my family. You ruined Jane's chance at a future with the man she loves!"

"Elizabeth, listen to me, I beg you. For however poorly I began, I love you and wish to marry you. I have tended to your reproofs, truly I have—"

"Have you? I think not. Indeed, I would say this is an exceedingly strong example of a selfish disdain for my feelings."

He ran a hand across his face.

"I have been ill, and recovering from a grave injury, and you have taken advantage of that weakness—"

"That was *never* my intention."

"But it is nevertheless what you have done!" she cried. "For weeks now, you have allowed me to persist under the belief that I accepted your offer of marriage! You never hinted that we had this contentious—"

"I told you we argued!"

"Argued! But not months of impassioned dislike! Not an entire acquaintance stained with rancour!" The words hung in the air as Elizabeth gathered her sensibilities. "You claim you love me and yet so much of me, of what I am, is abhorrent to you, else you could not have said it in a marriage proposal. And apparently, I had equal revulsion for you—and I must say it cannot surprise me. Arrogance and pride have long been the thing I can tolerate least in a person, to say nothing of deceitfulness!"

"I cannot disagree with you," he said finally. "My actions have been...I have erred. All I can do now is throw myself upon your mercy and pray you will permit us a new beginning."

Her insides shook as she beheld him, so handsome and yet capable of such cruelty towards all those she loved and yes, even towards her. Mercy? Where was his mercy when she was addled and sick and wholly dependent on those around her?

"How am I ever to trust you? It is bad enough that a man will so often mislead a woman as to his intentions and feelings. You have lied to me about my *own* intentions and feelings. And you think I can just wave it away like some little bit of nothing?"

"I do not ask you to merely wave it away but only to think of how wonderful these weeks have been and—"

"It has all been a lie!"

"If you will only consider this reasonably," he said urgently. "These last weeks, this time when all of our prejudices and preconceived notions about one another—"

"Reasonable?" Elizabeth gaped at him. "I should think it quite reasonable that I want no part of a man who would deceive me for weeks, allowing me to think myself engaged to him!"

"I have *never* once said we were engaged. You said it, and yes, I should have corrected your misapprehension. But I did not lie to you, nor have I taken any of the liberties that an engaged man might have."

"Liberties?" She laughed, bitterly. "What greater liberties might a man take than an attempt to force a woman to bind herself inextricably to him! I suppose you planned to tell me once the wedding was over, and I had no recourse?"

"No." He knelt before her, reaching to take her hands in his own. She pulled them away before he could. "Elizabeth, please, I beg you. Everything was done believing it was for the best. I was persuaded that it was what was best for you."

"I do not believe you," Elizabeth said softly. "How could I? I do not even know who you are."

He stared at her, the pain evident in his eyes; she swallowed and looked away from that. Lies, it was all lies, none of it meant anything. Darcy—no, *Mr* Darcy—was nothing at all like she thought he was. He was an arrogant, impudent, unfeeling, haughty, unkind stranger, the sort of person who thought himself so much better than anyone else. The sort of person accustomed to getting their own way, no matter the cost.

Well, *she* was not for *sale*. She thanked God for whatever interventions or coincidences had led her to discover the truth before it was too late.

She rose to her feet with the greatest amount of dignity she could assume, and without a syllable more, strode towards the door. She heard Darcy rise from behind her.

"Looks like I had the right of things the first time," she threw over her shoulder. "You *are* the last man in the world I could ever marry."

CHAPTER SIXTEEN

HEARTLESS

The maid was rapidly retrieved from where she had gone to have tea below stairs and joined Elizabeth in the carriage which had, thankfully, remained in front of the house. It was a vast relief that Elizabeth did not have to sit there battling the temptation to go back in to Darcy. Her body was fatigued but more so were her spirits. *I am too distressed even to cry. After weeks of weeping at anything and everything, in this, my eyes remain dry.*

She arrived at Gracechurch Street to find her aunt and mother sitting amid scraps of fabric in the parlour. "Lizzy! You are returned earlier than we expected," Mrs Gardiner said with a smile.

"And a relief it is too because I do not know how I am expected to choose everything she needs! Mr Darcy is a great man!" Mrs Bennet cried out. "You need a trousseau equal to your new station, and I surely cannot be the only one who cares—"

"You may rest your mind on that account, ma'am. There shall be no trousseau, no wedding, no marriage," Elizabeth informed them. "I am not going to marry Mr Darcy. Mama, let us make plans to return to Longbourn…tomorrow perhaps?"

Both her mother and her aunt stared at her briefly before Mrs Bennet began to fret. "Is it because he fears you have lost your wits? Oh, I knew we ought to tell you more, enough to make you pass muster! No man wants a witless wife!"

"In fact, I daresay Mr Darcy was depending upon me to remain witless," Elizabeth said, feeling the warmth of her ire returning to her. "It suited his purpose quite well, in fact!"

"It seems we need some tea," Mrs Gardiner said with authority. "Allow me to ring for some, and then we will have a good talk."

WHEN ELIZABETH HAD GONE, DARCY RETIRED TO his study to consider what next to do. He knew he ought to have explained everything to her! Accursed physician who persuaded him against what he knew to be right!

No, he could not wholly lay it at Dr Hughes's door. It was his own fault; the temptation to court Elizabeth, to bask in the glow of her approbation, her love, had been too much from which to walk away. He was weak, too weak to do it, and now the worst had happened: she had discovered the truth for herself.

Her distress, her anger, were both natural and just. But could he obtain her forgiveness? And how was it to be done?

I shall be required to go to Gracechurch Street.

He grimaced. He had no wish to present himself before Elizabeth's uncle. Mrs Gardiner had seemed pleasant enough, but Mr Gardiner was Mrs Bennet's and Mrs Philips's brother. He was probably as vulgar, crass, and irrational as his sisters were. Nevertheless, the man was his only hope.

"To Gracechurch Street, then," he announced grimly to the empty room.

He was relieved to find that he was not turned away from the door once he arrived at the commodious house on Gracechurch Street. There was some part of his mind admiring the fine furnishings and the butler who was well-trained and pleasant, even as he rehearsed in his mind what to say to a man like Mr Gardiner.

He need not have worried about that, for if he had been surprised by the genteel appearance of Mrs Gardiner, then it was an utter shock to see Mr Gardiner. Had he passed him on the street, he certainly would have believed Gardiner a man of fashion, and one not significantly older than himself. His accent was well-modulated and bespoke an educated man, and his study boasted nearly as many books as Darcy's own did. He was, in fact, so very agreeable and elegant that Darcy felt stupid for having ever thought otherwise of him.

Mr Gardiner welcomed him into his study, sent for coffee, and saw to it that he was seated in a comfortable chair. Then he took his own seat, and his own coffee, and stared at Darcy expectantly. Darcy found himself tongue-tied.

"Perhaps I ought not to have come here," he said at length. "Maybe once tempers were cooler—"

At that most inauspicious of moments, from elsewhere in

the house, Darcy heard the muted sound of female distress. He stopped speaking, listening as Mrs Bennet berated her daughter. It seemed that she would never forgive Elizabeth for jilting him and for having no care for her mother's nerves. Darcy swallowed hard.

Mr Gardiner decided to take the lead. "Mr Darcy, I have only just returned from my business, so I am at a loss to know what is happening. You and Elizabeth, it seems, have had some sort of disagreement?"

Darcy licked his lips. "'Tis more than a disagreement, if I am being perfectly frank." Speaking quickly, he related to Mr Gardiner how the deception of his niece had come about and why he had not corrected her misapprehensions. Mr Gardiner listened intently but did not interrupt with any reply, although Darcy could easily discern concern and genuine feeling in his eyes. They were the male version of Elizabeth's eyes, he recognised.

Mr Gardiner sighed heavily at the end of the recitation. "So, on the ninth of April, you proposed to her, Elizabeth refused you in no uncertain terms, you quarrelled and parted ways. You then wrote a letter, meaning to give it to her the next morning, the tenth of April, except that before you did, she had her accident and woke up with no memory of any of it."

"And someone—not I—had said something to make her think herself engaged to me. With no memory of the prejudices of our past together, we were able to get to know one another anew," Darcy said. "She permitted me to court her as I ought to have done last autumn."

"And you say Dr Hughes advised you not to tell her the

truth?"

"Each time I consulted him on the matter, he assured me that no good would come from shocking her with the truth of our past contentions."

"Alas, now she has learnt of it all herself, which is undoubtedly the most shocking way she could have."

Darcy nodded miserably.

"I suppose one can only hope it does not have deleterious effects on her health." So saying, he rose and went to ring the bell. The housekeeper appeared moments later, and Mr Gardiner asked her to send his niece in to him.

Elizabeth appeared in her uncle's study looking positively dreadful. Her eyes were red-rimmed and swollen, and her countenance bore clear tracks of tears. From the scent of her, Darcy deduced some foul liniment had been applied to her, likely for a headache. She was plagued by headaches in times of high emotion, he had noticed. She refused to look his way.

"Sit down, Lizzy," Mr Gardiner said gently. "Would you like something to drink?"

Elizabeth sat, turning her head away from Darcy's direction and shaking it slightly in reply to her uncle's question.

"Where is your mother now? Things have grown quiet out there."

"My aunt is with her and gave her something for her nerves," Elizabeth replied.

"Good, good," said Mr Gardiner in that same soft voice. "I understand, from Mr Darcy, that there was a misunderstanding—"

"A grievous misunderstanding," Elizabeth replied warmly.

"A deception, to phrase it more accurately. I was deceived into thinking I was engaged when in fact I had refused him."

"Refused him based on your former acquaintance, I believe?"

"Yes, of course. Evidently, we hated one another," she replied.

"I did not hate you," Darcy protested. "We argued, but never did I—"

She rounded on him immediately. "Oh, so it was only my family you despised, then? The people I love most in the world? Did you tell my uncle how every moment you have to sit here, in a tradesman's home, disgusts you?" Her eyes flashed with anger as she spoke, and he was reminded of that night in Hunsford Parsonage.

"Lizzy," Mr Gardiner inserted. "How Mr Darcy might feel about mixing with other circles of Society is not material at this moment."

"He ruined Jane's chances with Mr Bingley, you know," she said heatedly. "Had it not been for his interference, Jane might be married even now!"

"I made a mistake," Darcy said, wondering why on earth he had decided to come to Gracechurch Street. Had he imagined that Mr Gardiner could somehow help him?

"Jane has been in devastation for above six months and he"—Elizabeth thrust a pointed finger towards him without looking at him—"was the architect of her downfall. Do you think I am tempted in any way whatsoever to marry someone who has ruined Jane's happiness so heartlessly?"

It was uncanny, how near those words were to the ones she had uttered at Hunsford that night.

"What sort of sister," she continued, "would marry a man who termed their beloved sister *a certain evil*? Who would align themselves with a person who was so disgusted by everyone she was connected to? No one in her right mind, and so it was. I refused Mr Darcy's proposal, unequivocally, and yet, once I was enfeebled, I was persuaded to believe I had accepted him."

The weight of her charges was sinking him. For whatever guilt he had felt before, it visited itself upon him now tenfold. Nay, one hundred! He did not deserve her mercy and he knew that, but neither was he above begging for it.

"Dr Hughes persuaded me that it was for the best," he said, his voice sounding very meek. "I never intended to cause you harm, Elizabeth. I only wished for that which would aid in your recovery. Once I realised that you believed us engaged, I did think, often, of disclosing the truth to you. But we were happy…you were happy."

"I was not happy, I was insensible," she said with another glare.

"You were happy," he insisted quietly. "What I did cannot be undone. I was a party to your deception, and I cannot deny my guilt. I can only say that it was done for the best, with your best interests at heart, and I wish more than anything that I had told you the truth before you discovered it. The reproofs you uttered that night at the parsonage have been tended to. I have changed—"

"No, you have not," she retorted. "Not a whit. You behave even now as if the plague might come upon you. You did not even wish me to come to your home in my aunt's carriage, which by the bye is quite as fine as your own. You disdain them, these people who are very dear to me, such that my aunt felt it certain you would not wish me to associate with them once we had married."

"I would not do that," Darcy said, knowing full well that in fact he might have. He might have discouraged the Bennets from coming to Pemberley. He might have discouraged an association with the Gardiners and Philipses. He would not have forbidden her outright, but was that any better? He lowered his head, particularly ashamed to feel the calm gaze of her uncle upon him.

"Lizzy," Mr Gardiner interjected. "I understand very well what you feel. Your anger is not…misplaced. But the question now becomes, what is to be done about your engagement?"

"I have never been engaged, nor would I agree to one now," Elizabeth said firmly. "I will not marry Mr Darcy under any circumstances. I simply cannot bind myself inextricably to a man who has done this to me."

Her words were like a knife to Darcy's chest but still worse were the tears that rolled down her cheeks as she spoke. "How could I ever trust such a person to act in my best interests? What if I had another spell of memory loss and woke for him to tell me, no, we were not married, I was merely some hired prostitute or—"

Darcy gasped, then protested, "Elizabeth, I would never—"

"I think you are capable of anything," she hissed, dashing the tears away with her knuckles. "You gave a grand performance, I admit that much. Fitzwilliam Darcy in his acting debut as The Doting Betrothed! Also starring Elizabeth

Bennet as The Hapless Half-Wit. Uncle, may I please go now? My head is aching fiercely again."

She stood as if to leave, and a surge of panic enveloped him. He reached for her hands, sliding from the chair to kneel in front of her. Part of him was amazed that he cared not for how he looked; he was well prepared to beg and plead and kiss her feet if only she would marry him.

"Elizabeth, please. Please marry me. I will make this up to you, all of this and more."

She stared down at him and in her eyes he saw it, a small glimmer of love, a softening towards him.

"I love you. Please do not throw me over. I will make this up to you. I will amend all the dreadful things I have said of your family and give them, all of them, all due respect."

Her feelings warred within her; he could see it played out in her eyes, the smallest bit of thaw in her icy anger towards him. It was his only hope, and he pressed into it.

"I beg you to forgive me and marry me."

She yanked her hands from his. "No," she said. "I promise you that I will never, ever consent to be your wife." She then turned round and strode from the room.

Darcy stood and briefly could only stare at the door that she had closed behind her. He turned then to Mr Gardiner whose countenance was not encouraging.

On seeing Darcy's observation, he offered a nod, then said, "It seems the lady has made her choice, sir."

CHAPTER SEVENTEEN

AT HOME WITH THE BENNETS

There was little for Darcy to say or do following Mr Gardiner's pronouncement. He was correct: Elizabeth had made her choice. Twice, in fact, and the same answer both times.

He kept his mind on the banalities of getting himself back to Mayfair. Bidding Mr Gardiner a polite farewell and asking that his best wishes be given to his family. One foot in front of the other to go down the Gardiners' wide front hall, observing the quality of the furnishings and concluding that Mr Gardiner's warehouses, for all that they could be seen from his home—and actually, you really could not see them unless you went to a great deal of effort and craned your neck —were exceedingly profitable. Mr Gardiner was wealthy, perhaps not as wealthy as he was, but possibly as wealthy as Bingley.

His mind was then centred on the sights viewed from his carriage on the way home. A turn there, observe a fine pair of horses passing, consider the condition of the roads, calculate how many persons were walking along the streets. Thinking of anything but what had just happened and how he might have avoided it.

The evening was long as he thrashed about between his study and his bedchamber, eschewing human interaction to the greatest extent possible. To Georgiana, he penned a quick note of scant explanation, telling her more would come later.

He returned to Gracechurch Street the next day with a posy in hand and his heart pounding as if he had run the whole way there. Alas, he was too late. Elizabeth and her mother had evidently decamped from London at dawn. Mrs Gardiner was out, and Mr Gardiner was at his warehouses.

"Shall I fetch him for you, sir?" the housekeeper asked. "I can send a footman over."

"No, no," he said. "That is not necessary."

His demurrals were interrupted by the two girls he had seen previously. Curiosity had brought them to the top of the stairs, and when they perceived his notice, they came down to the door. "Lizzy went home," the elder informed him. "Her head is still sick."

"A snake bit her in the brain," the younger added. "It made her very queer."

"Enough of that," the housekeeper interrupted sternly. "Your cousin wants for nothing but a bit of time, and she will be right as rain."

A bit of time. Would time dispose her towards forgiving him?

Darcy recognised he had no reason to be still standing there, so he asked the young ladies if they would like to share the flowers he had brought for their cousin. They were absolutely delighted to divide the posy between them. He heard the elder tell her sister, as the door closed behind him, that she really thought Cousin Lizzy ought to marry the nice man.

HAVING SPENT MOST OF THE NIGHT CRYING INTO her pillow, Elizabeth began the next day with a throbbing headache that was not helped by Mrs Bennet's vociferous disapproval of what she had done.

"I could forgive you when you refused Mr Collins," Mrs Bennet proclaimed, her phial of salts held in three fingers so that the fourth might point at her daughter in an accusatory manner. "But to refuse such a man as Mr Darcy? Do you understand how rich, how great you might have been?"

Elizabeth only nodded. To tell her mother she did not care for such things would only lead to further lecturing.

"The pin money! The jewels! He very likely would have bought you a carriage. I should wager my own life on it."

Elizabeth nodded again, then rubbed her eyes which felt gritty and inflamed. Her head hurt, her chest hurt…she felt like her skin was on too tight. "I do understand, Mama, and I am sorry. But the lies—"

"Lies? Who cares about some silly little lies?" Mrs Bennet scoffed.

"I do. I care a great deal about lies. I was everyone's fool, including yours and Charlotte's."

"Charlotte and I were as deceived as you!" Mrs Bennet

protested. "It was that cousin of his who started the whole thing."

"And you did not think to doubt it?"

"No, Elizabeth, I did not," said Mrs Bennet in an uncommonly stern tone. "If a man as great as Mr Darcy took notice of you, I am sure I was too busy in my delight to doubt it. It was his cousin himself who told us of it! If I ever see that man again, I shall box his ears directly!"

Elizabeth sighed. It was no use being angry with her mother or with Charlotte. As her mother said, they were as wilfully misled as she had been.

"But who cares about a little falsehood here and there?" her mother continued. "I am sure he merely misunderstood it! It still gives no cause for you to wantonly put aside the attentions of a man of such consequence!" On and on she went, berating her until, thankfully, the rocking of the carriage caused her to fall into a doze. Then Elizabeth was left to stare out of the window and berate herself for such foolishness as falling in love with such a man as Darcy.

They arrived midafternoon. Jane uttered a cry of relieved joy and came to kiss her cheek, and Mary came from upstairs to do likewise. Kitty and Lydia wanted to know if she had brought them presents, which Mrs Bennet rapidly scolded them for, and Mr Bennet laid down his newspaper to enquire, "How are you feeling, my dear Lizzy?"

"Stronger every day," she told him, even if the journey had left her feeling rather spent. "Now if I can only manage to read again without a pounding headache, I shall be well satisfied."

"A pounding headache from reading! That is grievous

indeed," said Mr Bennet with a chuckle. "And what of young Darcy? Engaged, not engaged—shall I expect him to come thundering into Hertfordshire to rant and storm about his love for you?"

The way that he said so made Elizabeth understand that he thought her heartbreak a source of great amusement. Had she been in her usual spirits, she might have bristled at such levity, but she was too low to even summon up vexation. She felt only tired as she said, "No, Papa, I do not think we should expect to see Mr Darcy ever again."

Mr Bennet had raised the newspaper again. "We all thought him a proud, disagreeable sort of fellow, so no great loss there."

"We did, Lizzy, we all hated him," Kitty informed her. "No great loss, just as Papa said."

Elizabeth could think of nothing to say to that and merely nodded.

"How clever it was of me to ensure the neighbourhood would not know about Lizzy's engagement," Mrs Bennet announced, tossing herself into her usual chair. "I told Charlotte to say nothing of this to anyone and see that Mr Collins did likewise. I just knew that once Mr Darcy understood Lizzy had lost her wits, this engagement would go off like a puff of smoke!"

"There was never any engagement to go off," Elizabeth reminded her. Again, she was not acknowledged. It was a mercy. Mrs Bennet's harangue from the carriage still rang in her ears, and she imagined more scolding would come in the days ahead.

Jane had taken a seat near to her on the settee and

studied her with a worried crease in her brow. "But your health, Lizzy. How do you feel?"

"Sad," Elizabeth replied for Jane's hearing only.

"I thought she was well enough," Mrs Bennet interjected. "I was told there seemed to be no damage to her wits, but then this! She is clearly out of her senses! That snake! Why, I would like to wring its neck!"

"Do snakes even have necks?" Jane asked softly, an obvious attempt to make Elizabeth smile. It *did* succeed, if temporarily.

"Snakes," said Mary from her seat across the room, "have long represented the evil of temptation, the allure of what is forbidden to us, and their bite is the sting that represents the pain of spiritual warfare and—"

"In my case, the pain of the snake bite represented bruising and bloodshed," Elizabeth interrupted. "I think I ought to go to my bedchamber and rest. I slept very poorly last night and the journey was long."

She retreated to the bedchamber she had always known. Thankfully it looked as it always had, even if there was a shawl on the chair that she did not recognise. She did like it, however, and picked it up to wrap around her shoulders before reclining on top of her bed.

A quiet knock on the door came only minutes later, followed by a tentative opening of the door. Jane poked her head in. "Lizzy?"

"Jane, you need not knock at the door of your own bedchamber." Elizabeth smiled at her sister as she arranged pillows around herself.

Jane entered and took a place on her sister's bed, then

spent some moments fussing over Elizabeth's health, adjusting a blanket over her, and fretting that her pallor indicated a setback was afoot.

"The journey was...challenging," Elizabeth admitted. "But every day is a step forwards, I believe."

"You are home now, and I am determined to do my share in caring for you," Jane said with a firm nod. "I still cannot believe you lost your memory. An entire year, gone! It must be very distressing."

"I confess it was at first, particularly waking and finding that I was engaged...but then was not."

"I could not believe it when my mother told us what happened. But you must tell me everything in your own words, so I can understand it all."

Many, many letters had gone between Hunsford and Longbourn; any house boasting so many energetic females was bound to have a brisk correspondence abroad. Alas, Elizabeth had found herself unable to read many of them, and nevertheless, it could never be the same as hearing things firsthand. Elizabeth told Jane how it had come about, how she had not known Darcy at first...but had come to love him.

"He showed such diligence in caring for me! And the time we spent together was just wonderful—we have a similarity in our minds that I felt would serve us very well once we had married."

Jane pursed her lips. "And yet, you have jilted him."

"No! I did not jilt him—I never agreed to marry him. That is an enormous difference."

"Very well. So you have refused to marry him."

"Several times, in fact."

Jane said no words, but her countenance and her attitude spoke clearly.

"Jane, how could I marry someone who lied to me in such an egregious manner? I was deceived by every person who purported to care for me! Charlotte and Mama, I can forgive; they did truly believe I was engaged. But Mr Darcy?"

"Dreadfully distressing," Jane said sympathetically. "Only…"

"Only what?"

"You came to love him, I think? Is that not what you just said?"

Elizabeth sighed. "I did."

"And do you believe he loves you? Or do you accuse him of a lie there as well?"

"N-no, I do not think he is lying about that." Elizabeth pursed her lips. "If anything, his feelings were his motive. He wanted to have me and would stop at nothing to get me."

"Or he truly believed he was acting in your interests. Mama said that the physician warned him, warned them all, against shocking you or causing upset."

"I refuse to believe his motives were wholly altruistic, and do you know why? Because I have subsequently learnt firsthand how well he enjoys arranging people's lives to his own liking."

"Who else's life did he rearrange?"

"Mr Bingley's…and yours, in fact," Elizabeth told her. "Mr Darcy played a principal part in persuading Mr Bingley against returning to you."

Jane looked down, a frown marring her pretty face. Elizabeth cursed herself for being so insensitive; what angered her was fresh pain to her sister. "Forgive me. I do not mean to wound you further."

"It is no one's fault but my own. I knew it would all come to nothing, and did all I could to practise restraint, to guard my heart, but—"

"Practise restraint? How do you mean?"

"I did not wish to make it seem as if I had expectations of him, so I…I was careful with my own expressions of attachment. A woman can only show so much of herself. I did not wish to seem…brazen or forward."

And thus did Darcy conclude she merely tolerated Bingley. Pushing that thought away, Elizabeth asked, "But surely a man needs a little encouragement, does he not? You must have let him know how you felt at least a little?"

Jane was busy tracing a finger over the embroidery on one of Elizabeth's pillows. "Lizzy, I know how these things are. I am not so naive, am I? How does the saying go? The marriage mart is in London; the mistress mart is in the country."

"Jane!" Elizabeth laughed. "Where on earth did you hear that?"

"I cannot say," Jane admitted. "But it is true. No one comes into the country, into a leased house, because he wishes to find a wife. He was seeking diversion and a good time, and for me to behave as if I expected more would be the greatest presumption. It was too embarrassing to think of—me, making a cake of myself for nothing. A man like Mr Bingley is not seeking a wife with no fortune from an embarrassing family."

Elizabeth shifted her position on the bed. "Were they so very bad?"

"If you had only seen Mama and the girls that evening at the assembly! That is, you *did* see it, but I mean if you could remember seeing it. But perhaps it is all best forgot."

Elizabeth reached over and stroked her sister's hand for a moment, then withdrew.

"They were positively the worst I have ever seen them," Jane admitted. "Our mother allowed our younger sisters out as soon as Lydia turned fifteen last June—do you remember that assembly?"

"I do. And I remember thinking then, as now, that it was far too young, although I know Mama did the same for you and I, once I was fifteen. From what I remember the girls were very—"

Jane nodded vehemently and interjected, "Excessively silly, all giggles and running about wildly, and nothing had improved from June to the time when the Netherfield party came in October. Every time we were in company with them, Mr Bingley's sisters and Mr Darcy were aghast, and rightly so."

"It does seem that I am fortunate to have forgotten it."

Jane nodded. "That is why it is no surprise to me to find out Mr Darcy had a hand in keeping Mr Bingley away. How do you think he did it?"

"Well…" Elizabeth twisted her hands together in her lap. "In truth, Mr Bingley told me he readily withstood the protests of fortune and family. It was not until Mr Darcy said…he told him he perceived no affection on your side. Mr

Darcy believed you were only tolerating his friend, and given Mr Bingley's natural modesty...he believed it."

A weighty silence ensued. "Therefore, I have no one to blame but myself."

Heatedly, Elizabeth said, "Yes, indeed there are others to blame. Mr Darcy ought not to have presumed to know you. Mr Bingley ought to have discovered your affections for himself. He owns himself that he has, in the past, relied too heavily on his friend's judgment."

"Mr Darcy could not have influenced his present engagement." On Elizabeth's look, Jane added, "Yes, my mother told me."

Elizabeth did not know what to say for a minute. "He did not seem happy about it."

"I hope he is happy. I do not wish him ill, nor any of them. They do no worse than anyone else does. Everyone wishes to better themselves through marriage. Why should a young man of large fortune do differently?"

"Because he could have had something worth far more than gold," Elizabeth told her. "And that is you."

"Someone else will have me, then," Jane replied. Her eyes looked a little moist, but she seemed determined to put a brave face on it. "At least, I hope they will. Oh Lizzy, I do not wish to be four-and-twenty and unmarried!"

"You will need to be three-and-twenty first," Elizabeth reminded her.

"Which I shall be next week," Jane replied. "And you will be one-and-twenty the day following." It was a long-time jest at Longbourn that when Elizabeth had been born, one day after Jane's birthday, Jane imagined her sister to be a birthday gift for herself.

"I daresay we both still have a little bit of time to find husbands," Elizabeth teased. "No need to put ourselves in lace caps just yet."

Jane suddenly leant towards her, wrapping her in a hug. "I am so glad you are back, and so glad you are well. I am less glad you have managed to purloin my new shawl already."

Elizabeth was relieved by the little jest. "Is it yours? I imagined it was a gift to me for all of my many misfortunes." She paused. "May I ask you something?"

"Anything."

"When you learnt that I was engaged to Mr Darcy, were you...shocked?"

Jane pressed her lips together, then said, "In some ways I was."

"So you saw my dislike of him?"

"I saw how much you *wanted* to dislike him."

Elizabeth furrowed her brow. "What does that mean?"

Jane looked like she wished to smile. "You gave him a great deal of attention for someone you said you despised."

"I did say I despised him? Who heard me say it?"

Jane considered that. "In fact, I do not know that you ever said that you despised him, not to my knowledge in any case. You said he was proud and disagreeable—"

"Because he insulted me at the assembly."

Jane nodded. "I think the largest part of the problem was Mr Wickham's testimony against him."

"Which is not true," Elizabeth admitted. "Mr Wickham lied just like Mr Darcy did."

"Not exactly like Mr Darcy did," Jane said.

"What do you mean?"

"Mr Darcy hid information for your own good. Mr Wickham lied to make you feel sorry for him."

"Need I remind you that if I had not learnt the truth, I could have found myself bound to Mr Darcy for life!"

"Ooh!" Jane gave an exaggerated shiver. "How terrible! To marry a wealthy and handsome man who adores you! Yes, Lizzy, how good it is that you escaped *that* fate!"

Elizabeth rolled her eyes. "I have always said that, above all, I wish to look up to my husband, to admire him. I cannot admire a liar."

"It seems your decision was right, then, and you should be happy in it."

"And so I am," Elizabeth replied.

"Are you?" Jane kept her gaze steady on her sister. "You surely do not seem very happy."

Elizabeth sighed, absently running her hand over the coverlet on her bed. "You know me too well for me to prevaricate. I suppose I would say I wish to be happy more than I actually am at present. In time I do not doubt I will recover my spirits."

"Which no doubt would happen faster if you forgave him."

Elizabeth gave her sister a look. "Forgiving is not the problem. Trusting is. I loved the man I believed him to be—a man it seems he was not, not at all. It is *that* man I regret, a man who does not exist. But it will all be forgot, and I will be happy once again."

Jane looked doubtful as she leant over and kissed her

sister on the forehead. "For you to be happy is all any of us wants."

CHAPTER EIGHTEEN

A MAN ABOUT TOWN

Since his time in Kent, Fitzwilliam had been out on some sort of business with his regiment. Engaged as he was in his own matters, Darcy had paid little attention to the particulars of his cousin's whereabouts, but it was a relief to discover that the colonel was returned to London a few days after the disastrous scene on Gracechurch Street. Darcy found his cousin enjoying a hearty breakfast at his own breakfast table early one morning.

"There he is!" Fitzwilliam pointed towards him. "I was about to come up to your bedchamber and pull you out by your ankle."

Darcy sat at the table and signalled to the footman for coffee. While it was poured, he rubbed his eyes roughly. "Barely slept," he muttered.

"I am sorry to hear it," Fitzwilliam said gravely. "Georgiana told me about...Miss Bennet. Is there any way I can help?"

Darcy knew he was in dire straits if Fitzwilliam did not tease him about it. If Saye behaved kindly, then he would know he was well and truly doomed. "Yes, well…I hope to rectify matters once her health is improved."

"I am sure you will." Fitzwilliam signalled for more coffee, then asked, "How do you think you might go about it?"

Darcy shrugged. "Write to her? Send gifts? Arrange for time spent in Hertfordshire…Bingley has made a purchase offer for Netherfield, so it is possible—"

"That he will wish to invite you down for his honeymoon?" Fitzwilliam sniggered. "Even *he* is not so besotted with you as all that."

"After his honeymoon, I meant," said Darcy, although in truth, Bingley's wedding had not been a part of his calculations. It would mean a delay, but how long was one required to celebrate a friend entering into a loveless marriage?

The door opened then, and Saye entered, tossing himself into the seat nearest Fitzwilliam. "I need something to do," he announced. "There are no good scandals this Season! Nothing to gossip about, no one to cut. If someone does not jilt someone else, and soon, I shall go stark, raving mad."

He then paused and made a face. In his nearest approximation of an apology, he said, "Of course I did not mean *you*, Darcy." He then reached out to select a piece of bread from the basket on the table.

"Are people speaking of it?"

Saye gave a one-shouldered shrug, which Darcy took to mean yes, he was in fact the subject of gossip. Splendid.

"While we are on the subject of Darcy's lost love—" Fitzwilliam began.

"Which we are not. I do not wish to speak of any of this."

"You really shot into the brown on that one," Saye informed him, blithely disregarding Darcy's embargo.

"I disagree," Fitzwilliam said. "It was done for the best."

"If it was done for the best, our boy would not be sitting here all Friday-faced, would he?"

"He might be, if Miss Bennet had been so shocked that she had keeled over dead."

Saye scoffed. "I doubt the shock would have killed her."

"And with all your medical training plus the fact you scarcely know the lady, that is a very well-considered opinion."

"Enough," Darcy said tiredly. "If you two wish to bicker all day, pray do it somewhere besides my breakfast table. And pray, let us speak of *anything* else but Elizabeth."

"Fair enough," Saye announced cheerfully. "By the way, Darcy, you are not obliged to walk Anne down the aisle. My father will do it."

"I did not realise I was obliged, but I am glad to know it came to naught. I had not heard the plans were fixed."

"Lady Catherine has been in London since she left Kent," Fitzwilliam replied. "It seems she must have overcome her dislike for the notion of Anne marrying anyone besides you, for she has the nuptials all set at St George's and five hundred coming for the breakfast."

Darcy was relieved a lighter subject had been introduced. He did not much enjoy being an object of pity, even if his present state was pitiable.

"And they mean to take a wedding trip to the Lakes afterwards. Perhaps you might see them at Pemberley."

"No need to wait for an invitation these days," said Darcy with mild reproof. In a trice, a vision appeared in his head—he and Elizabeth receiving guests at Pemberley—and his cousin was forgot. *Elizabeth.* He needed to write to her, today, a perfect letter that would somehow set things to rights and make her remember the good times they had shared together.

With a sigh, he rose from the table. "Excuse me, I have some business to attend to in my study. You both know the way out."

The letter he needed to write was even more difficult than the one he had written after Elizabeth's first rejection. This time there was no misunderstanding. He had lied, and she had caught him in it. George Wickham was not at fault this time; it was his own actions and presumptions which had sunk him.

After almost an hour complete spent staring at the blank page in front of him, he began to write. The words came slowly, almost painfully, and in the end, it was a full day's work, crafting the best possible missive.

Dearest Elizabeth,

Pray know that above all things you are dear to me. Your happiness I hold well above my own, and the only thing I have wanted and wished for these months is your health and felicity.

I have erred, and there are no two ways to look at that. I own it completely. That I had the best of intentions, that I felt it was for your good, does not signify. I can well understand how very disturbing it has been to have lost the memories of almost a year of your life and regret deeply the role I played in your confusion. There is nothing I can say to any of this but to fall upon your mercy and beg your forgiveness.

I do not think you could justly say you were unaware of my love for you. From nearly the first moment of your awakening, your heart, unencumbered by the prejudices of our contentious past, knew it was for me, just as mine has long been for you. The days we spent in Kent, save for your illness, were nothing short of glorious, and they were made so because of the excellent harmony between us.

I beg that you would not throw aside our love for my error. You may feel you cannot trust me, but if I must prove my fidelity to you every day for the rest of our lives, I shall, happily and with gratitude.

My heart rests within your hands, my darling, and I pray you will not cast me aside.

I shall only add that I love you, deeply,

FD

As it was, it did not signify how long he had struggled over the exact right words and phrases to her. There was no reply, not to the first, not to any until the seventh letter was sent. Then he did receive a reply but not from Elizabeth.

My daughter has declined your proposal, sir, and as such I cannot condone the liberty you assume in writing to her. I thank you not to do so again.

Mr Bennet

"Think again, Bennet," Darcy replied to the page. "You have not seen the last of me."

CHAPTER NINETEEN

TO LOATHE AND LONG FOR A MAN

I t was easy to fall back into the routines of life at Longbourn. The months Elizabeth had forgotten were not mentioned overmuch—she had worried her younger sisters would tease her, but evidently their father had warned them against it.

In any case, the primary concern of her younger sisters appeared to be the imminent departure of Colonel Forster's regiment, which had been quartered in Hertfordshire all winter. Elizabeth remembered nothing of them, but apparently for her sisters, the loss could never be bemoaned sufficiently. They alternated expressions of agony with pleas for their father to take the family to Brighton, but Mr Bennet showed no signs of acceding to the scheme.

Gradually Elizabeth's rambles got longer, and her leg ached less; her tendency to tears and headaches and pique abated. In short, she became herself again and was much relieved for it. She and Jane passed into the ages of twenty-one and twenty-three with as much ceremony as any birthday was given at Longbourn, with Lydia informing them both that she would rather die of shame than reach such advanced ages without marrying.

Elizabeth did not know if it was her memory loss or her time away which had provided her some measure of clarity with regards to her family. In many ways, she felt all the justice of Darcy's censure, for her father was indolent and indifferent, the younger girls were spoilt, Mary was pedantic, and their mother was as silly as a child. She tried to view them all with amusement, but too often they made her cringe and wish they might all behave as she saw most families did.

One morning, Lydia burst into the breakfast room, wholly elated. "Mrs Forster will take me to Brighton!"

"What about me?" Kitty cried out immediately. "Surely the invitation includes me as well?"

"Only me," Lydia crowed triumphantly. "*You* are not her particular friend. I am, and I shall go! Oh, Mama! Just imagine the parties, the balls! I shall have to have at least three new gowns!"

Elizabeth and Jane exchanged looks. Their father, so far, had not looked up from his newspaper. Their mother was flushed with delight; her only reply was to begin to imagine what officers her youngest daughter might flirt with, and what gowns and accoutrements were needed. In a flurry of violent chatter and planning—punctuated by Kitty's peevish protests against her own exclusion—the three soon quit the breakfast parlour. Elizabeth and Jane were left in silence with their father and Mary, both of whom were reading.

It was Jane who spoke first. "Papa?" Once their father had raised his eyes, she continued, "Surely you do not mean to let Lydia go to Brighton on her own?"

"She will not be alone; she will be with Mrs Forster," their father replied.

This made Mary raise her eyes from her book and observe, "Mrs Forster is not even as old as I am, and I would surely not be able to manage Lydia in a seaside town full of army officers."

The fact that Mary had exerted herself to say as much alarmed Elizabeth. "Papa, perhaps she ought to be kept home."

"Do you even remember any of the persons we speak of?" he asked satirically, with one brow raised.

"I remember Lydia," she said, not at all amused. "And you must admit for any young lady, fifteen is full young to be roaming the countryside unattended."

Mr Bennet's eyes were returned to the newspaper. "Lydia will never be easy till she has exposed herself in some public place or other, and we can never expect her to do it with so little expense or inconvenience to her family as under the present circumstances."

Jane sighed and looked down. Then, not asking to be excused, she rose from the table and left. Elizabeth followed suit, and the two repaired to their bedchamber.

"What hope is there, Lizzy?" Jane demanded as soon as the door was closed behind her. "What man in his right mind could withstand such embarrassment?"

Elizabeth knew just what she meant. "They were right to hold us in contempt, then?" she asked softly.

Jane threw up her hands. "How could they not? We looked like the very worst sort of country bumpkins, ill-mannered first to last. I cannot blame Mr Darcy for warning his friend away from a permanent attachment. Who could? And now Lydia will go to Brighton, and who knows what might come of it! Nothing good, I shall assure you of that! Mrs Forster is scarcely older than Lydia herself and twice as silly."

"Perhaps Papa would send our mother with her?" Elizabeth liked that idea, not only to see her sister watched over but also to rid herself of a long summer of her mother's censure.

Jane shook her head. "Mama was adamant she was needed here, for you."

Elizabeth groaned. "That is precisely the opposite of what I need."

And in truth, she did not need her mother, or her mother's endless reminders of what Elizabeth had thrown away. Elizabeth felt, already, the loss of Darcy, of the life she had anticipated with him. It had nothing to do with his wealth—though that formed the chief basis of Mrs Bennet's complaints—but with him. She missed the times spent together in Kent, driving and walking and talking. She repined the loss of their plans for a future together, the loss of the children she might have had with him. She simply could not reconcile that man with the one who had so cruelly deceived her for weeks on end with no apparent plan to reveal the truth to her.

Never mind that. It is done. She had refused him bitterly, fought with him, and then rejected him again. There was no hope. No man would try a third time when a lady had made her answer so clear the first two times.

Would you wish for a third chance? She shook her head, hardly knowing what she wanted. *He lied,* she reminded herself continually. *You cannot trust him.*

THE WEIGHT OF FAMILY NONSENSE, COMBINED with her own regrets, began to sink her. She did all she could to keep herself busy, often walking into town with whomever asked her to accompany them. It was on one such excursion with Kitty that a handsome gentleman in regimentals was seen across the street. Kitty had no scruple in calling out to the man, who smiled and walked towards them.

"Kitty!" Elizabeth scolded. "You cannot be waving at men in such a bold manner!"

"Oh, dear Wickham is an old friend to us by now," Kitty said dismissively, not realising how the name fairly electrified Elizabeth.

"Mr George Wickham?" she asked softly, but not softly enough, for the man had drawn near to them then and replied, cheerfully,

"At your service, Miss Elizabeth. How wonderful it is to see you!"

"She has memory loss," Kitty told him blithely. "She has no idea who you are."

"Indeed?" Mr Wickham peered closely at her, and Elizabeth raised her chin, coolly evaluating him just as intently. Mr Wickham was an undeniably handsome man, almost as tall as Darcy was, but with an open artlessness in his manner that was baffling. This was Georgiana Darcy's seducer? He seemed almost...bashful. Sweet, even. *So do most devils,* she reminded herself. *They would be far less tempting otherwise.*

Kitty gave him a quick summation of Elizabeth's troubles, from the snake right up until she had broken things off with Darcy. Elizabeth might not have been so free with details, but as she was determined not to speak to Mr Wickham, Kitty's way was the way it was done.

"Engaged to Darcy, hmm?" Mr Wickham grinned. "My old friend has done very well for himself."

"I am not and was *never* engaged to him. It was all a misunderstanding." Though Elizabeth had been resolved to not speak, in this matter she felt obliged. "I refused his proposal. Twice."

Mr Wickham raised his brows. "Singular indeed. I do not know many ladies who would refuse Darcy's hand."

"Money and position are not nearly as important to me as...as...other things," she concluded. No matter how angry at Darcy she was, she would not defame him to his sworn enemy.

Mr Wickham chuckled. "Knowing Darcy as I do, I am not surprised. You are excessively ill-suited to one another."

Somehow this rankled. She and Darcy had been, in fact, exceedingly well-suited to one another. *Then why are you here instead of planning your wedding to him?* She dispelled that errant notion with a tight smile to Mr Wickham. "I forget, sir, that you know me better than I know you."

"It must be excessively unsettling," he said sympathetically. "Forgive me if I am too familiar."

His kindliness surprised her. "Um, no, not at all. Yes, in

fact, it is very unsettling, but I am growing accustomed to not knowing things."

"You are very fortunate to be alive," he said. "And in truth, memory loss is not as bad as some of the stories I have heard from those bitten by adders."

Begrudgingly, Elizabeth nodded. "I am fortunate. A washerwoman in Kent stumbled upon a nest last year, and she is wholly incapacitated now. She completely lost her ability to speak."

"Positively dreadful," Mr Wickham said with a click of his tongue.

Kitty had grown weary with the conversation, and with a quick look at her elder sister, indicated that she would go into the shop closest to them. Elizabeth nodded her assent and moved to accompany her but was stopped by Mr Wickham.

"A moment, if you please?"

CHAPTER TWENTY

ANOTHER SNAKE IN THE GRASS

M r Wickham appeared to be all humility as he said to Elizabeth, "I sense a coldness in your manner to me and it grieves me. We have been good friends in the past. I would hate to imagine that we could not be so now."

"Friends do not lie to one another," Elizabeth replied loftily. "And it seems you have spoken many lies to me, Mr Wickham, even if I do not remember them."

"I do not doubt that my old friend Darcy has blackened my name." He shook his head sadly.

Elizabeth gave a quick glance round them to ensure privacy before saying in a low voice, "I think any person who attempts to seduce the innocent sister of a friend, with the object of gaining her fortune, will be thereafter vilified by the family."

Mr Wickham's reply was not what she expected. He

merely winced and said, "Seduce little Georgiana? The very notion!"

Elizabeth raised her brows. "Do you deny it, sir?"

"With everything I have, yes, I do deny it. You must understand, Miss Elizabeth—growing up at Pemberley as I did, very nearly a son of the house, she was a sister to me. I assure you, when I met her in Ramsgate, I had *no* design on Georgiana Darcy whatsoever, save for friendship."

"Indeed?"

"I was excessively fond her of when she was a child, you see. I devoted hours to her amusement, but I had not seen her since Darcy's father sent him and I to school. I saw her as my *sister*, always," he said, very earnestly. "I could no more seduce her than I could seduce my own father!"

The manner in which he said it bespoke truth, yet it was very different to how Darcy had related the circumstances to her. "Mr Darcy thought otherwise. He believed he interrupted a near elopement and that your object was to obtain Georgiana's dowry."

Mr Wickham shook his head and sighed heavily. "Here is where I must admit some fault. I still looked at her as a child, just as she had been when she was toddling about, and we would laugh and play games together. I did not guard myself or restrain the ease with which I greeted her. I had no idea how that same friendliness might be...misinterpreted by a fifteen-year-old girl with a fondness for romance novels."

"Do you mean to tell me that Miss Darcy believed you were seducing her when in fact...you had no such intention?"

Very earnestly, he said, "I greeted her with all the old

fondness, never suspecting she might take it as anything besides *brotherly* affection. It was all a grave misunderstanding."

"I see." This was very different from how Darcy had viewed it, and yet, it made sense. Elizabeth did have experience with fifteen-year-old girls, had once been one herself. Well did she know how the slightest looks or most banal conversations could be conflated into grand romantic tales!

Her doubt must have shown on her countenance, for Mr Wickham leant towards her. "And with all due respect to your own charming sister—" He nodded to the shop Kitty had entered. She was visible in the window and had picked up a length of lace and draped it on her head like a bridal veil. "—I cannot look seriously upon a lady who is half my age. A mere child! As I said before...the very notion! It... well, if I am honest, it rather disgusts me."

With marked scepticism, Elizabeth asked, "Why do you not go to Mr Darcy, then, and explain your side of things?"

"I have tried," he said simply, and there was truth in his looks. "It was too late, unfortunately. Darcy and I have had our disagreements for some years now. I enjoy fun too much for his liking, and he is grown too serious for mine. I like to gamble, I like to drink, I stay out too late...these things I do not deny. But I am no seducer of children."

"Mr Darcy has had a great deal of responsibility thrust upon him," Elizabeth said, surprised herself by the impassioned manner in which she defended him.

"He has. I do not doubt he has heartily resented those of us who could enjoy our youth," Mr Wickham owned. "Who would not?"

Darcy does not, Elizabeth thought. *He accepted his burdens without flinching.* Oh, how very confusing it was to simultaneously loathe and long for a man! To admire what she wanted to despise!

"I suppose there are always two sides to every story," she acknowledged. Was it wrong of her to soften towards this man? Darcy had blackened his name, but perhaps—as it was in the case of her 'engagement'—it was all a misunderstanding. Of course, Darcy had also told her of Wickham's profligacy...but her own parents routinely overspent their income. She was the last person who should judge a man for that.

They were interrupted by Kitty who had returned from the shop and posed enquiries as to why Mr Wickham remained in town when the other lieutenants had already gone on to Brighton.

"I will only be here another week," Mr Wickham explained. "I am assisting Colonel Forster's removal from this fine place."

"You have enjoyed your time here? The country society is not agreeable to everyone," Elizabeth asked, surprising even herself with the friendliness in her voice.

"One cannot find the equal of the fine people of Hertfordshire so easily! I should say that there are none so welcoming, nor so friendly, most notably your own good family."

In the light of all her most recent realisations, it was soothing to hear someone say something kind about the Bennets. Elizabeth felt a faint blush colour her cheeks and murmured her thanks.

"But the seaside is sure to be very agreeable even for

those of us who must spend half the day marching about and performing military exercises."

Kitty let out a little cry. "I am sure the seaside should be very agreeable to me, too! I am still furious that Mrs Forster has invited only Lydia to join you all, and not me! I am just as much her friend and ought to have been asked along!"

"Miss Lydia is your youngest sister?" Mr Wickham looked to Elizabeth, seemingly for confirmation.

Elizabeth nodded. "Lydia is but fifteen. I understand Mrs Forster is quite young as well?"

Mr Wickham knitted his brow and nodded. "She is very young—seventeen, and only just."

"Seventeen...as am I," Kitty announced petulantly. Elizabeth ignored her.

"I daresay anyone within the household of the colonel must be afforded extra protection?" Elizabeth enquired.

"Something tells me that you have concerns about the scheme?" Mr Wickham tilted his head, looking thoughtful. "Perhaps you ought to accompany her? It would no doubt do you good as well. Some sea-bathing, to aid in your further recovery?"

"I believe my father has already put a stop to any hopes of a family sojourn to the seaside." Elizabeth smiled apologetically. "Travel is never very agreeable to him."

"If you feel you are well enough for the exertion, I may be able to arrange something with the Forsters," Mr Wickham said slowly. "I will speak to the colonel when I return to the regiment."

"Oh, no! I could not have you exert yourself on my

behalf," Elizabeth replied immediately. "Truly it...I am certain all will be well."

"Miss Elizabeth, if I might be candid with you?" On Elizabeth's nod, Mr Wickham said, very earnestly, "My particular regiment happens to consist of the finest fellows ever I knew, gentlemen in looks and comportment from first to last. But I fear it is not always so, and there are many different regiments in Brighton, men from many different walks of life. You are right to be concerned for your young sister. She will need more looking after than Mrs Forster will do, or the colonel *can* do, given the demands on his time."

Elizabeth met his gaze. Mr Wickham was very earnest, with warmth and genuine feeling apparent in his eyes. He seemed to truly have her best interests at heart.

"Allow me to speak to Mrs Forster on your behalf," he urged. "I do not doubt having another woman in the house would be enjoyable for her."

With much hesitation, Elizabeth agreed. "If it is not too much trouble for you, then yes, I would appreciate anything you might be able to do."

MR WICKHAM WAS TRUE TO HIS WORD, FOR scarcely half the day had passed when a note came from Mrs Forster for Elizabeth. Of course, Kitty could only grow more peevish at the notion that now Elizabeth—'who scarcely ever even spoke to Mrs Forster!'—was included while she herself remained excluded from the plans. Happily, she soon took herself to her bedchamber to sob out her indignation, leaving Elizabeth to argue her mother and father into agreement.

"Go to Brighton? Nonsense. You will stay right here where we can watch over you," Mrs Bennet said immediately.

"With all due respect, Mama, I do not think I am the one who most needs watching," Elizabeth said firmly. "And in any case, my health is almost wholly restored."

"You scarcely know your own name one day to the next!" Mrs Bennet cried out theatrically.

Elizabeth sighed and then appealed to her father. "I know you think it a fine thing that Lydia should expose her nonsense to the world, or whatever it was you said on that score, but I cannot be so easy about it. I would like to accompany her."

"You have only just got home," Mr Bennet replied. "I cannot like this, you always here and there. What is next? The Continent?"

"After Brighton, I have no plans at all," Elizabeth said. "I will be right here, snug at home, for…well, for all foreseeable future." The thought gave her a pang of hollow dismay, but she pushed it back.

"She is too ill. She will suffer a setback and then what shall we do? What if another snake bites her?" Mrs Bennet demanded.

"The sea air will be therapeutic," Elizabeth protested. "And I promise to avoid snakes at all costs."

Mrs Bennet seemed as if she wished to further argue the point, but Mr Bennet had grown weary of the subject. "Let her go then, Mrs Bennet," he said. "What harm could there be in it?"

CHAPTER TWENTY-ONE

HIGH-WROUGHT LOVE

Though he could not imagine Mr Bennet would permit Elizabeth to receive a gift, Darcy hoped that the man's naturally indolent nature might allow one or two things to slip through, perhaps believing them parcels, or things which she herself had purchased in town. Thus, did he take himself to the shops one summer morn, intent on purchasing something, anything to send to her.

It proved impossible. Nothing seemed quite right, not bejewelled combs for her hair, not a book, not a fan. It all felt horribly inadequate, yet what did feel adequate was too over-done, too much like he meant to flash his wealth at her—a strand of exquisite and perfect pearls, or a soft shawl from Kashmir. She was not the sort to be won over by expensive gifts, he knew, but he was at ends to discern what might do. *I need it to be something that would make her willing to see me, to allow me to woo her properly and hope it will be sufficient to earn her forgiveness.*

A tall order for any trifle. He had just left the fifth shop, nearly boiling with frustration, when he heard his name being called.

"Darcy!" Bingley waved to him with such enthusiasm that it drew the attention of the passersby on Oxford Street. He was accompanied by his ladylove, Miss Roberts, who was arrayed in all the finery one might expect of a bride about town. Her pretty face was wreathed in a delighted smile, but Darcy observed what could only be described as a rapid-fire snarl directed at Bingley that made him lower his wildly waving arm.

He was all dignity and decorum by the time Darcy approached and bowed. "Miss Roberts, Bingley. How do you do?"

"Oh, we are very well," said Miss Roberts. "Very well indeed! Mr Darcy, I understand you will be standing up with my dear Charles, hm? Allow me, if you will, to acquaint you with our plans."

With that, Miss Roberts was off and running telling him more than he wished to know about the plans for everything from the wedding breakfast to her renovation of Netherfield Park. Bingley stood by silently, with a fixed smile and glazed eyes as his lady rattled away.

"It all sounds charming," Darcy managed to say at last.

"My uncle, the duke, means to visit us at Netherfield," she said with a gleaming smile. "After we are settled."

"How delightful."

"He did say he knew you, Mr Darcy. I had to tell him, of course, that you would stand up with dear Charles, not

wishing to draw his disapproval with any of the arrangements!" She tittered madly.

"Yes, I do remember being introduced to him. I look
forward to seeing him at the breakfast." In truth, he barely
recollected the man, remembering only a reserved sort of
gentleman who had a fondness for horses.

There was, then, a group of two ladies and two young
girls who went by them. One of the girls, alas, had the
misfortune of bumping into Miss Roberts as she passed. The
girl was quick to beg Miss Roberts's pardon and curtsey to
her, but Miss Roberts only looked away, her nose raised.

"The absolute nerve," she spat angrily as soon as the
group had walked into a shop. "Charles, did you see that?
This place is becoming overrun by the lower class. It will not
be two years until decent people cannot even shop here
safely!"

"I believe people of all classes occasionally bump into one
another," Darcy said, not hiding the note of reproof in his
voice. "The street is full of carriages, and pedestrians must
be safe above all."

"Yes, dear," said Bingley. "One would rather the girl
bumped into us than be overrun by a carriage!"

Miss Roberts sniffed. "I do not know. Would it really be
tragic if there was one less tradesman's family? I mean,
really! Who brings children to Oxford Street! Positively
savage!"

"What made you think they were the family of a tradesman?" Bingley enquired.

Miss Roberts waved her hand dismissively. "The one is a
Mrs Gardiner. I have been to her husband's warehouses."

At the name Gardiner, Darcy felt a jolt. Elizabeth's aunt and cousins? He cursed himself for failing to recognise them, as Bingley did likewise, telling Miss Roberts he had once called at the Gardiner's home to see Miss Elizabeth Bennet. Miss Roberts was not pleased to hear of the acquaintance, her smile growing tight.

Darcy decided he had had enough of Miss Roberts and her ways, and that he would leave them. "Bingley, will you be at our club later?"

Bingley opened his mouth to reply, but Miss Roberts was quick to again insert herself.

"Not today! He simply has no time for it today! We have a list of tasks a mile long!" She tittered again. "This one seems to think a trousseau purchases itself! I told him, 'Charles, it is your wedding too. You simply must get new clothes!'"

Darcy had no notion of what to say to this. In truth, Bingley's attire did run to the shabby if he was not encouraged to buy new, so she might have been correct.

"Perhaps I will call on you tomorrow, then," he said, and Bingley, finally able to say something, urged him to do so, then took his lady and walked off.

AS SOON AS BINGLEY AND HIS LESS-THAN-charming bride-to-be disappeared round a corner, Darcy turned and entered the shop where, he believed, Mrs Gardiner still remained.

She was with the shopkeeper, settling a bill it seemed, for she laughed over her shoulder to the other lady and commented, "My husband will not be best pleased about this one!"

"Good day, Mrs Gardiner," he said, drawing near.

She turned and smiled, and to his relief, he found no apparent censure in it. "Mr Darcy, it is good to see you, sir."

"Pray forgive me for not greeting you properly out there." He gestured towards the door. "I did not recognise you and the Miss Gardiners when you passed."

Her smile dimmed slightly, and she inclined her head. "Do not think of it, sir."

He understood her immediately. She believed that he was as haughty as...well, not both his companions, for Bingley was never haughty, but as haughty as Miss Roberts. And perhaps at one time, he had been, but he would not continue in it.

"No, no," he said earnestly. "I truly did not realise it was you, else I should have been glad to greet you."

"Thank you," she said. "Elspeth was very sorry for running into your friend as she did."

"The lady is no friend of mine. She is merely the betrothed of my friend," he said. "Mr Bingley, who I believe you might know."

"Only a little," said Mrs Gardiner gracefully. "And I would not have imagined him to remember me, we were introduced only very briefly when he came to call on Elizabeth."

"He did remember," said Darcy. "But I believe his back was to you."

Darcy glanced towards the other woman and asked to be introduced to her. With a demurring sort of smile, the lady stepped back, but Mrs Gardiner said, "My maid, Mr Darcy, Miss Norris."

The younger of the two girls approached them, asking her mother if she could have a fan. Mrs Gardiner laughed and said, "Grace, you have no need of a fan."

The girl appeared to be crestfallen but obediently nodded and turned to walk off. As she went, Darcy was struck immediately by an idea. An underhanded idea, but an idea nevertheless.

"Miss Grace?"

Startled to be addressed by him, the little girl paused, then recognition dawned. "You are the man who gave us flowers!"

"I am. Mr Darcy is my name." He tried to look as agreeable as possible. "And I wonder if I might get some assistance from you and your sister? If you can help me, I should be well-pleased to buy you each a fan."

"Oh, sir, no, that is not necessary," Mrs Gardiner interrupted.

"Pray, madam, I assure you that what is very necessary is assistance. For me." Lowering his voice he said, "I find myself almost...desperate to rectify things between myself and Elizabeth. She is not the sort to be impressed by trifles, I know, but I should like to send her one anyhow."

The older girl came over to him and said, "Sir, my sister and I would be honoured to help you, but you need not buy us fans. You already gave us your flowers."

He smiled, and complimented Mrs Gardiner on the excellent behaviour of her children.

"Thank you," she said, her cheeks growing pink. "They

do have their moments, like most children, but their father and I are exceedingly proud of them."

"I thank you for your kindness, Miss Gardiner," he said, addressing the older girl. "But I am a man of my word, and I have promised you fans, so fans you shall have. Now my trouble is that I should like to purchase a gift for your cousin, Miss Elizabeth. Alas, I fear that as a gentleman, I really do not know what she might like."

Elspeth knew immediately what to do. "Perfume."

"Perfume?" Mrs Gardiner echoed. "My dear, I am not sure—"

"Lizzy spilt hers because she was crying," Grace informed them all. "While she was at our house. And she said a bad word, she said, 'Stupid fumble-fingers!' But she did not know I was there."

Crying because of me *no doubt.* Darcy inhaled sharply. "It seems we have our orders, then. Let us pick out the prettiest fans and then go to Floris's parfumerie."

WHAT FOLLOWED WAS THE PLEASANTEST HOUR that Darcy had spent in a long time. The girls had decided tastes in perfumes for their cousin and even encouraged him towards a scent for himself they felt certain 'Cousin Lizzy' would like.

"What you are wearing makes her sneeze," Miss Grace informed him gravely. "If you must know, it tickles my nose a bit, too."

"And mine as well." Saye had entered the shop unseen.

"Darcy, you were meant to meet me a quarter of an hour ago!"

"You are never punctual, so I gave it no consideration."

Happily, Saye immediately forgot his pique. Mrs Gardiner was a very pretty young woman, and one thing Saye never looked away from was a pretty woman. "And who is this charming creature?"

"Mrs Gardiner, if I may present my cousin, Lord Saye," Darcy replied guardedly. Surely Saye would comprehend these were the relations in trade? "Saye, this is Mrs Gardiner and her two daughters, Miss Gardiner and Miss Grace Gardiner."

"Utterly rapturous to know you," Saye pronounced, giving a none-too-subtle flick of his eyes over Mrs Gardiner's gown as she, in a very genteel manner, echoed his sentiments. Fortunately, Floris himself came to them then, offering Darcy a phial to smell.

"That is very fine lace on your gown," he heard his cousin remark to Mrs Gardiner.

"Thank you," she replied.

"Alençon?"

"You have an excellent eye for lace, sir," she said. "It is perhaps a bit extravagant for day, but I had some left from an evening gown and thought it ought not to go to waste."

"Just so," Saye agreed with a nod.

By the time they left the shop, Darcy had purchased a specially blended scent for Elizabeth, one for himself, and small bottles of a sweetly girlish fragrance for the two girls. The young girls held their new possessions tightly in their hands, but Elizabeth's would be sent to her directly from Floris.

"Like a Trojan horse," Saye muttered into Darcy's ear. "Sneaking in your love to the lady whether she wants it or not."

Mrs Gardiner, as was appropriate, protested wildly against the expense, but Darcy was adamant. He had enjoyed the time spent with them and regretted, painfully, that he had not been more agreeable to her previously. On an impulse, when parting, he asked her if she and Mr Gardiner would come to dine with him and his sister one evening soon, and after a short, surprised pause, she said they would be glad to.

CHAPTER TWENTY-TWO

EVER A FRIEND

When Mrs Gardiner and her small group were all safely tucked into the lady's carriage, Darcy walked with Saye down the street towards their club. They were silent as they went, which was extraordinarily uncommon for his cousin. At length, Darcy was compelled to say, "Well, then? Speak as you find."

"I am not sure I take your meaning."

"I am sure you have something to say about Mrs Gardiner, yes? Elizabeth's connexions in trade?"

Saye shrugged one shoulder. "If you say you are all eaten up with love for the girl, then you will need to countenance her relations." He sniffed. "Pray do not forget that we are related to Lady Catherine. She married a commoner, much as she should wish to forget that."

"Sir Lewis was knighted. And very wealthy."

"Knighted," Saye scoffed. "Shake a few pounds at old George, and he would have knighted positively anyone...and his son is no different. In any case, they must be quite wealthy, these Gardiners. That lace was not inexpensive, and she treated it as nothing. The carriage, too, was new and well sprung."

"You have formed quite an opinion on only two minutes' acquaintance! Do you have anything to say about her petticoats?"

"In fact, she had lace on them as well. I observed it when you handed her into the carriage, and she pulled her skirts in behind her. My *point* is that I would not be disgusted to know Mrs Gardiner. And you"—he pointed a finger at Darcy—"*you* ought to become a bit more broad-minded."

They paused, needing to cross the street, which was busy with carriages and people.

"That is something, coming from the haughtiest man I have ever known."

"If I lost the woman I loved over it," Saye informed him loftily, "I would change it. And in any case, I daresay I am more broad-minded than you are."

That comment did not warrant reply. "Then you will not mind coming to dine with us?" Darcy challenged as they walked across the street. "How is Thursday?"

"Are you making some attempt to call my bluff?" Saye chuckled. "Darcy, you will need to try harder than that."

"You said you would not dislike knowing Mr and Mrs Gardiner. Then…will you dine with us?"

"Darcy." Saye paused, shaking his head. "How many times do I need to tell you of my influence? I could have Mrs Gardiner at Almack's next Wednesday if I wished it to be so."

"No, you could not."

"Yes," said Saye in his maddeningly superior way, "I could. Pray do not test me on it, for in truth, I do not think married ladies find much to enjoy at Almack's unless they have a young lady to bring forward. Although..." He drew out the word. "There we have it! I shall secure a voucher for Mrs Gardiner to bring *Elizabeth* to Almack's and see if I cannot stir up a few rivals for you."

He chuckled at his own wit and gave Darcy a punch on the sleeve.

"And yet, all your boasting of Almack's aside, you still have not answered the question. Will you dine with us?"

"Thursday does not work for me. Make it Friday and..." Saye smirked. "I will bring my mother and father."

THE DINNER AT DARCY HOUSE PROVED A SUCCESS. Lord and Lady Matlock had come with Saye, and all of them, ladies and men alike, had had a splendid evening together. Lady Matlock had even said, afterwards, that she very much would have mistaken the Gardiners for people of fashion.

There was but one dissatisfaction in the evening for Darcy, and that was that Mrs Gardiner had little to tell him of Elizabeth beyond the fact that she was 'improving daily' in her health and planned to go to Brighton. It had shocked Darcy to imagine that she would again leave home to travel; but Mrs Gardiner informed him of her purpose, to watch over her youngest sister, and Darcy understood it, even if he believed it ought to have been her mother's duty. Well did he know what ills might befall a young lady at the seaside!

It was nearly a se'nnight until he was able to pin Bingley

down for a talk in Miss Roberts's absence. Darcy, along with Saye, called at the rooms Bingley kept at the Albany.

"What is this?" Saye enquired suspiciously as Darcy deviated from the route that would have taken them directly to their club. "I knew walking anywhere with you was a dreadful notion."

"I need to speak to a friend."

"What friend? Not Bingley?"

"Come!" Darcy ordered. "You dined with the Gardiners, did you not? And seem to have come through the experience well enough."

"The Gardiners are everything charming and clever," Saye replied. "Bingley is a pup. Too young and too eager by half. Were he a duke, I would still find him intolerable."

"The call will be short," Darcy promised. "He might not even be home."

In fact, Bingley was scarcely awake when Darcy and Saye arrived, but nevertheless received them happily, albeit in his dressing gown. A meal had just been brought up for him, and he invited Darcy and Saye to partake with him.

"Coffee will do," Darcy told him, and Saye, after a sharp poke to the ribs, mumbled something about needing nothing.

Bingley's man poured coffee, then left them to their conversation. Bingley did not appear enthusiastic about the eggs before him and eyed them briefly before preferring his own cup of coffee.

"Not hungry?" Darcy enquired. "Or do you fear a revolt of the gastric variety?"

Bingley chuckled lightly. "I confess it is the latter. Sophie does enjoy a good party, and I fear I am drinking too much and sleeping too little. My head and my stomach begin to protest against the revelry."

"Things will no doubt settle after the wedding," Darcy observed, taking a sip of coffee. "Do you mean to travel afterwards?"

"She wishes to go to Italy," Bingley replied with as much eagerness as one might display for a trip to the smithy for a tooth extraction. "She says people of fashion must go to Italy for at least six months."

"Six months?" Darcy raised one brow even as a sinking feeling beset him. Six months of Bingley on the Continent was six months that he could not expect an invitation to Netherfield Park.

"Sometimes a year," Saye offered brightly. "Unless of course she falls with child. When that happens, you will want to get back to English soil as soon as you can."

"With child?" Bingley looked as if the notion had never before occurred to him.

"You do know how all of that works, do you not?" Saye enquired. "Allow me to explain. First you will want to—"

Bingley was looking decidedly nauseated, and Darcy thus interrupted his cousin. "Of course he knows, Saye. Bingley—it seems the notion of a sojourn in Italy does not agree with you."

Bingley sighed and looked down at his plate. "Ah, Darcy, I cannot lie to you. You always feared I would show my affection too freely and find myself trapped in an untenable position, and here I am." He scrubbed his hands through his hair. "No, I do not wish to go to Italy with her. I do not wish to live with her or have children with her. I do not even much wish to dance with her."

Darcy heaved an unhappy sigh, an ache in his chest from his friend's torment. Saye said nothing but flicked a glance in Bingley's direction that might have been sympathetic.

"She was so sweet the first night we danced at Almack's. It is not my usual place, as you know, but Caroline somehow got a voucher and insisted I take her. I had met Miss Roberts before, and she seemed kind enough, but that night she was all that was charming and I…I asked her to dance twice."

"Twice, at Almack's?" Darcy exclaimed. It was well known that one did *not* dance twice with any one lady at Almack's. Not only did such behaviour displease the lady patronesses, but in a place known as the Marriage Mart, it was tantamount to a declaration. More than one breach of promise suit had arisen after two dances at Almack's.

"When she parted from me, after the first, she encouraged me to ask her again. I do not mean to blame her—I know the rules well enough—but I confess I was a bit overwhelmed by her charms and therefore did it anyway."

Darcy offered a sympathetic wince in reply. Saye, less concerned with Bingley's sensibilities, rolled his eyes and said, "Quite stupid of you, Bingley."

Bingley nodded glumly, then with a burst of desperation asked, "What am I to do about it?"

"Do?"

"Surely there is something?" Bingley begged. "I cannot go through with it. I cannot! I am twenty-three years old, and the most optimistic outcome I can think of is an early death."

"Ask her to release you." Saye leant towards Bingley, drawn into the drama despite himself.

"I tried to, once… She was having a tirade about the lower classes encroaching into Mayfair. She said if she saw one more matron in shiny new jewellery parading about as if she owned the place, she would not be responsible for her actions. I said that as my money comes from my father's work, she ought to reconsider my suit. It did not go well."

"What did she do?"

"Shrieked. Cried. Slapped me…twice. And said the only thing worse than a tradesperson was a jilt and she would not allow me to lower her. Would it truly be so terrible if *I* broke things off?"

"You would not be received again," Darcy told him gently. "Nor would Miss Bingley. The club would remove you, and there would be little hope of regaining any sort of position in Society for you."

"Nor your children," Saye added in with a sort of delighted foreboding. "You would do best to move to somewhere savage, America perhaps."

Bingley lowered his head into his hands and moaned.

"I am sorry. I wish I could offer some consolation," Darcy said sympathetically.

Bingley sat up straight, his countenance brighter. "What if I shot off my own leg? Surely she would not wish to marry a lame man?"

Darcy laughed but sobered quickly, realising that Bingley was not making a joke.

"Shoot the Earl of Tooleywag down there," Saye

suggested. "Perhaps once she knew you were unable to be a proper husband, the rest would follow naturally."

Bingley frowned and pushed his breakfast about with his fork.

Darcy rubbed his hand across his mouth thoughtfully. "Are her servants loyal to her?"

"I have witnessed her slap her maid on several occasions, and she abuses her coachmen something awful."

"Spread a few coins among them, see what they will tell you," Darcy advised, well aware that he was once again inserting himself into Bingley's affairs. "If you are certain you truly wish to know, that is! Do not do it unless you are prepared to discover the worst."

"You mean…a liaison?"

"A liaison, an affair de couer," Saye said. "A tumble in the hay at her father's estate. Anything at all."

"There might be nothing, but if something were to come to light, something which made you rightly doubt the lady's character…"

An expression of hope had come into Bingley's eyes. Leaping up, he clapped Darcy on the arm. "You are ever a friend, Darcy! Ever a friend!"

"I will keep my ear to the ground as well. One never knows what might come to light," Saye offered with an amiability that Darcy immediately mistrusted.

"Thank you, Lord Saye," Bingley said, seeming truly gratified by the idea. "You have no idea—"

"But once we see you sprung from this thing," Saye continued, with an innocent-looking grin, "you must promise to repay us with a house party! I cannot rest until I am a guest at the famed Netherfield Park!"

"Name the date and it shall be done," Bingley promised, his eyes bright.

DARCY AND HIS COUSIN LEFT BINGLEY AND HIS breakfast and went to their club. They had invited Bingley to attend them, but he had declined, being required as he was at Miss Roberts's mother's drawing room.

The day was fine, and Saye whistled as the two men walked.

"Unable to rest until you have spent time at Netherfield?" Darcy enquired of his cousin. "At a house party?"

"Indeed," Saye replied.

"Why?"

"Miss Lillian Goddard of Ashworth lives near there," Saye replied. "County does produce some beauties, does it not?"

"You wish Bingley to have a house party so you can do what? Make him host a ball so you can dance with Miss Goddard?"

"Dance with her? I mean to marry her."

Darcy gaped at his cousin, but Saye was not looking in his direction. "Have you been—"

"Alas, I find myself a tardy boy. The Season draws to its close, and I do not have time sufficient to properly woo her. Ergo—house party!" Saye paused on the street and turned to Darcy who halted as well. "This Italy thing. It cannot stand. I need Bingley in Hertfordshire in September, having balls and parties."

Darcy chuckled and began again to walk, as did Saye. "Persuasive as you are, Saye, you can hardly require a man to give up his Italian honeymoon so you can court a woman at his county house."

"It simply will not do. He will be gone for months and then, rest assured, she will be with child. Do not let his squeamishness over breakfast fool you. The boy will be riding neck or nothing in that saddle."

"Nevertheless, it is his life, and he must make his own decisions."

Saye chuckled. "That is rich, coming from you of all people."

Darcy rolled his eyes. "My past mistakes notwithstanding—"

"We must get him out of this marriage," Saye interrupted. "Absolutely must. If her people have nothing on her, then we will need to come up with something else. Keep me apprised."

CHAPTER TWENTY-THREE

ALL SWEETNESS AND AFFABILITY

"I cannot believe you are leaving again, Lizzy," said Jane as they stood in their bedchamber, overseeing their maid who was once again packing Elizabeth's trunk. They still had several days before they were due to travel, but Elizabeth imagined Lydia would consume the maid for most of that time with her endless indecision about what to wear.

"Nor can I," she said with a little sigh. In truth, as much as Elizabeth enjoyed travel, particularly to new places, it had begun to wear on her, all the to and fro. *If it saves Lydia from mischief-making, so be it,* she reminded herself.

Moving to her closet, she retrieved a wrapped parcel, and brought it to the maid, saying, "This too, Sarah, and I suspect it might be breakable so—"

"What is that?" Jane enquired, very nearly pouncing on the parcel as Sarah began to reach for it.

Elizabeth quickly retracted the parcel. "Nothing! 'Tis nothing!"

"The label says it is from Floris. Did you buy perfume? Can I smell it?"

"If I had wished to purchase scent, Floris is surely above my touch. I did not dare even enter the place, last I was in London," Elizabeth replied with a chuckle.

"Then how did you get it? Why have you not unwrapped it?"

Elizabeth sighed. "Because…I am afraid of what is in it."

"Afraid? You are making no sense to me."

"Sarah, will you leave us for a few minutes?" The maid nodded, and left the two sisters. Elizabeth sank onto her bed, the parcel still in her hands. "Aunt Gardiner wrote to me…"

After a pause, Jane said, "Yes, and…?"

"She met Mr Darcy while shopping and spent a little time with him on Bond Street. Evidently, she and my uncle were subsequently invited to dine at Darcy House."

Jane's hand flew to her chest, her eyes wide. "In truth?"

Elizabeth nodded. "She told me only the barest sketch of things but said she would be happy to tell me more as I wished it. I have not yet had the courage to ask more."

"Because you fear you might forgive him? Or miss him too much?"

Elizabeth did not reply to that directly. "Not only have I not had the courage to ask more, but I have also lacked the courage to open the parcel."

"Do you know it is from him?"

"Who else?" She gave her sister a look. "My aunt suggested that I might expect something, indicating I ought not to let Papa hide it away in his study. This was what came."

"I think you need to open it. Immediately," Jane said firmly. "I will open it for you if you would like."

"No, no, I...I shall open it. I shall." Slowly, she unwrapped the paper. A missive fell to the ground; Jane picked it up for her then sat down beside her while Elizabeth gazed at the treasure she had unwrapped.

It was a pear-shaped bottle made of rock crystal with an ornate brass covering over the glass, which looked like vines and tendrils. It was, simply, one of the most beautiful perfume bottles she had ever seen—not that she had seen very many. Beside her, Jane breathed a sigh of delight, her closeness meaning that her breath went directly into Elizabeth's ear.

"What does it smell like?" Jane asked. "Even if it smelt terrible, having this bottle alone would be well worth it!"

Elizabeth by then had removed the bronze-capped stopper. She held it to her nose, inhaling deeply of a fragrance unlike anything she had ever before smelt. "Exquisite," she said, passing it to Jane to smell.

"Ohh! It is really just indescribable, is it not?" Jane glanced at the folded note. "And is this Mr Darcy's hand?"

Elizabeth took the proffered note from Jane and glanced at it, then nodded.

Darcy had written her a number of letters, which she had publicly denounced but privately secreted away in her bedchamber. They had not been read, but neither had they been sent back or burnt. After the last had been received, she had told her father she wished him to write to Darcy and tell him to desist. She had not imagined her father would actually bestir himself to do it, but several days later, he informed her that he had done as she wished.

It seemed that Darcy had gone around that edict regardless. "High-handed," she murmured, but she could not deny that the gesture pleased her. "Perhaps I am more persuaded by his wealth than I had ever imagined."

"Persuaded or not, pray do open it," Jane urged.

Elizabeth unfolded the paper, taking a moment to bring it to her nose. Even the paper smelt delicious.

> *Elizabeth,*
>
> *I hope this small token will meet with your approval. The perfumer was instructed to concoct a scent that would answer some of your finest qualities—sweetness and light balanced with an agreeable piquancy of wit. What was created seemed very apt to me, and I hope you will enjoy it as well.*
>
> *I must confess that in this endeavour I received the aid of two young but expert perfumers, Miss Gardiner and Miss Grace Gardiner, who were quick to guide me away from any errors of choice. Miss Grace also urged me to alter my own tastes in cologne, telling me that something in what I presently wore made her favourite cousin sneeze.*

Elizabeth gasped.

"What is it?" Jane asked worriedly.

"Oh!" Elizabeth laid a hand on her head and chuckled ruefully. "Never tell Gracie a thing you do not want told to the entire world."

"What did she tell?"

"She told Mr Darcy his cologne made me sneeze!"

"Did you tell her that?"

Elizabeth sighed. "Yes...I...I did tell her so. It was a bit of exaggeration—it sometimes made my eyes sting and my nose become stuffy—only when it was freshly applied, I believe—but I never actually sneezed. He always smelt very nice, of course..."

Elizabeth drifted into a recollection of the one time he held her, the time she had not given him any choice, thrusting herself directly into his arms and feeling his embrace. It had been nothing short of heavenly.

Jane was peering over her shoulder, clearly attempting to read the note. "He had it custom-blended for you! Do you have any notion of what this must have cost?"

Elizabeth shrugged, attempting to be nonchalant. "He is wealthy, as we know. I am sure he only wished to remind me of it."

"Lizzy, stop."

"I am only teasing." She forced a chuckle and then returned to the page.

As I would not wish any part of me to be displeasing, I have forth-with had new cologne made for myself as well. Mr Floris assures me that my lady shall not be able to resist me with his latest concoction, and I can only hope, desperately, that it shall be one day true.

Until then, I remain yours — D

A contrariety of emotion beset her at the ending. *The man does know how to end a letter in a heartfelt manner.*

She took a deep, steadying breath and said, "I suppose I shall have to send it back."

"Lizzy! No! I forbid it in every way."

That made Elizabeth laugh. "Society forbids that I should keep it!"

"Society! Pah!" Jane cried out.

"We are not engaged, Jane. It would be highly improper, no matter how elegant the bottle or how delightful the scent."

Jane took the bottle and smelt again. "Yes," she said with an unusual note of satire in her voice, "do send it back. In any case, we can certainly make something of its like in our still-room, can we not? I shall go and see where Hill keeps the lily of the valley."

"A lady cannot accept a gift from a man," Elizabeth protested weakly over her laugh. "It would not be proper."

Jane handed the bottle back to her sister, with a gleam in her eyes. "Were it me, I should keep the perfume and the man along with it."

Elizabeth rolled her eyes. "My life long for a bottle of perfume. Am I really so cheaply bought?"

"It was decidedly not cheap. Perhaps you might at least forgive him?"

"On the basis of perfume?"

"On the basis of the fact that he loves you and would do anything for you."

"Except tell me the truth. Even in this he has not been truthful!" Elizabeth waved the perfume at her sister. "This perfume was sent under the guise of a parcel from a shop! I am sure if my father knew it was a gift from Mr Darcy—"

"He would not have done a thing and we both know it," Jane concluded. "The officers were forever giving our younger sisters little gifts, and there was nary a blink from the book-room."

Elizabeth winced. Was there no end to the examples put before her that Darcy had been, in fact, correct about her family? Then again, it was not his correctness in that regard that was in question, only his hurtful declarations about it.

"Do you truly think he was shopping with Mrs Gardiner?" she enquired. "I cannot comprehend that. He did not even wish to enter the house when he brought me to Gracechurch Street."

"Write to her," Jane suggested. "Then you will know."

ELIZABETH DID WRITE TO HER AUNT, GIVING HER direction in Brighton and saying she wished to know all. Mrs Gardiner responded with alacrity—evidently, she had wished fervently to write to her niece with the details of the events in London.

It seemed he had been searching for a gift for you, Lizzy, and had not met with success. Elspeth and Grace were quick to offer their opinions, and although I might have admonished them for speaking so decidedly to such a gentleman, Mr Darcy did appear to be grateful to them. I would not have gone into such a shop as Floris on my own accord, but it appears Mr Darcy thought it perfectly natural to escort us there and set about creating perfumes for not only you but the girls as well. And himself—I am afraid Gracie might have suggested you were not fond of his cologne.

Elizabeth, despite her prior intelligence on this matter,

found herself blushing anew. With a fond shake of her head, she continued to read.

> It was shortly thereafter when your uncle and I found ourselves invited to dine at Mr Darcy's home. We accepted, of course, and had a wonderful evening with not only Mr and Miss Darcy but Lord Saye and his parents, the Earl and Countess of Matlock. You might have knocked me over with a feather when I saw them all, but I found them perfectly amiable. Lord Saye has a bit of a flaming character, but he kept us all laughing even if he seemed, at times, to vex his cousin.

There was more—Mrs Gardiner gave a detailed account of what they dined on and how late they remained—but Elizabeth was not wholly persuaded by it. "All well and good to invite them to Mayfair," she scoffed. "See if he would dirty himself by going to Gracechurch Street!"

Then her eyes fell a bit farther down the page.

> …brought his sister to drink tea with me while he and Lord Saye called on your uncle in his office. Evidently, they mean to make some sort of investment…

Elizabeth could read no more. *Very well*, she told herself. *He has amended the part of himself that has unfairly judged the Gardiners. Who in their right mind would not like my aunt and uncle Gardiner! See how he enjoys an evening with the Philipses!*

Then again, she reminded herself, she herself did not particularly enjoy evenings with her aunt and uncle Philips, not due to their station, naturally, but rather their characters.

Her aunt was full of hilarity and high spirits, but when entertaining, she had a decided tendency to become vulgar. Even when not entertaining, the subjects she found suitable for polite conversation often provoked Elizabeth to blush or cringe. As for her uncle, he was stuffy and drank too much, though he could be depended upon to be silent.

Darcy probably would have met the Philipses in Meryton last autumn and perhaps had assumed the Gardiners would be much the like, she realised. He had probably imagined that the Gardiners would also be drunk, vulgar, and loud. But they were not, and he had revised his opinion when confronted with that truth—had even taken his sister to Gracechurch Street to call on them.

Reading on, Elizabeth learnt that Georgiana had been utterly charmed by the Gardiners' children and had kept little Henry on her lap nearly the entire visit. Even when the baby had spit up a little on her gown, she had waved off any attempt to remove him.

What does any of this signify if you intend to never see him again?

Never to see him again. Why was it that the thought of that left her feeling so hollow inside?

CHAPTER TWENTY-FOUR

HOISTED WITH ONE'S OWN PETARD

"Let us go down to Jackson's parlour," Saye proposed one fine summer morning at the Matlock town home. "I understand he has some fellows coming in today that mean to make the rest of us look like schoolboys."

His mother eyed him contemplatively over her teacup. Setting it down she said, "I despise all that sort of thing."

"They ought to allow the ladies their time in there," Saye proposed. "Perhaps there would be sweeter tempers in the ballroom if we permitted you to pummel one another occasionally."

Lady Matlock laughed. "Now that I cannot disagree with." Finishing the tea she had been drinking, she rose and excused herself from the men.

As the door closed behind her, Fitzwilliam said, "It seems a fine plan to me. Darcy? You will come, will you not?"

Darcy had remained silent through the exchange,

speaking only to murmur his thanks to the footman who poured him coffee. His initial hope that Elizabeth might somehow forgive him was fading; he had written many letters, had sent his gift, and it had all come to naught. He knew not what to do next. "I have nothing better to do," he said at length.

"Pray, dim your enthusiasm just a bit."

"No doubt you wish to be at Pemberley," Fitzwilliam said sympathetically.

Darcy made a noise of agreement but, though it was his habit to be at Pemberley in July, this year was different. He had Anne's wedding to attend, as well as his obligation to stand up with Bingley, to keep him in town. More than that, however, was a general reluctance to be in Derbyshire without Elizabeth. Therefore no, he had no urgent wish to go to Pemberley, nor a wish to be in town. What he wished was to be back in time, in Kent, with her, to have a chance to re-do much of what had been done.

"The shine of the Season has dimmed," Saye pronounced. "Nothing else to do but attend the inevitable weddings which result from the matrons' efforts."

"Our cousin's wedding is less than a fortnight away," Fitzwilliam said cheerfully. "When does young Bingley don the shackles?"

"I wish he would not don them at all," Darcy admitted to his cousins. "But it is a mere se'nnight away. It may be unavoidable now."

Saye was suddenly upright, looking startled. "A se'nnight? Good Lord!"

Darcy inclined his head but continued to speak to

Fitzwilliam. "I advised him to speak to her people. She is none too kind to those in her employ, and they might wish to give her up for bad behaviour. Alas, they had nothing to say against her save that which he already knew—she is unkind and ill-tempered to them."

"None too kind to him either," Fitzwilliam said. "And corrects him as if she is his governess. She was forever hissing instructions to him at Lady Cockfoster's dinner last week. One would have thought the poor lad was never in good company before."

"I believed his wedding was in August?" Saye enquired.

"No, next week," Darcy replied, then continued with Fitzwilliam. "She does at least seem quite enthusiastic about her new home."

"Evidently she likes the nearness of it to London," Fitzwilliam agreed. "No doubt poor Bingley has been tasked with buying her a new carriage for her travels."

"She can buy her own carriage," Saye replied. "Quite rich from all I know. And niece of a duke, as we are all reminded often."

"A very proud, very haughty girl," Fitzwilliam agreed.

"How can I reasonably support him entering into such a marriage? And yet when has he needed my support more?" Darcy asked rhetorically.

"If nothing else," Fitzwilliam offered, "you ought to be there in case he swoons, realising what he's just done."

Darcy shook his head, regret consuming him. If only he had stayed out of the business of Jane Bennet and Bingley! "They mean to be off to Italy for six months, departing in

August. Bingley is hoping the ship will go down or that he might be captured by pirates along the way."

Saye drummed his fingers against the table. "I cannot say strongly enough how inconvenient all of this is to my purposes. I *must* be in Hertfordshire in September, and if Bingley is not there… What of Miss Elizabeth Bennet?"

"You do not imagine she might invite you to Hertfordshire?" Fitzwilliam laughed.

"Elizabeth has gone to Brighton," said Darcy.

"Brighton?" Fitzwilliam grimaced. "With all those encampments down there?"

The word 'encampments' made him wince. "The notion has weighed on me."

"As well it should! Are there not packs of soldiers down there?" Saye asked blithely. "What of Wickham? He may try to—"

Darcy felt his gut clench. "If he dares try to insinuate himself—"

"You have told her about Georgiana," Fitzwilliam observed soothingly. "She will not fall prey to his wiles now, not when she knows the truth of him."

"I should hope that is true."

"There are so many people in Brighton, far more than were in Hertfordshire," Fitzwilliam added. "Wickham has no doubt found a greener pasture, if not two."

"And surely he knows she jilted you," said Saye with painful candour. "No doubt he imagines that you should be more than happy to leave her to the consequences of her own actions."

"Have I ever been so spiteful?" Darcy retorted instantly. "My temper is not so resentful as that, is it?"

Neither of the two brothers replied.

"It is not," Darcy insisted. "For those whom I love, there is little I would not do."

"I believe Wickham imagines you always resentful, always spiteful," said Fitzwilliam carefully. "Because he caused you to be so. No doubt he believes that any woman who has jilted you would receive the same feeling, if not worse."

"Let us hope that notion keeps him away from her," Darcy said. "I could not care less what he thinks if it keeps her safe from harm's way."

"When do you think you will have the opportunity to speak to her yourself?" Saye enquired.

"I do not know that I have any reasonable hope of seeing her again."

Saye leant forwards. "Which brings us round again to the subject of the house party."

Darcy took a long drink of his coffee. "There is no house party. At least not in the foreseeable future."

"Positively insufferable. All hope for my future felicity is pinned on Bingley's party." Saye grimaced and rolled his eyes. "There is a sentence I could not have ever imagined saying. And a mere week to act! What to do, what to do?"

There was a silence while Darcy and Fitzwilliam both observed Saye. At length, Darcy enquired, hesitantly, "You would not...make an attempt on Miss Roberts's virtue, would you?"

Saye abruptly brought his gaze from the study of the ceiling, his face screwed up with disdain. "What do you take me for? In any case, I am in love. All other women are abhorrent to me."

"You will not make Sir Frederick do it?" Fitzwilliam pressed. Sir Frederick was Saye's most intimate friend, and it was widely agreed that if Saye told him to jump, Sir Frederick asked him how high. "It would be cruel to the lady to engineer her ruination."

"That *is* an interesting possibility," Saye owned. "But I think not. Too risky. What if she slapped poor Fred? He would run off with his tail between his legs before his face showed the welt."

"You appear to be scheming," Darcy said. "Pray tell us what you mean to do."

"Do? What is it to me to *do* anything? What, pray tell, could I do with a situation so wholly unrelated to me?" Saye rose from the table, tossing his napkin onto his plate. "I must toddle off, fellows, important things afoot this morning."

"What about Jackson's?" Fitzwilliam asked.

"Too busy, little brother." With that he was gone, his boots rapping smartly down the hall until the sound faded.

Fitzwilliam turned to look at Darcy. "Do you think he is going to ruin Bingley's lady?"

"Where your brother is concerned, anything is possible." Darcy sighed. "Do you think Elizabeth is safe? Were it not for Bingley's wedding, I should be down there at once, even if she would certainly run the other direction the moment she saw me."

"I think I could ensure she is well on your behalf, if you would like me to?"

Relief swept through Darcy even as he said, "I could not ask you to go to Brighton—"

"As it stands, my general needs a favour, and while I do not usually enjoy being an errand boy, in this case, I might be persuaded."

"I would be in your debt," Darcy said.

"Well! Double the pleasure," Saye drawled in his most flirtish voice. He had just been shown into the drawing room of Lady Jersey's home where she sat with another of Almack's lady patronesses, Lady Emily Cowper. "If it is not the two most beautiful married women in London."

As he had anticipated, both ladies laughed and blushed.

"Lady Cowper, I understand your husband is ailing? When may I wish you joy?" Saye smiled broadly as he accepted a cup of coffee and refused cake.

"You, sir, are terrible to speak of my beloved husband in such a way," Lady Cowper scolded, the sparkle in her eye easily belying the truth beneath her words. Lord Cowper was stupid and dull and despised any sort of fun, and thus Saye had no use for him whatsoever. How the man had managed to connect himself to such a vivacious and sweet creature as Lady Cowper, he could not imagine, but so it was.

"You all but jilted me in favour of the scoundrel," Saye informed her. "You might have become the Countess of Matlock one day!"

"And instead," said Lady Jersey with the acerbic wit she was known for, "she is the Countess of Cowper, *today*."

DONE FOR THE BEST

"You wound me," he replied with an easy smile. "I suppose ladies are in scorn of viscounts these days, hm? Better an earl older than one's father than a lively viscount, is that the way of it?"

The ladies laughed. "Fortunately for the viscounts, the decrepit earls are declining in number now," said Lady Jersey. "Something to do with the war, I believe."

"Positively dreadful," Saye agreed. "But what do we do? Speaking of wars and death…too tedious by half. What news from the Marriage Mart, ladies? Tell me all that I do not know."

The ladies needed no more than that, quickly setting off to tell him who was marrying whom, who had jilted whom, and which hapless souls were presently in disgrace with them. Among them was a lady who had run off with her coachman.

"Convenient," Saye opined. "One does not have to worry who will drive to Gretna if the groom becomes the bridegroom."

"Yes, I am positive it was the convenience of it all which drew her," Lady Jersey said with a roll of her pretty eyes. "Nothing at all to do with his handsome face or figure."

"In any case, nobody cares who anyone marries anymore," Saye replied dismissively. "Why, I lately heard that the niece of the Duke of Rochdale is to be married to a tradesman. Such a notion!"

"Who is that?" Lady Jersey asked, suddenly all attentiveness.

Saye tapped one finger on his temple, both to build suspense and to seem unsure. "Miss Robinson? No—

Roberts. I daresay the entire thing happened at Almack's, so no doubt you already knew about that."

"A tradesman? And he was dancing with her at Almack's?" The two ladies exchanged glances.

"I am sure I scarcely know either of them," he told them in an affectedly weary manner. "That is only what I heard. My cousin Darcy, you know, is great friends with the man. Bingley is his name."

"Friend of Darcy or not," said Lady Cowper, "he had no right to be dancing at Almack's. How did he get a voucher? Whose was it?"

Saye examined his nails while replying, "I have not the least notion, my dear. Maybe he found it on the street?"

The two ladies gasped, but then Lady Cowper giggled. "You are ever so naughty, Lord Saye."

"Lord Saye raises an important point," Lady Jersey said earnestly. "If we do not maintain exclusivity for Almack's, then we might as well scatter vouchers about on the street."

"Too right," Saye said with an approving nod. "But I do feel terribly bad for Miss Roberts. Such a sweet soul! But merciful as you both are, *of course* you would not ban her simply for lowering herself. Bingley is quite wealthy—two or three thousand a year, I believe."

He knew, of course, that it was at least double that, but best to make this all as shocking as possible.

"Two or three thousand?" Lady Cowper enquired. "Surely she is not...I mean, it is a decent income, to be sure—"

"One cannot keep a house in town on that," Lady Jersey asserted.

Saye inclined his head in barest acknowledgement.

"There is always economy," he asserted. "A place in the City perhaps."

Lady Jersey frowned while Lady Cowper looked as if she had swallowed something unpleasant.

"On such an income, one could not afford the voucher," Saye added. "You would not even need to ban her outright."

"No. It must be done," said Lady Jersey firmly, and Lady Cowper murmured her assent, so vigorously that her turban nearly came off. "Otherwise, the whole thing becomes nearly farcical."

"If we do not continue to preserve the distinction of rank, who will?" Lady Cowper added earnestly.

Saye nodded. "We are of like mind in this, madam."

"Speaking of Darcy, I thought I had heard that he was engaged?" Lady Cowper enquired. "To some lady no one knows."

"No, not engaged, but he is quite in love with her. I do not doubt the matter will come to the natural conclusion shortly."

"In love?" Lady Jersey exclaimed. "Darcy? Why, how… unexpected. And who is the lady?"

"Miss Elizabeth Bennet."

"Who?" Lady Jersey asked abruptly. "I never heard of her."

"Have you not?" Saye raised one carefully shaped brow. "Lady Cowper, I should think *you* of all people would know the Bennets. They have been at their seat in Hertfordshire for above a century. Is not that Elizabethan monstrosity your husband has been remodelling in that county?"

"The Cowpers have extensive property in Hertfordshire,"

Lady Cowper agreed. "Where, precisely, in Hertfordshire is her father's estate?"

"I confess I do not know. Near to Ashworth, which is the Goddards' place."

"Oh, that is about fifteen miles—"

"There you go, then! You are neighbours. No doubt you will wish to host a dinner for her or something once they are wed."

Lady Cowper smiled uncertainly and agreed, and Saye was filled with all the contentment of having done a good turn for Darcy. *Where would any person in this family be without my efforts,* he thought with indulgent satisfaction. *If only they all realised what they owe to me.*

Saye spent another few minutes with the ladies, obtaining some last giggles and blushes before leaving them with grand bows and kisses on the hands of each. Then he left them, satisfied that his work had been done and done for the best. *Miss Roberts has been hoisted with her own petard. Let her uppishness be its own punishment.*

CHAPTER TWENTY-FIVE

A LITTLE SEA-BATHING

Brighton was an exciting place, thrumming with the activity of the military regiments that made it their temporary home and the ladies and gentlemen who came to the seaside on holiday. Elizabeth was intrigued by it from the first time she saw the neatly aligned rows of army tents on the very outskirts of the town. She could never have imagined such a variety of people, or such activity. Everywhere she looked, there were people gathered, talking, laughing, watching the soldiers on their exercises. How good it was, she thought, to be in a place rightly unknown to her, and be among people with whom she did not share lost memories.

Even though her heart would always prefer a ramble through the countryside, by the time their first se'nnight in Brighton had passed, she had fallen in love with walks along the Promenade and the coast. The variety of persons she beheld was enough to keep any student of character busy for weeks; she even caught sight of the famed sea-dipper Martha Gunn, now advanced in her years and yet still active in her trade. Elizabeth did think it might be nice to be dipped, but within a week of her stay she had already learnt of soldiers who lingered about to catch a glimpse of the ladies in their post-bathed state. She knew not if it was true, or if they ever actually saw anything, but she would not risk it.

Strangely, no matter where she turned, she was reminded of Darcy. She saw him in every man who passed, regardless of how slight the provocation. One man had on boots with a certain scuff, and she thought Darcy's boots had had a similar scuff once. Another gentleman she saw had a certain way of tapping his walking stick while he walked that was very much like Darcy's way of tapping his.

And with these thoughts always crept another: *Have I been absurd?* In refusing to forgive him, had she cost herself something very dear?

Though she could not remember her behaviour on the evening of Darcy's proposal, she had read and re-read his letter often enough to know that she had certainly not been a credit to herself. She had always been quick to anger, this she had long known, but she had learnt at an early age to control her tongue. Evidently that control had failed her on the night he proposed.

Even though he had angered her, his feelings were just. Jane *had* appeared indifferent, and her nearest relations, while dear to her, *had* behaved abominably. 'They were positively the worst I have ever seen them' was what Jane said of the matter, and for Jane to say so was remarkable indeed. Elizabeth was thankful *not* to remember any of it, but she could imagine enough to make her blush and to forgive Darcy his judgment of them.

But these things were all nothing to his deception of her. His deception which, most peculiarly, had begun to feel rather unimportant, no matter how it had struck her at first. In acknowledging the wisdom of his discernment in other matters, she began to own that he might have been correct. Perhaps it *was* best that she had been permitted to believe herself engaged. Perhaps it *would* have been too much a shock to learn the truth, especially since she had been occupied with falling in love.

A remembrance bestirred her feelings: the day she had nearly had leeches applied to her. The practice was commonplace, but no one from among her acquaintance had ever seemed to benefit from it. Moreover, common as it might be, the treatment had never happened to her before, and the intense trepidation she felt on beholding the jar of them had nearly made her swoon. Dr Hughes had meant to treat her aggressively; she overheard him telling Charlotte she would need to be bled thrice each day with as many as twenty leeches, for a week if not longer. Dr Hughes told her it would not hurt, but imagining sitting for as long as an hour, watching such ugly creatures feeding upon her? Even now she shuddered at the notion.

And then she had heard Darcy running through the house, footsteps like righteous thunder, to make the man stop. *My own Lancelot*, she had thought at the time. Charlotte had revealed later that Miss de Bourgh said he had run at terrific speed from Rosings the moment he felt Elizabeth needed him.

She considered the gentlemen she had seen earlier that day. Fine gentlemen, according to their dress and their carriages, who strolled about with equally fine ladies on their arms. She could not imagine those gentlemen so much as bending to retrieve a dropped handkerchief much less running full speed to argue with a country physician about his patient.

Seated at the dressing table in the bedchamber she shared with Lydia, she closed her eyes briefly. It was not wrong for her to have been distressed. It had been upsetting enough to discover that she had forgotten a year of her life. And on top of that, to find she had been wilfully misled? *'Twas agony!* And yet…

It had been done for her own good, or at least those who had done it had believed so. Was wrongdoing still wrong if it was done with good intention?

It made her head ache, merely trying to sort it all out, but one thing she knew for certain: the love she felt for Darcy was stronger than her dismay, and her belief in his goodness held sway over all.

Into this reverie, Lydia intruded, flinging open the door to their bedchamber and standing with her mouth theatrically agape. "You are not even dressed! Mrs Hamilton means to take us to the party in half an hour!"

THE SOCIAL ENGAGEMENTS OF BRIGHTON ARE POSITIVELY WEARYING, Elizabeth mused a short while later. She had dressed herself with due haste, knowing how Lydia could be if she felt any sort of fun was happening without her. Her hair was nothing to be proud of, and she wore simple jewellery better suited to daytime, but in truth, she could not much care. What did it signify? She wanted none of these soldiers, did she?

The ladies—Elizabeth, Lydia, Mrs Forster, and Mrs Forster's mother, Mrs Hamilton—attended balls, sometimes more than one, every night save Sunday, when it would have been unseemly to hold a ball even in Brighton. There was the theatre and concerts, but Lydia had little interest in those, and Elizabeth did not press the point. As it was, she attended her own sort of theatre, sitting among the matrons and spinsters on the side of most of the ballrooms, watching people. It was drama enough to see the lovemaking and the quarrels and to hear gossip about persons wholly unknown to her. There was never any shortage of gossip; Brighton was every bit as wild as rumoured, and she heard tales of ruined reputations almost nightly.

Elizabeth saw Mr Wickham once or twice, and although he had been the architect of her stay in Brighton, he did not behave in any sort of overfamiliar way. It was to his credit, she thought, that he did not presume too much on an acquaintance that she did not remember.

Almost as if her musings had summoned him, he came to her, two other soldiers in tow. Of the three, Mr Wickham was undeniably the handsomest, but the other two—one tall with almost black hair, the other short with pale brown hair— looked well enough, too.

"Miss Bennet, how are you tonight? I must say the sea air seems to be agreeing with you."

"Good evening, Mr Wickham, and yes, I daresay the reports of the charms of the seaside have not been conflated.

I find it very healthful." She eyed his two companions and then enquired, somewhat sheepishly, "Will you introduce me to your friends? Or do I already know them?"

The men chuckled and the taller one spoke. "We are already acquainted, Miss Bennet, but we have heard of your illness and wish only to express our sympathy and become reacquainted."

Mr Wickham presented them then as a Lieutenant Denny and Captain Carter. Elizabeth found them to be very pleasant men and much enjoyed the conversation—until Mr Denny mentioned Darcy.

"I understand Mr Bingley has lately purchased Netherfield for his home. I do hope it will not require you to spend more time in the company of his friends!" He chuckled.

"I do not remember Mr Bingley's friends or sisters," said Elizabeth with a smile. "But I do hope his wife will be an agreeable addition to the ladies of the neighbourhood."

"You do not remember his friends? But I had understood that Mr Darcy rather—oof!" Mr Denny grunted as Mr Wickham gave him a sharp elbow to the ribs, followed by a few hushed words. Mr Denny looked immediately abashed.

"I do not know what you might have heard, Mr Denny," said Elizabeth evenly, "but Mr Darcy and I are merely friends."

"Of course," said Mr Wickham warmly. "Darcy would not know what to do with such a vivacious beauty as yourself."

"He always looked to me as if he might like to try though," said Captain Carter in a voice he no doubt believed was low enough for Mr Denny's ears only. When he perceived that Elizabeth had heard him, he flushed and said,

"Forgive me. His interest in you was apparent to many of us last autumn."

Elizabeth had no idea what to say and merely nodded.

Mr Wickham shook his head and shot a look at Captain Carter that seemed disgusted. Turning back to Elizabeth, he said, "I am going to take these fellows off before their wagging tongues get us all into trouble."

The three men all bowed and left her to her thoughts. It had pained her a little to admit that there was no connexion between herself and Darcy. Her eye drifted across the crowded room. She could still see the top of Mr Denny's dark head—his hair was darker than Darcy's, but he seemed to be of similar height, at least enough that she could imagine looking across a crowded room and seeing Darcy standing there. Standing there, and perhaps turning, seeing her, and smiling. Or doing that thing he did where he did not quite smile, but just sort of...warmed. Somehow it had always seemed more special.

So even the soldiers had observed his attentions to her last autumn. Attentions which had been met with spite, if her sister's report was accurate. Mary, who often sat unnoticed on the edges of ballrooms, had told her that at the ball at Netherfield, Elizabeth had agreed, unhappily, to dance with Darcy. According to Mary's report, Charlotte had tried to console her, telling her she might find him agreeable, and Elizabeth had replied by saying, 'That *would be the greatest misfortune of all!—To find a man agreeable whom one is determined to hate!—Do not wish me such an evil.*' Mary had added, very primly, that Elizabeth ought not to be determined to hate any person.

You were evidently determined to hate him then and still carry your prejudice now.

Her musings continued late into the night. While Lydia slumbered, Elizabeth crept from the bed and went to the closet, withdrawing her valise. Within was the perfume, as well as a small packet of unopened letters, letters sent by Darcy. She first indulged in a smell of her perfume, then took up the few on top, carefully tucking the others away.

Happily, the moonlight was sufficient for her to read by, for Lydia would have thrown a fit had she lit a lamp. She sat on the floor, her back to the window, and began to read.

My dearest, loveliest Elizabeth

I write with little hope that this missive will be read more than any other, but alas it seems there is little else for me to do. I do not imagine you would see me if I travelled to Longbourn, nor do I think an invitation to come to London as Georgiana's friend would be accepted.

Thus, again do I write to plead my case, and to beg your forgiveness. It was not my object to deceive you into marrying me. I cannot tell you how many times I thought, 'Today, today shall be the day that I tell her.' And yet one obstacle after another arose, and before I knew it, it was too far gone.

I will never deny that the leanings of my own heart were part of this. The physician was asking me to do that which I already wished to do; that is, to be your suitor. There was nothing I wanted more, save to be your husband. To be as we were, in the country in spring and in love—could anything be finer? 'Yes', I can almost hear you say, 'there could be something finer, and that is for all parties to have had a complete understanding of the business.'

And to this I can only reply, forgive me. I never intended you any harm, only good.

You say you cannot trust me, but that is not true. You can trust me to always have your best interests at heart. You can trust that I will always love you. You can trust that given any chance to make you happy, I shall do it.

My heart resides within your hands, and I remain, faithfully yours,

FD

She sighed. *For however he might say the wrong thing when he speaks, he surely can compose a lovely letter.*

In another of the letters, he spoke of his treatment of the Gardiners.

As a child I was taught what was right, but I was not taught to correct my temper. I was given good principles, but left to follow them in pride and conceit. I was spoilt by my parents, who allowed, encouraged, almost taught me to be selfish and overbearing; to care for none beyond my own family circle; to think meanly of all the rest of the world; to wish at least to think meanly of their sense and worth compared with my own. Your lesson in this regard shall not go unheeded. Even if I never see or speak to you again, you have humbled me, and taught me a lesson, and I shall be forever grateful to you for it.

She looked at the date on that one; it seemed it was the last that had arrived before the perfume. It sounded as if he had begun to resolve himself to their separation, to regard it as permanent. *And is that what you want? Truly?*

At once a yawn overtook her, and she realised she must go to bed, else suffer dear consequences the next day. *Another day, another party,* she mused and got to her feet. Returning Darcy's letters to their hiding place, she climbed into bed next to her sister, and hoped sleep would find her quickly.

CHAPTER TWENTY-SIX

A VISITOR IN BRIGHTON

E lizabeth entered yet another assembly hall for yet another assembly on yet another Tuesday night. It promised to be a crush, but then again, the assemblies in Brighton always were. Even as she thought it, Lydia, walking ahead of her, yelped as someone jostled her roughly coming from the other direction. "Are you injured?" she said into her sister's ear, but Lydia did not reply, her attention seeming to be fixed on the dancers.

For as much as the diversions of Brighton tired Elizabeth, Lydia was positively in raptures. Everywhere they went, she flirted and flounced to her heart's content, and more than once was Elizabeth required to intervene in some scheme or another that would surely have brought shame to them all. She once woke to find Lydia in the midst of dressing, having evidently planned a clandestine tryst outdoors. Another time, Elizabeth was made to stop her going off to the closet in what was meant as a 'kissing game'.

"That man is thirty if he is a day," she had scolded her sister. "I assure you he is not going to settle himself for a few kisses from a sixteen-year-old girl."

Lydia overspent her allowance, drank too much, slept too little, and in no way behaved as a gently bred young woman. Mrs Hamilton was certainly incapable of keeping her wild animal spirits in check, and Mrs Forster had no wish to do it. Mrs Forster was the sort of friend who admired effusively, and Lydia's antics were spurred on to great heights under her regard.

In all, Elizabeth felt that the dangers of Brighton far outweighed the pleasures and hoped, rather than believed, that they would end their stay with no significant damage to Lydia's reputation. Despite her tiredness and ennui, she was always glad she had accompanied her sister, laying down in her bed every night thankful another day had passed without incident.

"Pray tell me you will dance tonight, Lizzy?" Lydia abruptly turned her attention to her elder sister. "I cannot think why, with so many eligible gentlemen about—"

"Because I cannot," Elizabeth said with gentle firmness. "Go on and enjoy yourself, and I will satisfy myself with the pleasures of observation."

Elizabeth had discovered an impediment heretofore unrealised: the dances confounded her. As she watched from the side, she felt bewildered by patterns she knew she must have once mastered. She would study Lydia—no matter what else might be said of her, Lydia was an expert dancer—but her movements did not make sense to Elizabeth, the steps remaining unpredictable in her mind. She hoped if she continued to study them, she might re-learn them.

In truth it was no great loss to her, for the more she was in Brighton, the more that thoughts of Darcy came upon her. She knew not why—as far as she knew, she had never been in his company by Brighton or any seaside town for that matter. And the more she thought of him, the more she began to think that perhaps her painful rejection of him had been too absolute. She had always wished her expressions were more moderate but never more than now, sitting in a comfortable chair among the matrons and chaperons, longing for a man who might hope he never saw her again.

"Miss Bennet? How do you do this evening?"

Elizabeth looked up to see Mr Wickham standing before her.

It had been a relief to find that he gave them no particular notice since their arrival in Brighton. He was friendly but not too much so. They were not always at the same parties, nor did he always ask her sister to dance when they were. Towards herself, he betrayed no undue interest. They were passing acquaintances; she had no desire for more and was happy to find that he did not seem to either.

"Very well, sir, and you?"

With a little gesture, he asked if he might sit on the chair next to hers, and she agreed. He sat, smoothing his coat behind him. They chatted, briefly and civilly, about the little goings-on of the evening, after which he said, "I had hoped that I might tempt you away from that chair of yours tonight. Just one set?"

"I am afraid, sir, that I do not mean to dance this

evening." Elizabeth gave Mr Wickham what she hoped appeared a regretful smile. "My injuries, as you know."

"Oh! How stupid of me," he exclaimed. "Then I shall sit this one out with you."

"No, no," she said. "Pray do not sit out on my account. There are so many pretty girls to dance with in Brighton!"

"Aye, there are pretty girls aplenty," he agreed with a nod, his gaze moving absently over the crowd. "But prettiness and charm are so rarely united, that when one finds it, the appeal of dancing grows dim." He turned his eyes on her with a smile that left her in no doubt of his intention to compliment her, and she felt equal parts discomfiture and warmth spread through her. Discomfiture because of what she knew of him and pleasure because…well, it was pleasant to have the attentions of a handsome man, even if privately she thought him much less handsome than Darcy.

There you go again! Why must you always think of Darcy! To cover her consternation, she said, "And tell me, sir, how have you been spending your days? I hear that there are—"

She stopped as Mr Wickham abruptly stood. With a hasty "Excuse me," he strode off into the crowd. Her amazement was such that she could only stare after him, wondering if he meant to return. It seemed he did not, for he disappeared from sight without a look back. *So much for my charm and wanting to converse with me!*

His actions were not at all injurious to her; they were merely a source of bafflement. In any case, she had little time to think about it, for moments later, a man in the regimentals of a colonel in the regulars approached her.

"Miss Elizabeth Bennet!" he exclaimed. "May I join you?"

He did not wait for her reply, but sat himself beside her, grinning broadly. Despite the intrusion, she felt comfortable. Was this a friend? She would need to explain to him that she did not know him and why.

"Oh Lord!" With great theatricality, he lightly slapped a hand against his own forehead. "How stupid am I? You have not the least notion of who I am, have you?"

Elizabeth gave a relieved laugh. "I am afraid I do not, sir. I had an accident while in—"

"Kent. Yes, I know, I was part of the party that searched for you," he said with a laugh. "I am Colonel Richard Fitzwilliam. Darcy's cousin, Lady Catherine's nephew. Although with luck, you might have forgot her as well?"

Darcy's cousin! The thought electrified her, and she longed to ask about him even as she struggled to speak of Lady Catherine instead. What a relief that he had not come upon her speaking with Mr Wickham!

"That is true, I do not remember the lady, though I was told I dined with her on several occasions."

"And became something of her favourite, I must tell you. She told me she thought you were too clever for your own good. That is high praise, indeed!"

Elizabeth laughed again.

"Of course, you must know—or perhaps you do not—that her approbation must end with Darcy's avowal of his wish to marry you. She had hopes he would marry her daughter, even if her daughter had no wish to marry Darcy!"

He chuckled again, but Elizabeth, hearing reference to Darcy's wish to marry her, grew awkward and lowered her head to study her hands.

"There I have gone and done it, have I not? My mouth gets ahead of my brain box, I fear."

"No, think nothing of it," she murmured.

"It is precisely how everyone came to think you and Darcy were engaged, you know," he informed her. "The fault, wholly and completely, sits beside you."

She peeped up at him, and he nodded earnestly.

"I cannot remember Darcy's exact words to me—I believe he told me that he had proposed to you, and knowing him as I do, it did not once occur to me that he might have been refused—"

"Because he is so rich?" Elizabeth challenged.

Looking surprised, the colonel said, "No. Not at all. In truth, my cousin has a great deal to offer a lady and the least of it is his fortune." Leaning almost into her, he said, "You yourself have seen how he cares for people. There is nothing he would not do for those he truly loves. No person under his care suffers, not servants, not cousins, not creatures, not if he can help them in any way. Darcy never loves anything or anyone by halves, so if he loved you, well, I simply could not imagine you would not love him back. Any woman's heart, greeted with such devotion, must surely yield."

The force of that struck her so that she had to look away, feeling that the emotion in her eyes would surely give away all that she felt. The colonel seemed to sense her awkwardness and happily moved them past the uncomfortable moment.

"But, I see by your face that I have made you uneasy, and that was surely not my intention. I wished merely to renew our acquaintance, so let us speak on subjects less fraught. How is your health? Are you wholly recovered?"

A very agreeable half an hour was spent in conversation with the colonel. She did make the awkward mistake of asking—twice—whether his family were all in good health; he answered with the same geniality twice as well, saying everyone was busy preparing for Miss de Bourgh's wedding.

The colonel was very much the gentleman, telling her that she and he had taken more than a few walks in the groves of Rosings Park and relating to her the substance of some of their conversations. Elizabeth could see how she might have spent a good bit of time with him; he had just the sort of easy disposition she found agreeable in a friend. It was no surprise to her to learn that he was Darcy's dearest friend, for she had always heard it said that two men, so near in age and raised as brothers, would either become bitterest rivals or dearest friends. In the case of the colonel and Darcy, it had been, apparently, the latter.

As the conversation flagged, she enquired, "Are you staying long in Brighton?"

"No, my position mostly requires me in London. I came for only a few days."

He did not indicate why he was there for so short a time, nor did she ask.

CHAPTER TWENTY-SEVEN

A CHANGE OF CIRCUMSTANCE

Darcy did not often accept invitations from Saye's friend, Sir Frederick, but one evening several days after the breakfast with his cousins at the Matlock town home, he found himself with nothing better to do. Desirous of entertainment of any sort, he went.

Sir Frederick was fond of cards and frequently hosted evenings of gentlemen-only card parties at his house in town. They always played low, because everyone tended to get very drunk, and Sir Frederick did not wish anyone to lose a house or a carriage at one of his gatherings. That night's event had only just begun when Darcy arrived, the first hand not yet dealt. He was doubly surprised to see that not only was Bingley there, but he was looking excessively foxed, his eyes unfocused and his countenance slack despite the good cheer about him. Darcy took a seat beside him.

"Began early, did you?"

"Darcy! The most extraordinary thing happened to me today."

Bingley turned to look at him, and Darcy realised he was not drunk at all but perhaps merely shocked.

"What?"

"She released me! It is done!"

"What? Impossible! I thought she...she said—"

"Trust me," said Bingley with a laugh. "I am having considerable difficulty myself accepting such a change in fortune. Her father came to me at our club and said his daughter wished to exercise her prerogative and that he was mightily sorry for it. I was so shocked, I nearly could not comprehend him. He took this to mean that I was taking it hard, so we returned to their home to discuss it further. She would not speak, would scarcely look in my direction, but confirmed that yes, it was done, she would not marry me and released me from my obligation to her."

"With no true reason given?"

"She began to say something about circles of Society, but her father put a quick stop to it. I could not have cared less, of course, but evidently the gentleman thought I might."

"He was not concerned for his daughter's sensibilities? Her reputation?"

Bingley dismissed that notion with a little wave of his hand. "I daresay Miss Roberts is accustomed to having her way, and her father is accustomed to ignoring it."

Darcy sat back with a thud against the back of his chair. "Extraordinary!"

"Is it not? I have no idea what caused it. It almost feels

too wondrous to be real, but…" He shook his head, the same vacant delight in his countenance. "I daresay it *is* real."

"The marriage articles? What of those?" Darcy asked.

"Burnt. I watched it happen."

Darcy whistled low and long. Then he clapped his friend on the back and rose from his seat. "We must toast you, my friend. I shall return with something appropriate shortly."

On the other side of the room, near the windows, was the sideboard bearing any and all drink a young man might desire. Saye stood with a glass of brandy, his back to the window, as Darcy approached.

"Have some of this," he instructed. "Lovely stuff."

Darcy poured two generous glasses. "I must take one to Bingley."

"Toasting his change in circumstance?" Saye smiled like the cat that had got the cream.

"What do you know about it?" Darcy shot back immediately.

"What should I know?" Saye took another sip. "I am scarcely acquainted with Miss Roberts, and not much more with Bingley. Though I do look forward to being better friends with him, you know, after his house party. I thought September would be an excellent time for it, do you not think so?"

Darcy only gazed at him, amused and exasperated both, and wholly unable to think what to say. "Is there nothing you will not do to get what you want?"

"In principle, no," Saye replied. "But in this, I cannot think what you accuse me of doing? What could I do with two persons so wholly unrelated to me? No, by my accounting, it is only *you* who has ever truly intruded into Bingley's affairs. Not I." He smirked and then resumed his customary world-weary air.

Darcy studied him a moment, then raised one glass slightly. "I cannot think whether I should scold you or toast you, but my friend is excessively happy so I suppose I choose the latter. Shall I lay wagers tonight, or do you have the games all arranged to benefit you too?"

To this Saye only chuckled, but he followed Darcy across the room to where Bingley still sat, apparently eager to join in the happy drinking. "Now that the pup is off his chain, let us discuss this house party he has agreed to throw for us."

THE WEDDING OF ANNE DE BOURGH BORE EVERY mark of Lady Catherine's delight in the excess. Anne's gown was better suited to a court presentation than a simple wedding ceremony, and the breakfast included nearly every person of consequence known to any of them. Lady Catherine had even invited the Prince Regent, to her family's mortification.

"Surely she realises she is not a royal?" Lord Matlock grumbled.

But Anne was happy, in a manner that Darcy had never before seen of her. Her cheeks were girlishly pink, she smiled, and she gazed at her bridegroom with pure adoration shining forth from her eyes. Yardley was no different; he, too, was the very embodiment of a lover's devotion, beaming as proudly as if he was the first man ever to take a wife.

The breakfast, held in the de Bourgh town home, was the

first opportunity Darcy had to see Fitzwilliam since his travel to Brighton. His cousin appeared wearied by the return journey which had, Darcy learnt, been undertaken only the day prior.

"I understood, naturally, that the King's commission would not excuse me from attending this grand spectacle," said Fitzwilliam with a grin.

"Too right," said Darcy as two of the Prince's mistresses pushed by him. "Did you see her?"

"Anne? Yes, she was the one at the front of the church this morning."

Darcy gave him a look and Fitzwilliam chuckled.

"Yes, I saw your lady, and she appeared in good health."

"Was she enjoying herself?"

Fitzwilliam shrugged. "She was looking after her younger sister which was, she said, her purpose in being in Brighton. She did not dance with anyone, including me."

"And Wickham?"

"He was about, but I saw no evidence of undue interest in either of the Miss Bennets." Fitzwilliam grimaced then and added, "The younger Miss Bennet certainly requires looking after."

"Is she in danger from him? If he knew of her connexion to me, he would not scruple to inveigle himself with her."

"I would not worry about it. Her sister was keeping good watch on her and she knows all, does she not?" After Darcy nodded, his cousin continued, "There you are, then."

"Yes, she could not be taken in by him, now that she understands his character." Darcy toyed with the drink in his hand, trying for nonchalance before asking, "Did she enquire after me?"

"Yes, she did," Fitzwilliam confirmed.

"Did she? What did she say exactly?" Darcy could not care in the least for how ridiculously eager he sounded.

"She said, 'are all your family in good health?' and I said 'yes, they are'."

"Good health! Good Lord!" Disappointment was like a heavy stone in his gut. "That is not asking about me!"

"Yes, it is. You are part of the family."

Darcy rolled his eyes. "I do not wish to be asked after in the same breath as my aged relations, or my stupid cousins. I want to know if she asked about me and me specifically."

Fitzwilliam scratched his head, seeming uncomfortable. "I was already speaking of you, so she did not need to. I told her what a good character you have!"

"A good character." Darcy shook his head with disgust. "Excellent. Next time she needs a footman, I am sure she will send me a note."

Saye approached from across the room. "That Yardley is something else entirely. Can you believe he and Anne anticipated their vows months ago? Right under Jenkinson's nose too!" He shook his head admiringly.

"The notion of that makes me wish to drink heavily," Fitzwilliam said. "Shall we go to the club?"

"No," Darcy replied. "I must accompany Georgiana home and have promised to spend the remains of the day with her."

DARCY LEFT THE BREAKFAST FEELING LOWER THAN ever before. Anne, who had scarcely ever even left the drawing room at Rosings, had somehow managed to find love. How was it so impossible for him?

I daresay I found it easily enough, only that losing it was even easier.

He and Georgiana walked the short distance back to Darcy House. Georgiana had been enthralled by the whole of the affair and chattered happily about it as they walked and entered the vestibule.

"I do not think I shall eat again today, to be sure!" she told him. "I never saw such an array of dishes."

"It was undoubtedly the heartiest breakfast I have ever seen for any wedding. I am rather full to bursting myself."

"Three pieces of cake will do that to a fellow," she teased.

"Three? Only two!"

"Two and the remains of mine!"

"Sir?" Danforth, Darcy's butler, interrupted them. "Forgive me, but a letter came that I thought might require your immediate attention."

Darcy took the missive, seeing at once that it was in Wickham's hand. All teasing and levity fled, and he barely restrained a curse.

"Is that from Mr Wickham?" Georgiana asked, her cheerfulness of seconds prior gone.

"Maybe. Likely not."

"I think it is," said Georgiana worriedly. "Do you think... is he writing something about Ramsgate?"

"If it is from Wickham, I doubt it has anything to do with you, darling. In fact, I am certain of it." Darcy forced a smile to reassure her. "But I daresay I ought to attend to it. Excuse me."

He strode through the hall, pausing only to ensure Georgiana was on her way elsewhere and would not follow. He hoped that she had accepted his prevarication, but he himself was wholly persuaded it was never a good thing to receive a missive from George Wickham. From Brighton no less, where Elizabeth and her sister remained.

Scarcely had he taken a seat in his study before he tore open the letter and began to read.

Darcy,

Unhappily I find myself in Brighton, having come up against some debts to the fellows around me. Very fortunately, however, I find myself in the company of the very delightful Miss Elizabeth Bennet, in whom I understand you have some interest.

What a comely girl she is! Those lips fairly beg to be kissed, do they not, old man? And one need scarcely mention how the lady's figure cries out for a man's touch. But perhaps you have not yet indulged in her...you never did comprehend how a lady might say no but in truth mean yes. She and I may need to have a carriage ride together this Thursday to see if the rule proves true in her case.

If I had a sum of say, three thousand pounds, I might be better able to overlook her charms.

GW

Darcy cursed, then lowered his head into his hand. It seemed he was for Brighton.

Blast, but he was quite wearied with the manner in which Wickham forever intruded upon him. He wondered, looking back over the note, if the terms indicated would be sufficient for a conviction of abduction.

Very well, George, he thought. *You have sent your summons, and I shall come, for Elizabeth's sake not yours. And I shall bring the constables with me, and God preserve you if you have harmed one hair on her head.*

Elizabeth was on the Promenade one cloudy Thursday morning, idly wondering if there might be rain, when she saw, in the distance, Mr Wickham. He never had offered any explanation for his peculiar behaviour at the assembly, but Elizabeth did not much care regardless. Amiable as he was, she had no idea of any particular friendship with him, because if nothing else, it would displease Darcy. And with each day's passing, she found more and more that she wished to please Darcy and perhaps find some way to sort out the tangle between them.

Mr Wickham appeared to be searching for something or someone, and he seemed to be hurried as he did it. To her surprise, she perceived that when his eye met hers, he had found what he sought. He came towards her with rapid, long paces, raising one hand to hold his hat on his head so that a sea breeze might not catch it and toss it away.

"Miss Bennet!" He was out of breath by the time he drew near. "I have been looking for you!"

"You have?" She drew back. "Whatever for?"

"Forgive me," he said hurriedly. "I am...I am loath to tell you this, but I have great concern for your sister at present."

"For Lydia?" Her heart plunged. "What has happened? Is she hurt?"

"She is gone down to East Blatchington," he began, but stopped at Elizabeth's gasp.

She had heard of the wildness of the men stationed in East Blatchington. There had been a mutiny there, and those convicted were flogged and, in two cases, executed. If Brighton had, generally, a reputation for wild parties and debauchery, those in the East Blatchington encampment held it tenfold.

"What on earth can she wish to see there?"

"There is a rumour of a flogging," he said. "But pray, I can acquaint you with the particulars once we are there. I have a hack waiting."

"A hack?"

Mr Wickham took her by the elbow. "Yes, for I feared she would not heed me if I went myself to persuade her against going. I hope she will listen to the wise counsel of her sister."

Elizabeth walked faster, trying to keep apace with Mr Wickham. A glance at his countenance revealed genuine alarm on her sister's behalf. Dread and dismay commingled washed over her, along with a sense of inevitability. Had she not been certain that Lydia would get up to no good, led astray by something or another? She supposed if anything she ought to be shocked it took her this long!

Lydia was too easily led, too curious, and too lacking in good sense—and where had Elizabeth been? Rambling about, thinking of Darcy instead of watching over her sister which was the whole of her purpose in coming to Brighton!

Mr Wickham helped her into the carriage and then climbed in behind her, taking the seat opposite. She paused; what would it do to her reputation to be in a closed carriage with him? Then she decided there was no time for such foolishness. She needed his protection to go into the encampment and, in any case, it was broad daylight.

Surely all would be well.

CHAPTER TWENTY-EIGHT
ABHORRENT DISGUISE

The carriage went off at a rapid pace, and Elizabeth, leaning forwards in the small space, urged Mr Wickham, "Pray, tell me what you know."

"In truth, I do not know very much," he replied regretfully. "I heard there was more trouble among the men down there. Their colonel is a dreadful man, heartless and very cruel, so it does not surprise me. Several of his men got into an argument with him—again I do not know why, but they were brought up on charges and at least one of them is to be flogged today at the hour of three."

"And Lydia needed to be a part of it." Elizabeth sighed and just barely restrained a sob. "What can she be thinking?"

"She is thinking with a young girl's curiosity, a girl who knows not how bad things can be."

"How far is it, exactly?"

Mr Wickham winced. "Above ten miles. But I hope we may come upon them along the road."

"Who is with her?"

"Denny, Captain Carter... Mrs Forster may have gone as well, I know not."

Elizabeth pressed her hand against her forehead and closed her eyes, sighing deeply. "I suppose I must take consolation in knowing she is not alone."

"No," said Mr Wickham, and Elizabeth startled, opening her eyes. He had changed seats to be next to her on the small bench. She instinctively moved to put some space between them.

"She is not alone, and neither are you," he finished. There was something odd in the way he said so, and the peculiarity was reflected in his countenance as well.

"Th-thank you," she said.

They had left the road that went along the contour of the seaside and appeared to be driving off into the countryside. Elizabeth knew she was not familiar enough with Brighton to understand its geography in full...but it seemed to her they were not moving in the right direction. "Does the driver understand where we are going?"

"Oh yes," said Mr Wickham, sitting back a little to Elizabeth's relief. "He is well aware. He must know a quicker route."

Quicker than directly up the coast? Elizabeth forced an uncertain smile and was reassured by Mr Wickham's easy smile in reply.

HAPPILY, FITZWILLIAM HAD SUPPLIED DARCY WITH the exact address where the Forsters, with Elizabeth, stayed.

It was a neat little house not a mile north of the coast. Darcy did not hesitate, going there directly and presenting himself at the door. He was shown into a small drawing room wherein sat an older matron with Miss Lydia Bennet and Mrs Forster. The older lady looked at him appraisingly while being introduced as Mrs Hamilton, Mrs Forster's mother.

"I am looking for Miss Bennet," he began.

"Out wandering round the Promenade, no doubt," Miss Lydia replied immediately. "Or sitting in one of the benches. That is all she does all day long."

Carefully, Darcy said, "I have reason to believe she may have gone…somewhere…with George Wickham. In a carriage. Do you know anything about that?"

"Oh yes, now that you mention it," Mrs Forster said. "Mr Wickham did say something about an excursion to… Mother, do you recollect what he said?"

"When a man is that handsome," Mrs Hamilton declared, "an old lady like me finds it difficult to care about what he speaks of."

Miss Lydia and Mrs Forster both burst into giggles. Darcy clenched his jaw briefly, then forced himself to calmly ask, "Do you think Miss Bennet went off with him, then?"

"Stammer Park!" Miss Lydia exclaimed. "I remember it now, because I thought it was such a funny name! Who would call their house Stammer Park?"

"*Stan*mer Park?" Darcy clarified impatiently.

"Oh yes, he said there were some of them going to see the woods. Sounded ghastly dull," Miss Lydia opined.

"But Elizabeth was not here at the time, so we can only

presume he found her and persuaded her to go with him," said Mrs Forster.

Darcy thought it extraordinary that she had no notion of the whereabouts of a young lady who was a guest in her home in a place such as Brighton, who may or may not have got into a carriage with a reprobate.

But he said none of that, only thanked them and set off to find Elizabeth.

It was not long before Elizabeth's concern had blossomed into full-blown fear. They were headed away from Brighton yet nowise driving in the direction of East Blatchington. She was positive they were headed north, and yet Mr Wickham reassured her often that it was a shortcut, and all was as it should be.

"Sir," she began again, "I really cannot think that the driver understands—"

To her astonishment, Mr Wickham shushed her, leaning over her and bringing his face far too near to her own. Was it brandy on his breath?

"Elizabeth, do not worry."

She drew back as much as she could. "I am excessively worried about my sister."

"You need not be," he said. "She is safe in the Forsters' house, no doubt drinking sherry and gossiping the day away."

Elizabeth stared at him, unable to comprehend him. "Then why—"

"You know why." He levelled a serious look at her that

she hoped was not meant to be seductive. "I thought it would be nice for you and me to have some time...to ourselves."

"But the flogging..." she said stupidly.

"There is no flogging. I daresay those fellows are just as wild and happy today as ever they are." He reached over and trailed a now-ungloved finger alongside her cheek. "Thank heavens you did not marry a dullard like Darcy. I see your fire, darling Elizabeth. I think you like to be a little wild and happy yourself sometimes."

"You are incorrect." She moved to the backwards-facing bench. "Mr Wickham, I am afraid you have this all wrong. I do not, in any way, wish to be in an enclosed carriage with you and am very concerned for my reputation. Pray, turn the carriage round and let us return to Brighton."

"Cannot do that, my sweet." He smiled and moved to join her on her bench. "Come now. You have nearly driven me mad with your...lively spirits. Your smiles have made me promises that I should now like to collect on."

"Please take me back." She hated how weak and tremulous her voice sounded. Oh, of all the stupidity! That *she* should be the fool to be taken advantage of, while Lydia was safe at home!

He laid a hand on her knee, squeezing lightly, and she jerked away from him. He smirked at her discomfort.

"I cannot tell you how many people in Hertfordshire told me that your sister was the beauty of the family, but I always told them I could not agree. For it was you who stirred my blood—but I have always enjoyed a more sensual beauty."

What was the expected reply to such words, so obviously

intended to seduce? Did he think her so stupid that she would fall into his arms on this bit of flattery? *Then again, you fell into his carriage with a bit of a falsehood.*

She looked out of the window at the passing landscape and considered the mad notion of climbing out of it, or at least yelling up to the coachman for help. But Mr Wickham had hired the coachman. Perhaps he was in on the scheme himself. If word got out about this, would she be ruined?

Mr Wickham leant across her and pulled down the curtain. He then did the same on his side, plunging them into shadows. "No one will ever know," he murmured into her ear, his breath hot and moist. "A few kisses, and then we will turn back."

CHAPTER TWENTY-NINE

THE CAVALRY

When Mr Wickham leant over her, eyes half closed, appearing to intend to kiss her, Elizabeth acted by instinct, an instinct that was fuelled by rage. She was mightily tired of being the helpless, hapless female, chasing forgotten memories and dissolving into tears. Enough with all of that. Mr Wickham would not take that which she had not given him.

She drove the heel of her palm up into his nose. He yelped and reared backwards, even as his nose became a veritable geyser of blood. He recovered from his shock quickly, beginning to curse her and call her vile names while reaching into his pocket to withdraw a handkerchief that he pressed to his nose to stanch the flow of blood.

As he did, she noticed a glint of metal and, while he was distracted, snatched it, happy to see it was a blade. Her cousin Philips had once taught her how to stab, using a reverse grip so it was more difficult to take away from her.

She did not think she would have the courage to actually stab Mr Wickham, but she would certainly try her best if he attempted to take further liberties.

"Give me that." Mr Wickham's voice was stuffy and much less assured than it had been before.

"No. Let me out of this carriage."

He called her a name, and Elizabeth replied by leaning over and pressing the blade against his bottom eyelid. Her hand shook a little, but she supposed that might add to the effect. In any case, Mr Wickham froze, barely breathing.

"Let me out of this carriage," she said, proud of the steadiness of her voice, "or I will cut your eye out."

She pressed just slightly, horrified and yet somehow pleased with herself to see a small dot of blood appear. Mr Wickham cried out, then grew mean, cursing her and calling her an unthinkable name that made it easy to press a bit more.

"Let me out," she repeated, not letting up on the pressure against his eye. "A one-eyed man does not appeal to many ladies, does he?"

What his reply to that might have been, they would not know, for they were interrupted by the sound of a man yelling some sort of order from a distance. Very strangely, the sound brought a smile to Mr Wickham's lips. "Your cavalry has arrived, it seems."

She had no idea what he meant by her 'cavalry', but the carriage slowed and then came to a halt. Elizabeth waited for nothing, simply flung the door open and leapt out, falling onto the ground just as a horse came thundering abreast of them, stopping just short of trampling her.

It was Darcy, looking rather mad himself, his hair wild beneath his hat and his countenance grim as he ordered the coachman to stay where he was. Nevertheless, he was gentle as he leapt from his horse and bent to help her rise to her feet. She dusted herself off, trembling with relief.

"Was this Wickham?" he asked quietly. "Are you hurt?"

She shook her head. "A bruise or two, nothing serious."

"You are certain?"

She nodded.

Mr Wickham stepped out of the carriage, holding a handkerchief to his eye. "I wondered when you would get here, Darcy. Took you long enough. You have my money?"

Elizabeth, baffled, looked between the two men. "Go over there," Darcy whispered to her and used his chin to indicate a tree at some short distance. She obeyed unquestioningly. As she went, she heard Darcy say, "Some. Not all. I wish to ensure she is unharmed before you see the whole of it."

"Let me have it, then," said Mr Wickham, "or I will make sure every man in Brighton knows I had a bite of Darcy's pie."

Elizabeth arrived at the tree and turned to look at the two men. Darcy stood between herself and Mr Wickham, but a step to the side showed her that Mr Wickham had a pistol aimed at Darcy. As she watched, Darcy reached into his greatcoat and removed a small pouch. He tossed it at Mr Wickham who lowered the gun as he caught it, a smile on his face which now, she reflected, was actually quite ugly.

Mr Wickham's smile grew as he pulled bank notes, a great many of them, from the pouch. From her position, she could not see how much it was exactly...but it looked like a lot. *I was kidnapped*, she thought numbly. *Mr Wickham abducted me, and here is Darcy to ransom me.*

A wave of shame at her own foolishness crashed over her. She had come to Brighton to keep Lydia from mischief and had instead landed in her own massive heap of trouble. *Foolish, foolish girl!* And now Darcy was forced to pay a sum to save her reputation. *You will have to marry him now*, she told herself. *One cannot be so obligated to a man and continue to refuse him.*

She had very little time to consider it as just then two more men came round the bend on horses. Mr Wickham nonchalantly tucked the gun away and seemed unconcerned, but his countenance did grow wary as the other men stopped.

The first, an enormous broad-faced man, said, "This him?"

Darcy nodded, and Mr Wickham, his countenance changing from curious to alarmed, said, "What is this, now?"

"George Wickham," Darcy said, pointing towards him, "abducted and assaulted this young lady, and sought ransom from me for her safety. I mean to see him swing for it."

Mr Wickham gave a little yelp, then took off running, but he did not go far before the two men apprehended him. There was a scuffle—Mr Wickham cursing Darcy and yelling out that he had abducted no one, that Elizabeth had come willingly with him—until one of the men reminded him it was hard to talk with a noose around your neck. Then he grew silent as they tied him and shoved him back into the carriage. He made a pitiable sight, still covered in his own blood, but Elizabeth thought he was despicable.

To her very great relief, Darcy's purse was returned to him, and the two men were off, riding beside the carriage, after having instructed the coachman that he now transported a prisoner. The coachman did not appear to have any great feelings on the matter and was only really interested in the coins Darcy handed to him.

Then they were all gone, leaving only Darcy, Darcy's horse, and Elizabeth to determine the way back to Brighton.

CHAPTER THIRTY

UNEXAMPLED KINDNESS

It was not until Darcy saw the men and their prisoner disappearing round the bend that his fear began to seep away from him. Turning to Elizabeth, he enquired, again, "You are not injured?"

"No, I am not."

Darcy looked about him. He was not familiar with the area, having only been to Brighton once before, many years previous. Nevertheless, the road they travelled seemed like it might lead to a larger, more travelled one, and on that one, he believed they might find what they needed. The sky was cloudy, but there was no rain for which he was thankful.

"I believe we might find a posting inn not much farther down that road over there," he said. "It cannot be more than a mile. Let me assist you onto the horse, and I will walk him."

Elizabeth glanced over at the horse, and Darcy understood her immediately. He was a large beast, one Darcy had chosen for his speed, not his suitability for a lady frightened of horses.

"I could always wait here," she suggested. "Then you could ride him to find the inn. It would be faster."

He shook his head. "We can both walk, if you feel you are equal to it?"

"Yes, I think I am."

"You did not injure yourself when you leapt from the carriage?"

"Nothing of consequence," she said, offering a smile.

They began to walk, and Darcy allowed them to gain a short distance before enquiring, "And how is it that you found yourself alone in a carriage with George Wickham?"

Elizabeth flushed and cleared her throat, suddenly very interested in her shoes. "I-it was very foolish of me."

Darcy waited for more.

With her eyes lowered, and her face thus hidden by her bonnet, she said, "Mr Wickham told me that Lydia was going off on some excursion to see a man flogged in East Blatchington. He said they were very wild down there and that he was concerned for her whereabouts and urged me to come with him to retrieve her."

Darcy scoffed. "A likely tale. And did you verify your sister's whereabouts? When I came into town, I saw her at the Forsters' house, and she certainly seemed as though she had been there all day."

"You went to the Forsters' house?"

"Did you think it a coincidence that I came upon you?"

Elizabeth looked over, seeming like she had more questions, but he forged ahead. "The Forsters believed you were off to see some woods, then, but you believed you were off in rescue of your sister?"

"Yes, um, I thought…" She paused. "Mr Wickham showed great concern when we met in Hertfordshire…rather, when I met him, for he remembered me from…from before, obviously. He was concerned for Lydia. Said she was far too young. I believed we were of like mind in our understanding of what a young lady ought to be allowed to do. Clearly it was a mistake to believe him, else I never should have found myself in the predicament I was in."

Like mind? Rage, held in check all this time, began to overcome Darcy. "So, without question, you entered a closed carriage with a blackguard?"

His tone made her stop and stare briefly, eyes wide. "I—"

"The first time you believed George Wickham's lies," he said tightly, "I could understand it. You had been flattered by him and insulted by me, so naturally you accepted his appearance of goodness for truth. You heard and believed his lies readily. But now? How could you so endanger yourself knowing what you knew, what I told you about Georgiana?"

She turned to face him; the expression in her eyes nearly did him in.

"You are angry with me," she said softly. "And I cannot blame you. I am angry with myself for being so stupid. Forgive me for having put you to so much trouble."

"Put me to trouble!" His anger made him sputter out the words. "Elizabeth! Are you mad? Has nothing I have ever said to you sunk in? I love you. Of course I want to trouble myself to see to your well-being and yet you…you… You put yourself into that blackguard's power!"

"I did not intend to—"

"I must wonder, did you think all I told you about Georgiana was untrue? Do you think me such a liar, that I would contrive such a tale about my sister?"

"Of course not!" she cried. "But Mr Wickham, he said… he told me that…the whole of the matter between him and Georgiana was a misunderstanding. He said that he was too friendly, too brotherly, and that she had misinterpreted it as a romance."

"Misinterpreted?" He spat the word.

"He said he had never had any wrong intentions, but it was Georgiana who—"

"She was seduced," Darcy said, biting off each word. "You *do* comprehend me, I hope? She told my aunt that she was not forced, but I am unsure whether a girl of fifteen is capable of consenting to any such thing with a man of twenty-six. I daresay he had her alone and did what he could to carry things along without her truly knowing what he was about until it was too late."

Elizabeth's blush was now a deep red. "Oh."

"He then tried to extort more money from me by implying that he had got her with child. Thankfully that much was untrue, but I assure you, *Miss Bennet,* his interests were very far from *brotherly.*"

His use of a formal moniker stung her; he could see it in the way she flashed a hurt glance at him before lowering her eyes again.

He fumbled in his coat for the letter he had received from

Wickham, the letter that had brought him to Brighton with the greatest expedience possible. "It seems in this case, his interests were very much the same."

Handing it to her, he watched her gasp and grow mortified. When she next looked up at him, he saw every bit of the fear and shame that was flooding her.

"I hardly know what to say. I am stupid, and George Wickham is evil. Pray forgive me for having involved you in my foolishness. I-I am thankful to you for your assistance."

It was the last two sentences which angered him most of all. Who but he should be her rescuer? Why did she continue to *thank* him, as if he had no interest in the matter, no stake in her welfare?

Because you do not.

Fury moved him forwards with lengthy strides, and very shortly thereafter, they arrived at the Royal Boar. Elizabeth sat quietly on a bench while he made the necessary arrangements, and before long she was in a carriage which he rode beside, returning to Brighton and the Forsters.

He was angry with her, very angry, but it was the rage of a wounded lover. *How can you trust Wickham and yet doubt me?* was the question he wished to shout at her. He had been injured by her mistrust, by her betrayal, and yes, by her *gratitude*.

He and Elizabeth had scarcely spoken on the return, and when Elizabeth invited him in, he declined, knowing he sounded terse. "I must be for London."

"At this hour?" she exclaimed. Then her face fell, understanding, no doubt, that he only wished to be away. Far, far away. From her.

And yes, it was true. His sense of injustice would not allow him to view her with equanimity at the moment. His temper burned too hot at present. But there was one thing he needed to know.

"How was it that he came to be so bloodied?"

"Mr Wickham?"

He nodded.

"I fought back. As best I could," she said. "I knew not what he meant to do to me, but I knew I wanted no part of it. My cousin has taught me how to defend myself, a little."

"Then my thanks to your cousin," he said.

"My thanks to *you*," she said earnestly. "It is *you* who I owe much. I could not have extricated myself, had he decided to overpower me. You own my gratitude, sir."

Little could she have known that such words were like twisting the knife in his chest. *Owe me? Own her gratitude?* He would rather be burnt alive than have her imagine she *owed* him anything. "I want nothing from you," he said curtly, then turned on his heel and went to find his way back to London.

THE HORROR OF WHAT SHE HAD DONE, WHAT HAD nearly been done *to* her, struck Elizabeth as soon as she entered the Forsters' house.

"Elizabeth?" Mrs Forster had heard the door and come into the vestibule. "What is it?"

"You look like you saw a ghost," Lydia added, following her friend. "And your hair! I never saw it so! It looks like squirrels tried to make a nest in it." She laughed, and Mrs Forster laughed with her.

"Then I had better go and tend to myself." Elizabeth forced a smile. "If you will excuse—"

"Is that blood on your glove?"

"Oh! Um…" Elizabeth looked down. "No, I was, um, painting earlier and must have got it on there."

Lydia looked at her dubiously. "Painting with your gloves on? At Stammer House?"

"Stammer House? What do you speak of? No, I mean to say I was watching someone paint by the sea," Elizabeth said with a laugh. "The gloves were haplessly nearby."

"Did you not just say you were painting?" Lydia asked. "I thought you went to—"

"I misspoke. Pray excuse me, I must go and refresh myself." She hurried off, saying nothing more. Thankfully, Lydia was the sort of person who had limited interest in things not directly pertaining to herself, and Elizabeth had no doubt that her strange appearance would be forgot before she was next in the drawing room.

She was thankful to the maid-of-all-work who tended the Forsters' house, for a fresh ewer of water awaited her. Glancing up into the mirror, she was horrified by what she saw; wild eyes, pallor, and yes, hair that looked like a squirrel had nested in it. Her bonnet had gone missing at some point. "In the carriage, mayhap," she mused aloud.

This would be Darcy's last look at her. *'I want nothing from you'.* Could she blame him? His words were hard and exquisitely painful, but she did not doubt the truth of them.

She dipped a cloth in the cool water and passed it over her face, feeling a sting in the areas where the wind off the sea had chapped her skin.

One thing had become painfully certain to her, on her seeing Darcy again: she wished to be with him. Forever. With no thought for any nonsense before them, any misunderstandings, any deceit. She cared nothing for any of it. She wanted only him.

Alas, this escapade of hers must have done the precise opposite for him, for he left her with nary a look behind. *'I want nothing from you'*—those parting words rang again through her mind, again cutting like a knife, and she knew they were due to be repeated often in her memory in the coming days.

Her power over him was sunk, perhaps gone, under the weight of her stupidity. To believe Mr Wickham! After all she knew! She had willingly put herself in the power of Darcy's sworn enemy, trusting in a wicked man who wanted to lie and cheat and steal from the family who had nearly raised him.

But it was the pain she had caused Darcy that brought a wave of agony over her. She had seen the wounded rage in his eyes when he tasked her for believing Mr Wickham. The rage she could countenance; the wounds she could not, particularly knowing, as she did, that she could not provide consolation. Never had she so deeply felt that she wished to marry him, as now, when all hope must be vain.

Will I ever even see him again? There were faint hopes that his friend might invite him down in the autumn…but likely not, for Mr Bingley would be newly married. He would wish to be alone with his wife. Then again, Mr Bingley did enjoy a party above all things…so maybe something would be planned for later in the autumn. And if so, he would invite Darcy.

Who might not come. Who *surely* would not come.

Elizabeth swallowed and ran the cloth over her face again. Tears formed a hard knot in her throat but would not fall, not while she washed her face and not while she changed her gown. While she brushed her hair, she attacked her head viciously, mercilessly yanking the brush through wild tangles in a manner that made her eyes sting. Nevertheless, the relief of a good cry eluded her.

DARCY CONSIDERED, STRONGLY, THE NOTION OF riding through the night, but the possible danger of it dissuaded him. Instead, he rode only enough to remove him from Brighton and its environs and find a suitable-looking inn where he ordered a simple meal and went to bed early.

He awoke early, too, the sun shining directly into his rooms, but laid abed for a short while thinking of Elizabeth. She had been left in no doubt of his anger, and part of him thought that perhaps he ought to return to Brighton and mend fences. He had deceived her, and she had betrayed him. Was it enough? Could they put their missteps aside for one another at long last? Or was it all hopeless?

What is this dance we do, he mused. *One hurts the other, misunderstandings arise and flourish. Can we never just be happy?* Except that yes, he knew they could and would—had not the time in Kent taught him that much?

But he would not take her love if it was given for any cause but...well, but love. Not for gratitude, not for obligation, not for prudence. It would be too bitter to even think of it. Nothing but love would do.

And it seemed he could not have that, so instead he would ask for nothing.

Go back to London, fool, he told himself and then removed from the bed to do just that.

CHAPTER THIRTY-ONE

MR BINGLEY RETURNS

Elizabeth's foolish escapade, which she was ever more certain had cost her the love of her life, cast her into a lowness of spirits from which there appeared no relief. She attempted to persuade Lydia to cut short their visit and go home, but Lydia looked at her as if she were mad.

"Go back to Hertfordshire? For what, I might ask? Dull assemblies with people we have known all our lives?"

"In fact," Elizabeth said, trying to sound delighted, "I believe Mr Bingley means to soon be in the neighbourhood, and he is sure to have a party or two if only so that we can meet his bride."

"Soon is a relative term," Lydia announced with maddening superiority. "What is soon to you is dreadful far off to me, and I already know from Mama that Mr Bingley will not be at his house until the end of September. So there, Lizzy, no need to rush home on that score!"

With that gambit failed, Elizabeth resolved herself to a fortnight of melancholic tedium. She trudged about like Lydia's governess or paid companion, dutifully watching over her while privately acknowledging that perhaps it ought to be the other way round. Perhaps Lydia should have been given charge of her, keeping her from being led astray.

Even before his arrest, it seemed Mr Wickham had been in his regiment's bad books. Rumours swirled about regarding bad business schemes, gambling, debts, and a lady of consequence from some other town who found herself with child and laid it at Mr Wickham's door. With no thanks to precaution on Elizabeth's part, she gratefully found herself absent from these wild tales. As despairing as she was, it could only be worse to imagine herself the talk of the regiments for succumbing to one of Mr Wickham's schemes.

The fortnight at last came to its natural end, Lydia growing more peevishly despairing with every passing day, bemoaning the tedium of Longbourn and the unfairness of her having to leave the seaside when she was so very popular among the officers. A scheme began to emerge in the Forster house whereby she might remain, but fortunately Colonel Forster put a swift end to it. In his usual kindly way he said, "I could not think of it, not when I promised to return Mr Bennet's daughter to him safe and sound."

Elizabeth hid a small smile. She had begun to suspect that Mrs Forster might be with child, and while she doubted the lady's capacity to take care of even a kitten, it seemed to be the natural order of things. She and Lydia would only be in the way.

They returned from Brighton in early September, when the

days had begun to shorten and the nights to lengthen, and a bite came into the air in the evenings. Elizabeth did not speak to her sisters or parents of what nearly befell her in Brighton— although of course she told Jane, who fretted over it as if it were an error ongoing. To her father, she only mentioned how very glad she would be to remain at home for a good long while.

"I am glad to hear it," said Mr Bennet, peering over his spectacles at her. "For as much as I am no great mathematician, my calculations have shown that you have only spent about a se'nnight complete with us this entire year."

"That is not true," said Elizabeth with a laugh. "But nevertheless, the feel of my own bed and my own coverlets about me at night is a relief. But what news here? I understand we have cause to believe that Mr Bingley and his new bride shall be in residence soon?"

"I believe they shall." From his tone, Elizabeth deduced that Mr Bennet had no great interest in whether Mr and Mrs Bingley came or not.

From Jane's letters, Elizabeth knew that Netherfield had undergone quite a few renovations. Paint, wall coverings, rugs, even some of the furniture had been altered. 'On the orders of the new Mrs Bingley, no doubt,' Jane had remarked in almost every letter she wrote, always adding on, 'as a new bride ought to, of course!'

"With the renovations complete, surely they mean to move into the place," Elizabeth remarked.

"Better for the neighbourhood that they occupy it than let it sit there."

"I only hope for poor Jane's sake that it is—"

"It is what?" Mrs Bennet bustled into the sitting room, unhesitatingly leaping into Elizabeth's tête-à-tête with her father.

"We were speaking of Mr Bingley's near-inhabitation of his rightfully purchased home."

"You will not see me calling on her," said Mrs Bennet scornfully, lowering herself into a chair. "That is one bridal visit she shall have to do without."

"Pray do not be silly, Mama," said Jane as she entered the room. "Of course we will call on her."

"I have heard she is not at all amiable," Mrs Bennet announced.

"I did not know, Mrs Bennet, that you had so many connexions amongst the *ton* as to determine such things," Mr Bennet teased.

"If you will know, I had it from Sir William Lucas, who does have his connexions," Mrs Bennet retorted.

To this Mr Bennet only scoffed, then rose to open a window nearby. The drawing room, facing full west, had not yet learnt that it was nearly autumn, and continued to build to an extraordinary heat in the late afternoon. Very idly, he remarked, "My understanding is that Mr Bingley's engagement went off."

Shock descended upon them all, and Mrs Bennet began to proclaim that she had known it all along and was not surprised in the least. It was Elizabeth who gathered her composure enough to enquire, "Who might have told you such a thing, Papa?"

"Mr Darcy."

"Mr Darcy!" Elizabeth and Jane exclaimed it in unison. Elizabeth continued on to ask, "When did you speak to—"

"He wrote to me," said Mr Bennet. "And I should have you know that I am seriously considering replying."

"What did he say?" Elizabeth asked, suddenly filled with dread that Darcy might have told him of her escapade in Brighton.

"Nothing very particular," said Mr Bennet. "Only that Bingley would still be coming to Netherfield at the end of September and that he hoped the neighbourhood would receive his friend agreeably, and not hold past errors in judgment against him. I am sure I do not know what he meant."

"You will write to Mr Bingley himself," Mrs Bennet declared. "And tell him that he absolutely *must* dine here straightaway when he comes into the county."

Elizabeth glanced at Jane who was pink-cheeked and bright-eyed. Jane observed her notice and immediately said, "Lizzy, do not look at me, please. Just because he has ended his engagement, it does not follow that he would wish to pay any particular attention to me."

"Oh, but I think he will," Elizabeth teased warmly.

"How did he do it, though?" Jane asked. "For a man to end his betrothal would be enormously scandalous."

"If Mr Darcy was in the matter, you can be sure all was done with a gentleman's honour," Elizabeth assured her, believing that with every fibre of her being.

"I hope so." Jane added hastily, "For his sake, not mine of course."

"I do not doubt it was all for you, Jane!" Mrs Bennet exclaimed, having overheard only part of the conversation.

"Now, we must begin to plan, for it would not do at all for him to have his head turned by some other dreadful lady!"

Mrs Bennet then tugged Jane into plans and schemes for Mr Bingley's return, evidently wholly believing that Jane would be engaged within the first full day of seeing him again. Elizabeth remained quiet beside her sister, wondering and hoping whether Darcy would be coming to Netherfield, too, and if so, what she might have to hope for in it.

CHAPTER THIRTY-TWO

THE SWEETS OF AUTUMN

Darcy did not come to Netherfield.

According to the reports of the town gossips, Netherfield boasted only a small family party—Mr and Miss Bingley and Mr and Mrs Hurst. Elizabeth did her best to hide her disappointment from Jane, wishing to allow her sister all the delights of a hopeful heart.

On the day appointed for Mr Bennet to call at Netherfield and welcome Mr Bingley back to the neighbourhood, it was reported that he had immediately gone away again. Mr Bennet was relieved, but the Bennet ladies were confused. Happily, he returned almost immediately—again alone—but unhappily, Mr Bennet refused to go and see him.

"He will call on us soon enough," Elizabeth assured her sister as they walked into Meryton one afternoon. "He must! He is desperately in love with you!"

"Lizzy, I do not forget that *you* do not even recollect the whole of the autumn. You can have no idea of whether the gentleman ever even liked me."

"I do recollect when he called at Gracechurch Street, though, and the man was positively miserable at the notion of marrying another. And even *more* miserable that you might marry another! It would be extraordinary to think such a man would not be running here at his first opportunity."

"It is vexing, this dance of courtship we are all required to dance. Why can it not be easy? Why cannot a lady go to a man and say, 'I am in love with you and think we ought to get married'. Easy as that!"

"I am not sure I would be able to be so brazen!" Elizabeth mused, her thoughts, as ever, on Darcy. "And in any case, imagine the horrors of being rejected. A lady can only have the power of refusal, it is true, but at least we have not that sorrow, the burden of being the one who must ask."

A familiar pain thrust into Elizabeth's heart, thinking of how Darcy must have felt after his first proposal was so cruelly rejected. She still could not remember anything about it but knew from his letter how vitriolic she must have been. Was it any wonder he stayed away? If nothing else, the time since Brighton had wholly convinced her that he was right to despise her, a woman who rejected him a multitude of times, who had tossed aside all his kindness in Kent, and who concluded by nonsensically running off with his sworn enemy. It was not a flattering portrait he had of her, and she knew that if she ever did see him again, mortification would be her primary feeling.

The ladies had no true object in coming into town, other than the wish to be out of the drawing room for a while. Jane wished to go to the draper's, so they went, but her sister's interest in fabrics and trim was always much in excess of Elizabeth's. At length, she said, "I believe I might go over and see what is new in Mr Hatchard's bookshop. I imagine very little, but he might surprise me."

"Mm," Jane said. She was holding a length of palest blue silk up to her skin.

It suited her very well, and Elizabeth told her so, then added, "I shall return shortly I am sure, but if you finish before I do, come to the bookshop."

Jane nodded, her attention now fixed on a different length of pale blue silk, and Elizabeth chuckled and went to see the books. She spent a quarter of an hour browsing, taking up one book and then another, none of them interesting her in the least.

She was in the midst of the first chapter of *The Age We Live In* when a male voice interrupted her browsing. "Shall you pay for that or just stand here and read it for free?"

Whirling round, she beheld Saye, leant against the nearest bookcase and grinning. "I have been standing here nearly ten minutes complete, and you have scarcely done more than open and close books, all with a little frown."

She laughed, a little weakly. "I am afraid I can find nothing to suit me, but I must credit it to my own inability to concentrate. I am sure the books themselves cannot be held to account. W-what do you do here?"

"Bingley has invited some of us down." With an easy grin, he added, "As for why I am in the shop, I suppose I just wished to poke about and see what's where."

Her pulse quickened a little, and before she could stop herself, she said, "Is Mr Darcy with you?"

Saye shook his head, then tilted it and said, "Do you not think you might have noticed a tall, glowering man stamping about?"

Elizabeth laughed, but it was more the sound of discomfort than amusement. A sinking feeling pervaded her. *He is not here. He did not come.*

"I have been over by Hatfield. A lady I know lives over there."

Elizabeth forced herself away from the thoughts which would give her pain for many weeks. "In Hatfield? Is it Miss Goddard?"

"You know her?"

"No, not really. Only a little," Elizabeth admitted. "My sister knows her much better than I do."

"You simply must tell her how wonderful I am next time you see her." He yawned. "I have a new curricle, very fast, and my horse has been eager to stretch his legs. Should you like a ride? Or do you mean to shuffle disinterestedly about these heaven-forsaken shops all day?"

The shopkeeper looked up at this pronouncement and frowned in their direction.

Saye smiled at him. "I did not mean your shop of course, good sir. I will take six of them, how is that?"

"Six…books?" The shopkeeper looked interested if dubious.

"Dealer's choice, but do let us include this one for Miss Bennet," he said with a smile. Walking towards the man, he slid one hand into the pocket of his jacket, withdrawing a handful of coins. "Ten guineas should cover it, I daresay."

The shopkeeper's kindly face had moved from astonished doubt to delight, and he bowed. "Yes, sir. Thank you, sir, you are too good."

"Pray select some good ones for me," Saye ordered. "Nothing of the pious variety, now!"

So charged, the shopkeeper set to work and in short time had the books wrapped in a neat bundle. He offered to take them to Saye's curricle, and while he exited, the open door revealed Jane.

"Lizzy, there you are. I began to think you would never…" Her words died upon her lips as she beheld her sister's companion.

"This is one of your sisters, I suppose?" Saye asked. "I should like an introduction, if you will do the honours."

Jane took a few more steps towards them, and Elizabeth introduced her. She saw that Jane's beauty was not lost on Saye, but his interest was more of the connoisseur than the lover.

"Your sister has been plaguing me for a ride in my curricle," Saye informed Jane. "It only seats two, but as the pair of you are small, I daresay we can make it work if someone holds Florizel."

"Who is Florizel?" Jane asked as Saye began moving their little group onto the street where they beheld a curricle, Prussian blue with cream and gilt edges. A charming sight greeted them: a fluffy white dog, wearing a blue velvet collar that matched the curricle.

"Here you see my absolute dearest friend in the world," Saye pronounced. "Florizel! Bow!"

Elizabeth and Jane both laughed delightedly as the dog, who had risen up on all four legs to wag his tail and greet them, lowered his head between his two front legs. He then looked expectantly at Saye who slid his hand into his pocket, producing some sort of dried meat. He broke off a piece and handed it to the dog. Noting Elizabeth's curiosity, he offered her a bite as well, then Jane.

"I thank you, no," Elizabeth said with a laugh. "What is it? Dried beef?"

"Venison," he replied with a sniff. "He does not care for beef. He thinks it too common." Taking a bite himself, Saye assisted both ladies up, then walked round to the other side of the curricle and climbed in.

Elizabeth sat, drawing Florizel onto her lap. The pup curved his head back to look at her and then looked ahead, ready to depart it seemed.

"I ought to tell you, sir, that our home is but a mile that way," Jane said, gesturing towards the lane that would take them to Longbourn.

"Then I shall just have to take you to Netherfield instead. Twice the ride, twice the fun."

"Netherfield?" Jane asked, her voice sounding very high and anxious.

"Charming place," said Saye. "Acquaintance of mine called Bingley bought it, intending to get married, but it seems the lady reconsidered her options."

"Is that how it was?" Elizabeth enquired. "My father had

heard that Mr Bingley's engagement went off, but we knew not how."

"Bingley is unmarried, unengaged, untangled. By the very skin of his teeth, I might add!" Saye laughed and gave another little flick of the reins. "We all thought, how better to cheer him than to have an excellent party! Though in truth it is less consolation than celebration. Miss Roberts is a termagant, and I loathed her exceedingly."

The horses, which had been moving out of town at a more sedate pace, took off. Elizabeth had never ridden in such a conveyance and found the experience of racing through the countryside exhilarating, even if she had to raise one hand to hold her bonnet in place. In very short time, they were turning in to the lane to take them to Netherfield's door. Elizabeth thought how anxious the sight of it would make her if she knew Darcy were within.

Mrs Nicholls answered the door, smiling as she greeted them and quickly divesting them all of gloves, bonnets, pelisses, and Saye's greatcoat and hat. She handed them to a waiting maid beside her and then said, "Mr and Miss Bingley are with Mr Darcy and Miss Grantley in the drawing room."

She set off at a sprightly pace, Florizel trotting beside her, evidently well-accustomed to the house. Jane turned to her sister, looking pale and anxious. She had not uttered a word since Saye told them Mr Bingley was not married, and Elizabeth could only imagine what contrariety of emotion her dear sister must experience. Jane followed Mrs Nicholls, shoulders straight and head high, evidently prepared to confront things head-on.

Elizabeth had no such courage. The very word 'Darcy'

had set a great stone of mortification upon her head, and she nearly turned around and ran. *How can I face him? How can I face his coldness?* She was not prepared to truly comprehend the love she had lost from him.

"You will find it easier to get to the drawing room if you move your feet, Miss Elizabeth," Saye said gravely.

She allowed herself to be moved towards the drawing room. "Forgive me, I-I am only a little surprised."

Saye looked about the hall. "Yes, I understand a great deal of work has been done to the place."

"No, not by Netherfield itself." She lowered her voice. "You said he was not here!"

"What? Did not."

"You did," she insisted. "You said I would notice a tall fellow."

"I thought you wished to know whether he was in the shop. Which he was not."

Elizabeth huffed. "Obviously that was not my meaning."

"Am I to know your mind?"

They had come to the drawing room door, but she held back, whispering, "Surely you must be enough in Mr Darcy's confidence to know that neither of us wishes to see one another?"

In a customary, if perhaps loud, voice, Saye enquired, "You mean to avoid Darcy? Why?"

"Shh!" she hissed, feeling colour flood her cheeks. "That is not what I said. I said we, each of us, has no wish to see the other."

Mrs Nicholls had seen Jane into the drawing room and now turned back, walking a few steps to just outside the door where Elizabeth and Saye lingered. "Miss Elizabeth? Is there something wrong?"

"Forgive me. I…n-no, only, I am intruding. I did not mean to, um, intrude upon… Mr Bingley has guests, and I ought not to…to intrude."

"If I am understanding you," Saye said satirically, "you feel like an intruder?"

She shot him a look.

"Mr Bingley will be glad to see you here," Mrs Nicholls assured her. "As amiable as he is, he is always glad for more to join the party."

The drawing room door remained open from Jane's entry, and Elizabeth peeped through the opening to see Mr Bingley, his complexion ruddy and eyes bright, greeting her sister. Her heart sank knowing she must make a good show of things, for Jane if no one else. *Into the breach, then*, she thought and, with an uneasy smile at Mrs Nicholls, entered the drawing room.

It was both familiar and not. There were a great many changes, but as Elizabeth did not recall the prior autumn, she knew not whether Mr Bingley's former betrothed or someone else had made them. In any case, the entire room was rearranged from that which she remembered, and thus Elizabeth did not immediately see Darcy, not until she had walked farther in the room and looked to her left. He stood near the couch on the proximal wall, partly obscured by the opened door. He was not looking at her, having evidently found something of keen interest on the floor by his feet. There were two very pretty ladies, both dressed very finely, both still seated on the couch; they must have been flanking him. Closely. Mr Bingley's sisters, she supposed.

"Miss Eliza," drawled the one with darker hair. "How wonderful to see you and so well recovered. What an ordeal you have had!"

Without looking up, Darcy murmured something to her that made both ladies break into laughter. "Oh, dear! Still?"

Another murmur.

"Miss Eliza, Mr Darcy thinks it possible you do not even know me. Surely that cannot be?"

Elizabeth offered an uneasy smile that faded as she watched Darcy abruptly leave the room. Saye, still near her side, said, "Excuse me," and followed him. She turned her attention back to her hostess.

"Forgive me, but yes, that is true. Might I presume that you are Miss Bingley?"

This led to another round of titters and expressive glances between both ladies. At last, the presumed Miss Bingley rose and came to where Elizabeth still stood awkwardly in what felt like the middle of the room.

Taking both of Elizabeth's hands, she spoke very slowly, with condescending solicitude. "Yes, my dear, I am Miss Caroline Bingley. That is my friend Miss Julia Grantley, but fear not! This is your first meeting of her."

"Thank you," said Elizabeth, and Miss Bingley dropped her hands and returned to the couch. She did not invite Elizabeth to join them, or even to take a seat, and Elizabeth knew now why Darcy had told her, so long ago, that Miss Bingley was the sort of woman who was only truly a friend to herself. She glanced over and saw that Mr Bingley and Jane were talking, their heads bent towards one another. *If I must endure torture, at least Jane will benefit.*

Not knowing what else to do, she crossed the room and took up a position by a window. In truth, it suited her to leave the ladies behind—she would much rather think about Darcy. *'I want nothing from you.'* Evidently that included her very presence. Had her mistake with Mr Wickham made him despise her? He certainly seemed as though he did.

Such fits and starts between them both! Contention had led, somehow, to his first proposal; then an all too short period of exquisite felicity, after which they had more contention, her thinking him untrustworthy. Then him thinking her silly and untrustworthy as well. And now? Painful awkwardness.

She chanced a look over her shoulder. Miss Grantley and Miss Bingley were tittering over something, Miss Bingley's fan raised to cover their undoubtedly gossiping mouths. Elizabeth felt as though she might be the object of their amusement but could not rouse herself to care. She hoped Darcy would return to the drawing room even as much as she dreaded it. It was wonderful to rest her eyes on him, even if his lack of warmth towards her was agonising.

Saye did not bother knocking before shoving open the door to Darcy's bedchamber.

"Not now," Darcy said immediately. "I am in no humour—"

"What in the blazing ballocks of Napoleon are you about?" Saye demanded of him, one hand on his hip. "I ought to knock you right on the skull. I bring her to you on a platter—"

"By tricking her into believing I was not here!"

"And?"

"And she loathed the very sight of me!" Darcy shouted back at him. "I heard you, Saye, I heard you both in the hall, and I know how little she wished to see me!"

Saye glanced up at the ceiling briefly before admitting, "She may have been somewhat reluctant, 'tis true—"

"Thank you for admitting that much at least!"

"—but I know just what you need to do now. First you must—"

"No! No more schemes, no more plans, no more trickery. Elizabeth Bennet and I are a hopeless cause." Wearily he sank into a chair, the truth of that statement seeping into him.

"You surely do not mean to give up?"

"What else is there to do? Over and over again, she makes her feelings known to me. Her reply to my first proposal was that I was the last man in the world she would ever marry, and despite a dreadful injury and illness, despite having no recollection of nearly a year of her life, in this she remains true to herself."

He waited for Saye to argue it, to say something pithy or annoying, but Saye did not, and somehow his spirits sank even more. A lump, like a hard ball of lead, sank into his gut, and he followed it by lowering his head into his hands. "It is time for me to accept things the way they are."

There was a short silence, then Saye offered, "What if she

were to be knocked on the head again? Not enough to gravely injure her, just enough to—"

Darcy gave his cousin a look meant to quell his nonsense.

"What I mean is that if we could get her to forget again the whole deception thing, then you could—"

"I do not think amnesia can be tailored in such a way."

"You could make her jealous. Make her watch you make love to Miss Grantley."

Darcy did not even reply to that.

"If you were to get her alone, you might be able to—"

"Pray stop, Saye." He again lowered his head into his hands. The worst of it was that Saye's outlandish schemes truly were all he had left. Everything else had failed. *He* had failed.

He heard Saye sit in the chair opposite him and draw a deep breath. After several long, silent minutes, his cousin cleared his throat. "It is perhaps a bad time to mention this, but you do owe me ten pounds for getting her here."

CHAPTER THIRTY-THREE

THAT'S WHAT SHE SAYED

Saye descended the steps slowly, the ten-pound note from Darcy held loosely in his hand. The whole of the performance this afternoon had been dissatisfying and nonsensical. Miss Elizabeth hung back like a skittish pony in its first bridle, and Darcy had stormed off like his rear end got chapped. Utter rot, first to last.

Entering the drawing room, he saw a sight that displeased him further. Miss Elizabeth Bennet had seated herself at the far end of the room at the escritoire and was staring at the wallpaper. *Making a brown study of it too, by the looks of it.* She glanced at him when he entered, quickly searching behind him; she was unable to hide the look of disappointment on her face on observing Darcy's absence. *Bloody hell, Darcy, come to the drawing room, you fool.*

Saye then cut his eyes towards the little sofa where Miss Bingley lolled with her friend, both of them murmuring and giggling over *La Belle Assemblée* and ignoring the other two ladies in the room. Excessively rude.

There were those who found Saye himself rude, and he would not argue the point. He *was* sometimes rude, frequently unfeeling, generally insensitive—but not towards people he might actually injure. And mostly towards those who deserved it. Which Miss Elizabeth Bennet did not. She appeared rather pitiful, in fact.

He approached her directly. "Something tells me you might like a ride home."

She looked relieved and rose. As she did, she took up a folded page that had lain in front of her but said nothing about it. "If it does not inconvenience you too greatly, I would much appreciate being escorted home."

"Consider it done," he proclaimed gallantly and told her he would send the nearest footman to call for the carriage while she informed her sister that she was prepared to leave. Bingley looked terribly disappointed at the notion that Saye would take his lady back to her home.

"But surely we will all meet tonight?" Saye said. "At the assembly?"

Bingley's face brightened. "Oh yes! Surely all the Bennet ladies will be in attendance there?"

"Yes, we will," said Miss Bennet. "To be sure. Lizzy?"

Miss Elizabeth echoed her sister's sentiments, but Saye observed that she looked rather ill at ease.

It was a thankfully quick business to get the two ladies back home. Miss Elizabeth was silent throughout the short journey, and Miss Bennet, while lovely, was no conversationalist. It was a relief to enter the drive. Saye handed Miss

Bennet down and then thought frantically of what he might say to Miss Elizabeth to learn something of her mind in regards to Darcy.

As it transpired, he did not need to. As soon as he had her down, she reached into her pocket and slowly withdrew the folded page. Without meeting his eye, she asked, "Would you please give that to Mr Darcy?"

Although Darcy did not precisely recollect wagering Saye ten pounds to get Elizabeth to Netherfield, he paid him. Always easier to pay than argue with Saye, and in any case, it made him leave faster.

Darcy then took a book and sat by the fireplace, feeling as empty and hollow as it was. The book remained unopened on his lap while he sat and bemoaned the pitiful state of things, the opportunity that had come and gone from him. He requested, and received, dinner on a tray in his bedchamber, fully intending to spend the night indulging in the blue devils.

His reverie was interrupted by the arrival of his man, Fields, who bustled in speaking of baths and pomade and preferences in waistcoats.

"What on earth do you speak of, Fields?"

Fields stopped. "The assembly, sir."

"An assembly? No. Send my regrets."

"As you wish, sir." Looking like he had more to say but knowing it was not his place, his man bowed and left the room.

Darcy turned determinedly to his book but had managed

to read nothing by the time Fields returned looking distinctly uneasy. "Your cousin has sent his regrets about your regrets, sir."

"What does that mean?"

"It means he does not excuse you. He said either I see you dressed or lose my position."

Darcy rolled his eyes. "Happily, Saye has nothing to say about your position, so you have my permission to tell him to go and flog himself."

Fields permitted himself a small smile before again quitting the room. He returned only minutes later. "Lord Saye said he means to come up here and bathe you himself if needed and went so far as to enquire of Mrs Nicholls where he might find the buckets."

"Good Lord!" Darcy tossed his book aside and went to berate his cousin. Fields mentioned that he would find him in the billiard room. His strides echoed in a satisfying manner as he went through Netherfield's halls, indeed finding Saye and Bingley playing billiards.

"Not only am I not going to the assembly, I fear I must depart in the morning," he announced as he came through the door, in a tone that he hoped would not beltray the fact that the idea had only just occurred to him.

"What?" Bingley looked up from the shot he had been about to place. "Darcy, pray do not—"

"Urgent business calls me to London," he said firmly, glaring at Saye. "I will be gone at first light."

Saye was standing on the side, drink in hand, presumably awaiting his turn at the table. After a noisy slurp of his drink, he said, "On the *Sabbath*? A gentleman would not do such a savage thing, and as your superior in consequence, age, and good looks, I cannot allow it."

"He is right," Bingley said urgently, leaning against his stick. "You would not wish to travel on the Sabbath."

Sunday. Of all the luck! Darcy closed his eyes briefly. "No, um, I had forgotten what day it was. Monday is when I mean to go."

"Then you can easily attend the assembly this evening!" Bingley concluded happily. *Easy to be happy now that all of* his *romantic struggles are set aright*, Darcy thought sourly.

Saye took another disgustingly loud slurp that Darcy did not doubt was designed to vex him—he loathed mouth noises and Saye knew it.

"Monday does not work for me, old man," Saye announced setting down his drink and moving to the table. "On Monday, Miss Goddard is coming to Netherfield, and I will probably end the day an engaged man."

"I hope she refuses you if only to teach you some humility," Darcy informed his cousin.

"She will not refuse me, and in any case, I am already as humble as someone of my privilege could be. Furthermore, as my tedious brother is not here, I fear the family welcome falls to you, sir," Saye informed him as he set himself up for a shot. "Leave your business until Wednesday or so, and I can accompany you back to London."

"That will not do. I am afraid it is more urgent than that."

Bingley nodded sympathetically, but Saye looked sceptical, glancing up from the shot he was setting. "Sounds very important," he said. "What is it, then?"

"Alas, I cannot divulge it."

"In other words," Saye shot, the balls cracking loudly against one another, "it is nothing. Do not turn tail, Darcy. Stay."

"Turning tail? I have no idea what you mean. I have urgent business and must leave."

"If it is so urgent, surely it would be easy enough to tell me the substance of it?" Saye straightened and placed one hand on his hip. "And I am curious as to why, between two men of business, a secretary in London and a steward at Pemberley, it cannot be managed by someone else? If these people cannot do their duty and leave you to enjoy yourself, I say release the lot of them."

"If you need a new secretary," Bingley began, "I have recently learnt that Mr Edmund Williams—"

"I do not need a new secretary. My people do their duties perfectly well," Darcy retorted, then rubbed his temple. "But it is something that requires—"

Saye strolled over to him. "If you would simply tell us what it is"—his cousin put an arm about his shoulders—"we could surely come up with a solution that does not require you to abandon your dear friend and even dearer cousin and scamper off to London."

"I am not scampering anywhere."

"What say we send my father an express?" Saye offered brightly. "He is in London even now and can surely be prevailed upon to be of use to you in this *desperate* time, hm? And the rider could be there yet tonight! An even better solution to this very plaguing business of yours."

"Very well," Darcy said in a low, angry voice. "I shall see what I can do by letter."

"Splendid!" Bingley cried out.

"Oh, speaking of a letter…that reminds me." Saye made a great show of patting himself all over his coat, as if he was searching for something. His bit of theatre done at last, he extracted a folded page. "For you."

"From whom?" Darcy asked as he took it. "What is it?"

Saye shrugged. "From a friend. Now off you go, I am trying to run up your ten pounds here by beating your friend at billiards."

THERE WAS NOTHING ON THE OUTSIDE OF THE folded page, and it was not sealed. He peeked inside only enough to see a feminine hand, then set off for his bedchamber at a rapid pace. As he went, he absently wondered whether Saye had read its contents, for he never was one to restrain his curiosity. He could scarcely manage to restrain his own feelings on it—curiosity, hope, dread, anxiety. He knew not which should be taking the chief seat within him as he took the stairs two at a time to get to his bedchamber.

He was unfolding the letter before the door was fully closed behind him. There was no salutation, only a quick entry into the thoughts of her heart.

I hope not to pain you or to force you to review feelings that you would much rather forget, but it seems that if I remain silent, I run the risk of losing you forever. Perhaps I already have, and these words are written in vain, but I could not allow it to be without at least trying.

I have never said these words to another, nor do I think I ever shall, save for to you, but I must tell you that I love you. I know not when I began, for I have forgot all of our beginning, but I am in full comprehension of my heart as it is today, and it is wholly yours.

You may be too angry with me to receive these sentiments gladly. I know I pained you by acting so foolishly with regards to Mr W, and in this I can only beg your forgiveness. We have many mistakes and misunderstandings between us, and my resentment in the matter of our presumed betrothal has been, to this point, implacable, but my heart is no longer hardened. I wish only that we might discuss what troubles have arisen between us and, I hope, lay them aside.

If your affections and wishes are unchanged, I daresay I will understand it by your manner towards me. But do know that if not, one word from you will silence me on this subject forever. I do not mean to plague you with love that is too late, and too little. Only for this once will I plead with you to relieve my suffering and ask me again to be your wife.

Either way my heart will remain as yours,

EB

Elation made Darcy dizzy and warm, and he sat on his bed and then stood and paced too many times to count. He read and re-read and then read it some more, then recognised he was grinning like a madman over it. *Shall I go to Longbourn now? No, the assembly—I must dress. Where is Fields?*

He rang for his man who came at once, well prepared for the task ahead. Darcy had never been so eager for an assembly in his entire life, fairly twitching in anticipation. More than once, Fields had to ask him to be still while he shaved him.

Darcy wondered whether Mr Bennet would go to the assembly. Could you ask a father for his daughter's hand in marriage at an assembly? How he longed for the hour to pass quickly!

Just as Fields had handed him his waistcoat, the door opened without a knock, and Saye entered, a gimlet eye upon his cousin's attire. "Is that your notion of polished shoes?" he asked Fields. "Let me get some Champagne."

"Yes, sir," Fields said agreeably.

"No, sir," Darcy interjected. "My shoes will do, Saye. Worry about your own attire."

"My shoes are already shined," Saye replied blithely, as he took a seat in Darcy's chair. He held up one foot to exhibit the gleaming shoe. "Is that the new perfume you wear? I like it. Fields, is there something you can put in his cravat that will sparkle? I think it helps draw a lady's eye."

"My cravat pin will do well enough," Darcy replied. "Do you need something?"

Saye languidly crossed one leg over the other, withdrew a small mirror from his pocket, and began to examine the condition of his teeth. "What did the letter say? Does she still wish to marry you?"

Darcy raised his chin to allow Fields to tie his cravat. "She cannot *still* wish to marry me because she never *before* wished to marry me."

"Yes, Darcy, do concentrate on the grammar of the situation," said Saye. "You know my meaning."

"Things are as yet undecided. Will Miss Goddard be at the assembly this evening?"

"I doubt it, but one can always hope. If she is, I will know it is wholly for me."

Darcy rolled his eyes.

"You tell me what else would bring her here," Saye retorted indignantly. "If she is here, she is mine. I will know it. But we are speaking of you! Are you not glad I kept you here?"

"I am."

Fields finished, and after asking Darcy if he required anything else, quit the room.

"Will you propose again tonight?" Saye enquired. Darcy responded with a maddening—he hoped—shrug.

"Good Lord, man! Tell me something! I tell you everything, likely more than you wish to know!"

"Decidedly more than I wish to know," Darcy agreed. "And I can tell you only this: she loves me, and I love her. The rest will be sorted out naturally."

CHAPTER THIRTY-FOUR

THE WISEST AND BEST CONCLUSION TO THE AFFAIR

E lizabeth had never fumbled and fudged as much in her life as she did in the hours after giving her letter into the care of Saye. She tripped going up the stairs and slipped coming down again. She dropped her book so many times that her mother accused her of shattering her nerves. She was inattentive at the dinner table and ate next to nothing yet still managed to get a stomach-ache from it. Mrs Hill was quick with a remedy for it, but there was one perilous quarter of an hour when her mother considered keeping her home.

She regretted giving the letter as much as she was relieved to have given it. She could not envision it, how Darcy might be. Would he ignore her completely? Treat her coldly? Would it at last put the misunderstandings and mistakes of the past behind them?

A row between Kitty and Lydia, and Mary's reluctance to attend, made them late. It afforded Elizabeth ample time to decide that her hair looked worse than it ever had and that her gown was unflattering. Alas, just when she had resolved to go back to her bedchamber and put on a different gown, everyone was ready to leave.

"You do look terribly pale, Lizzy," Jane fretted as they all climbed into the carriage, and Elizabeth could give no reply but to squeeze her sister's hand with her own ice-cold fingers.

The carriage ride was interminable, but at last they arrived at the Merry Fox where the assembly would be held. Elizabeth ascended the stairs behind Jane and her mother, with her younger sisters coming behind her. Because Jane and her mother were both taller than she, and ahead of her on the stairs, she could see nothing until she had finished climbing.

Darcy was standing near the door, and he looked so very handsome, so serious, that it made her breath stop. Then their eyes met, and time itself seemed to stop until he smiled at her. With no regard to any person ahead of her, Elizabeth flew to him and he to her; he took her hands and gazed at her warmly, but they could do nothing more beyond that as she felt the eyes of those within upon them.

"A walk?" she murmured, and he agreed. Elizabeth quickly went to her mother and informed her of her intention to walk outside with Darcy. To this her mother replied with a smirk and a "I knew you would come to your senses," which might have vexed her another time but could not—not when filled with the relief of Darcy's continued devotion.

She turned back to him, and they descended the stairs and went outside. The harvest moon lit their surroundings, and the autumn air was still and scented with the pipe smoke of the various coachmen who lingered a short distance away. Darcy guided her around a corner so they would be unobserved and then took her in his arms, bringing her close to his chest. "May I kiss you?"

Unable to speak, she looked up at him and nodded.

His kiss was like nothing she had ever known or imagined, and it was perfection. He took her face in both hands, beginning with a gentle touch of his lips on her own but quickly deepening it to a true lover's kiss that might have made her swoon had she not been holding onto him so tightly. One of his hands eventually dropped so his arm could circle her waist, and one of hers moved into the curls at the nape of his neck. She hoped and prayed it might never end.

"Was that our first kiss?" she asked, her voice sounding strangely husky when they at last parted.

He chuckled then said, "Our first, yes, and then a second —" He kissed her lips again. "—and our third—" He kissed her once more then pulled away and merely looked at her. She returned his gaze until it made her shy and then tried to look down, but he would not have it. With one finger beneath her chin, he tilted her face towards him. "Will you marry me?"

"Yes," she replied. "But only if you promise to kiss me like that every single day."

His laugh made his chest rumble. "You have my word on that."

"How can you continue to love me?" she asked quietly. "I have occasioned nothing but pain upon you! I first recognised it one afternoon when Jane and I were speaking of how she wished a lady could simply say what she felt to a gentleman. And I replied that, yes, but then we would have also the horrors of rejection to face as well."

She swallowed, then added, "The last hours have been abysmal. I cannot imagine how you must have felt the night of my first rejection, or all the days since."

"It has not been easy," he confessed. "Deserved though much of it was. There were lessons, hard-learned, but necessary, particularly in regards to my treatment of your family."

"I love my family very dearly," she said. "But I confess that I do see why others might be dismayed by them."

"Nevertheless, I will show them due respect as I perhaps did not before. And in the Gardiners, I perceive people I might truly form deep and lasting regard with. They are charming people."

She could only smile warmly in reply to that, then added, "When you went off this morning, when I appeared so suddenly at Netherfield, I thought the very sight of me was abhorrent to you."

"Of course not," he said. "I was only distressed by my belief that you despised the sight of me. Saye had tricked you into coming. I could hear you in the hall, not wishing to enter the drawing room, reluctant to see me. You wished to avoid me."

"I could not bear to meet your indifference or your anger."

"Indifference and anger?" Now he looked at her searchingly.

"You were angry with me for the matter with Mr Wickham. You cannot deny it."

"I do not wish to deny it. Yes, I was angry at you for trusting him when you did not trust me. But being angry with you did not mean I should stop loving you."

"You said you wanted nothing from me." Her heart ached with the remembrance of that, his words, and his looks.

"No," he said. "I could not have."

"You did," she insisted. "Believe me, the words have echoed through me ever since."

He gave her a gentle kiss on her forehead. "Yes, perhaps I did, but I said it only because I despised hearing your gratitude. I hated that you thanked me for coming to your rescue."

"Hated that I thanked you?"

"Who but I should be troubled on your behalf? Who but I should be your rescuer? Had I not told you a multitude of times by then how I loved you? How much I wished to care for you?"

"Yes, but it does not follow that you should need to scamper about the countryside, offering bags of money to reprobates, because of my foolishness!"

He closed his eyes briefly. "The last thing I should ever want is your gratitude for anything. Your forgiveness, yes, your love, completely, but do not be grateful to me."

She was so astonished that she was silent until a giggle broke forth. "Never? So whatever you give me, henceforth, I should receive as my due? Perhaps a small grunt of acknowledgement would be permitted?"

He chuckled with her, then said, "If I have your love, I will have everything I need, everything I want from you. When you would look at me, back in Kent, with all you felt showing in your beautiful eyes, I could never have wished for anything more." He touched her nose with his finger and added, "Just as you look now."

To this she could only smile, thinking that with as much smiling as both were doing in that moment, she would surely wake in the morning with sore cheeks...and gladly so.

"Speaking of Kent," she said, "I do not wish to revisit painful subjects, but honesty is of critical importance to me. I know that I can trust you—"

"Elizabeth, what was done was done for the best, on your behalf."

"I know."

"Disguise of every sort is my abhorrence. I have always been taught that complete honesty is the only way. It was why, the night of my first proposal, I said such...cruel things to you about your family, rather than speaking the words of love you deserved. I believed it was honesty that was required. To deceive you as I did went against my reason and my character, but I believed it was best for you. And I confess I would do it again. Anything that brought you back to good health, to your vigour as you stand here today, I would have done."

"But henceforth...will you be completely honest with me?"

He considered that briefly before saying, "No."

"No?"

"I think we all must be a little dishonest to those we love, for the sake of kindness."

"I do not think that is sound at all," she replied.

"If you wear a gown I think suits you ill, I will still tell you that you are beautiful. Is that objectionable to you?"

"Yes," Elizabeth insisted. "Otherwise, I will keep wearing it and looking ugly in it."

"And what if someone said something cruel about you. Shall I tell you? My inclination would be to keep it from you, for there is no good to come of it."

He did have a point there. Elizabeth never did see the point of needlessly hurting people with gossip. "I suppose if it was someone I thought was my friend—"

"Let us say, for the purpose of discussion, it is not. Someone you already dislike."

Slowly, Elizabeth admitted, "I suppose I need not know that. No doubt Miss Bingley has already said a great many things I would never wish to hear."

"There are a myriad of little things that I might not be wholly honest about because I do not wish to see you hurt. And I give you leave to do the same for me. It is what people who love one another do." He paused. "You can trust me to always have your best interests at heart. You can trust that I will always love you. You can trust that given any chance to make you happy, I shall do it."

She had no idea how to answer any of that, but there were two things she did know. The first was that she did trust him, enough to put her heart and her life in his hands. The second was that she wished to kiss him again. Rising up on her toes, she placed a gentle kiss on his lips, revelling in her right to do so. Barely had she returned to a usual position before he claimed her lips again but not with the passion she might have anticipated. He was gentle, tender, offering her three caresses on her mouth with his own. Then he pulled back and brushed away a curl from her temple. "I love you."

In a voice barely above a whisper, she replied, "I love you too. And...and I wish to make you happy, too."

"Then tell me again you will marry me," he said. "That would make me the happiest man alive."

She looked up into his gaze, so steady and warm upon her. "I cannot wait to be your wife."

The smile of true, heartfelt delight which came upon his countenance made him look different to how she had ever seen him, and she squeezed a tight hug upon him, feeling his kiss on her head before he pulled back.

"My mother has been understanding, allowing us to hie off so long out here. I fear if we linger too much longer, she may come to find us."

"Or worse, my cousin, although Miss Goddard has seen fit to grace the assembly tonight. He may have found his own corner to kiss her in."

She laughed and they linked arms and moved back towards the entrance.

"It has been nearly a year since we danced together," he mentioned. "I confess I am eager to dance with you."

"Oh." She stopped in her tracks. "I do not think I can."

"Why not?"

"I cannot remember the steps," she said with a light laugh. "Of all the silliness."

He considered it then asked, "Will you trust me to lead you?"

She did not hesitate when she replied, "Always."

CHAPTER THIRTY-FIVE

POSITIVELY MEDIEVAL

Elizabeth again ascended the stair into the assembly room with Darcy hard on her heels, his hand laid with gentle possessiveness on the small of her back. She was glad for it; the fact that after all the contentions and confusions between them, they were acknowledged lovers, betrothed did not seem real.

The murmur of conversation and the strains of music from a quadrille got louder as they neared the door. Miss Goddard lingered at the edge, almost out of the door. She turned and smiled as they approached.

"Mr Darcy and Miss Elizabeth," she said warmly. "How good to see you both."

"We have been outside," Darcy blurted, somewhat awkwardly. "We are engaged."

Elizabeth laughed, as much from the impulsiveness of his declaration as the relief of knowing it was true.

"How delightful!" Miss Goddard exclaimed and threw her

arms around Elizabeth. "Do you mean just now? He has only just now proposed?"

"Only just now," Elizabeth confirmed with a nod.

"What is this?" Saye appeared suddenly from behind Miss Goddard. "Engaged? Ask a girl to dance first, Darcy." His teasing words were mollified by a clap on Darcy's back.

Before long, a knot of well-wishers had formed around them. Sir William Lucas informed Darcy that he had obtained the jewel of the county. Mrs Bennet told everyone she always knew it was going to be so and that Elizabeth needed only for time until her wits came back to her. Jane hugged her sister over and over again with tears in her lovely eyes, and Mr Bingley stood by his friend, smiling more broadly than Elizabeth had ever seen anyone smile.

Miss Bingley approached Elizabeth. "Miss Eliza, do allow me to offer you my warmest congratulations. You have certainly made an exemplary match."

"Yes, I have." Elizabeth cast a warm look behind her to where Darcy talked to the men of the group. "I count myself very fortunate."

"Mr Darcy moves in the highest circles. If I may be of any use to you in selecting your gowns or accoutrements, pray do not hesitate to consult me." With that, she moved off.

At length, Saye proclaimed, "Are we here to dance or discuss wedding plans? Miss Goddard, I believe you promised me the next?"

Growing pink, Miss Goddard nodded and allowed Saye to lead her away. Mr Bingley, Elizabeth saw with satisfaction, also took Jane away.

Darcy's voice, low and reassuring, came from over her

shoulder. "It seems it is time for the dance you promised me."

"Very well, but I might make a fool of us both," she said lightly.

"I do not care in the least what you do," he told her, "so long as you are with me when you do it." He took her hand and placed it on his arm and led her towards the set.

Happily, it was one of the easier dances, and to Elizabeth's relief, even if her mind did not recollect the movements, her legs did, instinctively taking her into the patterns she had once known well. She made one or two wrong turns, and stumbled once, catching her foot on the hem of her gown, but Darcy's hand was immediately there to steady her, and she did not think those around them noticed.

"You are doing perfectly well," he told her when it was their time to be still in the pattern.

"I remember more than I thought I might," she said. "But my mind still feels as though I am spinning about like a madwoman. I think that might be because of you."

"Me?"

"Us," she said. A little shyly, she added, "I am very, very happy."

"No more so than I," he assured her. "When might we do it?"

"The wedding?"

He nodded.

She pretended to ponder the question. "I am not busy tomorrow."

"Pray do not tempt me," he replied, his voice feeling like

a caress. "I have waited a long, long time for you and would move Heaven and Earth if it were possible."

"Then let us move Heaven and Earth, as least as much as we can," she said and he, happily, agreed.

To Darcy's dismay, Mrs Bennet was violently opposed to any sort of haste with the nuptials. "How would it look?" she demanded in the drawing room the next morning. "It makes it seem like there is a *reason* that the nuptials must occur with haste."

Shockingly, it was Darcy's own aunt who concurred. Lady Catherine, flush with the success of her daughter's wedding, insisted on a proper feting of her newly engaged nephew in London. "It will take away any gossip about Anne jilting you," she insisted via letter.

"Anne jilted you?" Elizabeth enquired. "You know, for such a handsome and eligible bachelor, you have suffered a great deal of romantic tribulation!" She accompanied this tease with a kiss and thus Darcy did not mind it in the least.

"No one knows what I have suffered," he said, with a purposely woebegone countenance that he hoped would garner him more kisses. Happily, it did and thus it was some minutes before he could explain to her, "Lady Catherine had a notion of Anne and I marrying, to unite the fortunes of Rosings and Pemberley. Neither Anne nor I agreed to the idea, but that did not discourage her whatsoever. Only Anne marrying Yardley put an end to her hopes, but she still likes to pretend Anne jilted me."

Mrs Bennet quite liked the notion of Elizabeth being celebrated in London by Darcy's elevated relations, and a happy fortnight was thus spent, in November, in parties, shopping, and a ball given by Lady Matlock. Darcy permitted Georgiana to be in attendance at each and all of the events, even if she did not dance at the ball. Between Elizabeth and Georgiana there was a growing regard that Darcy delighted in. It was what he had always hoped for and was grateful to see it happening naturally.

Elizabeth was also quickly growing very fond of Miss Goddard who continued to torment Saye with seeming indifference. She had told Elizabeth, privately, that she meant to accept him eventually but thought it good for his pride to suffer a little.

Bingley, too, was suffering romantically. Jane, once in London, was the subject of much interest. Her beauty, in combination with a connexion to the Darcys and Matlocks, made her an object of desire for many gentlemen. Having no fortune of her own was some little detriment, but did not seem to deter anyone at Lady Matlock's ball where Jane had more offers to dance than were even planned for the evening.

"She still loves Bingley," Elizabeth told Darcy as they sat at the supper observing Jane talking to the Duke of Ogden. "Jane is not the sort to have her head or her heart turned by a title."

"One thing I know for sure," Darcy replied to her, "is that I will not insert myself into the matter. Your sister may do as she pleases, as may Bingley. Ogden too for that matter."

Elizabeth married Darcy, at last, on a winter's day in December 1812.

It was a day when nothing went according to plan. The parson, Mr Willingham, became ill the day prior, and his curate was required to come from two towns away for the ceremony. This would not have been such a difficulty, save for the fact that a sleety, rainy kind of snow began to fall, making the roads treacherous.

Darcy was staying at Netherfield, where a new laundry maid took it on herself to press his waistcoat, burning it in the process. Darcy told Elizabeth later that he quickly conscripted Saye's new waistcoat to his own purpose, offering his cousin one of his older ones to wear. Shockingly, Saye did not offer much protest. "Well, it does not match *your* eyes, does it? Mud brown," he said with a sniff. "But I daresay the bridegroom deserves the new waistcoat."

One of the guests at the breakfast knocked the best dish off the table, sending it flying all over the rug, and one of the Goulding boys stuck his finger in the marzipan on top of the wedding cake. Fortunately, Lady Catherine—who had a previously unknown fondness for gin, and a lot of it—only laughed at the chaos, and Lady Matlock kindly set about soothing Mrs Bennet's nerves.

Saye was discovered kissing Miss Goddard in the west parlour. It was Jane who discovered them, having been in the process of sneaking Bingley in there for the very same reason. And Lydia became violently ill and nearly vomited on Colonel Fitzwilliam, only being hustled away by Mrs Hill at the very last moment.

"Were I not so full of felicity," Elizabeth told her new

husband, "I might find some of this a source of dismay. But I am Mrs Darcy; I have no cause to repine."

"You might," he said, "when I tell you the next calamity."

It seemed his coachmen did not think it sound to carry them off in the weather to London. "It seems unlikely we should make it to Watford, much less London."

This intelligence did give Elizabeth some pause. Their little village was full to bursting with wedding guests, a fact which had delighted her. It was not often that people would travel to a simple country wedding, and the honour of Darcy's relations giving her such distinction was much appreciated. Such a display of familial approbation would go a long way towards easing her way in Society.

Mr and Miss Bingley had graciously offered Netherfield Park for the convenience of Lord and Lady Matlock, Saye, Colonel Fitzwilliam, Georgiana, and Lady Catherine. Miss Goddard and her mother were being urged to join them there.

Elizabeth went to the window, gazing out upon a wintry wonderland. It was pretty, for anyone who had no intentions of travelling. Darcy came behind her, laying one hand on her waist as they both looked out. Elizabeth had hoped for some sign of lessening snowfall, but it seemed dishearteningly steady.

"What if..." With a deep breath, she enquired, "What if we are stuck *here*?"

"At Longbourn?"

Elizabeth's shudder was her only reply. It was her wedding night, and at the risk of being indelicate, she wished to be alone with Darcy. Finally alone.

"I cannot think Netherfield ideal either," he mused. "Not with so many people there."

"Netherfield has the advantage of lacking my younger sisters," she reminded him.

"But has the decided disadvantage of my cousins."

Elizabeth pursed her lips, staring out of the window into the squall and wishing she might see some sign of the clouds dissipating. In truth, it looked like one of those snowstorms that would last for days. Privacy, of any sort, was seeming like an increasingly distant prospect.

It then that Saye sidled up to them, sniggering as he came. "Poor Darcy. Tonight will be positively medieval."

"Whatever do you mean?" Darcy asked.

"Oh you know, Henry the Eighth and so forth, consummating the marriage while the courtiers cheered him on." Saye laughed while Darcy gave Elizabeth a look.

"Longbourn it is, then," Elizabeth said grimly.

Saye wandered off, while Darcy leant in and whispered into her ear, "I hope that before too long neither of us will remember exactly where we are."

"As long as I am in your arms, I will never need anything more," she replied and was rewarded by a kiss.

The End

GET A FREE BOOK!

The Course of True Love, a contemporary Pride & Prejudice variation is free for subscribers of the Quills & Quartos newsletter. CLICK HERE to join us today!

ALSO BY AMY D'ORAZIO

A Fine Joke

A Folly of Youth

A Match Made at Matlock

A Lady's Reputation

A Short Period of Exquisite Felicity

A Wilful Misunderstanding

Cads & Capers

Cursing Mr Darcy

Heart Enough

Of a Sunday Evening

So Material a Change

The Best Part of Love

The Happiest Couple in the World

The Mysteries of Pembcrlcy

Without Vanity or Pride

Wits & Wagers

RAGS TO RICHMONDS REGENCY ROMANCE SERIES

Get the Prequel Free!

The Maid

The Spinster

The Foundling

The Heir

ABOUT THE AUTHOR

Amy D'Orazio is a longtime devotee of Jane Austen and fiction related to her characters. She began writing her own little stories to amuse herself during hours spent at sports practices and the like and soon discovered a passion for it. By far, however, the thing she loves most is the connections she has made with readers and other writers of Austenesque fiction.

Amy currently lives in Myrtle Beach with her husband and daughters, as well as three Jack Russell terriers who often make appearances (in a human form) in her books.

For the latest information on new releases and sales please follow Amy on Bookbub or her Amazon Author Page.

Printed in Great Britain
by Amazon